THE SIEGE OF RAVENS

ABELIA SUMPTER

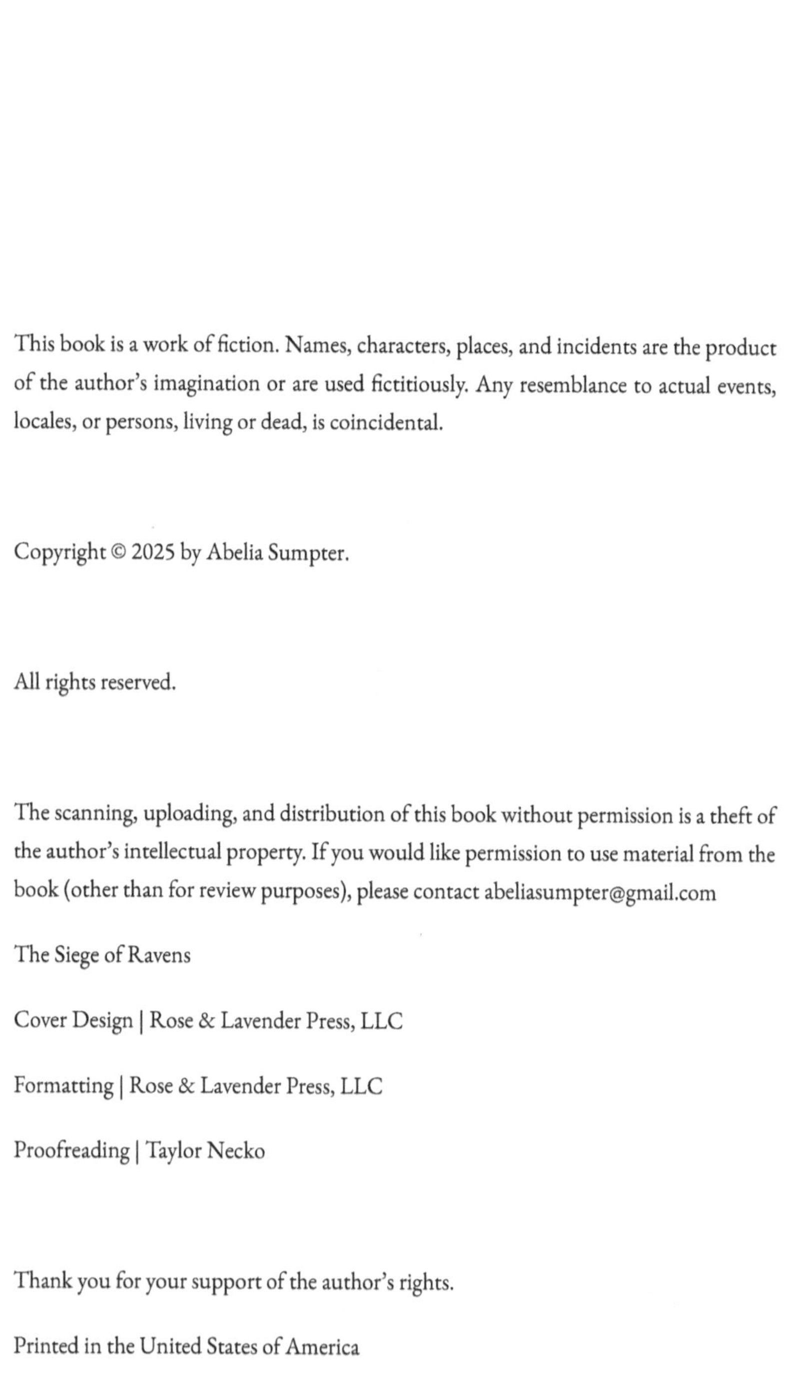

Note from the Author

The Siege of Ravens is not suitable for those under 18 years of age.
Please see abeliasumpter.com for a full list of content warnings.

Chapter 1

Margot

The engine of Milo's ship thrums as we pass through the vastness of the solar system. Stars glitter, each light-years apart, but from our eyes, they could reach out and touch each other. Lucinda used to tell Dimitri and me that the stars represented the souls of those who have long passed and those yet to be born. Hundreds of thousands of souls, burning bright, watching us. Watching me.

I try not to let the expanse of space through the transparent ceiling distract me as I make my way into the small privy in the back of the ship. Fumbling for the lock, my fingers barely hit the latch before I double over the sink, an indescribable pain seizing my abdomen.

By the love of the gods . . .

Before we escaped the Imnicus, one of my last memories was of being trapped in a recreation room, subdued by proditors, then becoming Knox's plaything for the hour. There were times during his ambush that I saw past the stars and into the depths of my own soul, begging for it to give it out.

I recovered enough to escape with the others, and at the time, I had hardly noticed my lightheadedness and pounding headache. There was too much adrenaline to sort through. Now it demands to be acknowledged.

I lift my tank top and am greeted by a bruise that spreads from my side all the way to my front rib. Knox didn't only use mind games on me. He beat on me the same way he would a man of much greater strength.

It's deep and not the kind of wound I can put antiseptic on, but the kind that will have to heal over time with rest. At least, that's what I deduce from my limited medical knowledge.

Right now, I'll have to bear it until we're safe from Knox. At any moment, he may pick up on our trail and have us arrested as traitors to the Arris Reign. There's no time for pit stops or detours.

A sudden nausea takes over me.

I drop to my knees and claw for the toilet, barely making it as my stomach empties itself. My head throbs like someone is beating on drums from within my skull, and a cold sweat breaks out on my forehead.

It seems like my crows don't like the uncomfortable sensations in my body either, and they retreat back into their nests. That in itself brings me more relief than relieving my stomach. Ever since I gave into them by choking out Crux in self-defense, they've become more incessant than ever before, defying everything I thought I knew about them. It was only a few seconds of obedience, but it didn't matter. A line was crossed, and I enjoyed those fleeting moments of watching Crux's face turn blue.

It pleased them. Every second since, they roam deeply within me, attaching themselves to my neurons and my secrets. They peck, slowly chipping away at the walls I've put between them and me.

When I'm pretty sure I've expelled all my insides, I reach for the handle to flush.

Then a knock resounds at the door.

"Margot?"

"Just a second!" *Dammit.* I wipe my lips and wash my hands, then practice putting on my smile in the mirror.

When I slide the door open, Lleu stands on the other side.

"All yours," I say nonchalantly.

"I heard you vomiting." Lleu folds her arms. "You look terrible."

Shit. "Aerial sickness."

"You've flown before and never had issues." Her eyes dip to my stomach suspiciously and then back to my eyes.

I throw my hands up defensively. "No, it's not *that.*"

Due to the injections the rebellion gave me after I returned from the Imnicus the first time around, nothing is habitable inside this body. And morning sickness doesn't come with expelling small amounts of blood.

"Still, it sounds like you need something to ease your belly." Lleu laughs, but it's not exactly the laugh I remember her having. Yes, she seems to have perked up since takeoff, but there's something more behind it. A shift in the girl she once was. Knox hijacked

Alarik's crows and invaded her mind. That's not something someone gets over for a long time, if ever.

If helping me keeps her mind busy, I'm glad to accept. "A
first-aid kit would be nice."

"It should be further back." Lleu links her arm with mine, and
we move through the narrow hallway together. I prepare for her to
start skipping, as she often does, but it never comes.

In the back of the ship is a small kitchen that doubles as a
miniature infirmary. I sit on the counter while Lleu digs through
the cabinets.

"You know, when Milo first took me, I had to go to the most
boring Imnicus training classes known to man. A lady's maid isn't
just for show, apparently. I learned all sorts of things like first aid,
wound binding, even care for gravity sickness. Guess it wasn't
completely useless."

"When I was undercover as an Imnicus soldier, I took the same
classes," I say. "Can't say I absorbed them to the same degree."

Lleu finds a large metal case and sets it on the counter next to
me. "Of course not. You were up to trouble." She opens the case to
reveal rows of medication. "Hmm . . . nausea medicine . . . nausea
. . ." She moves a few pill bottles around. There's a small tremble
in her hands that I'm not sure she's even aware of.

My eyes land on one medication in particular. I remember Lucinda telling me how well it can work for emergency wounds. How
it can make someone on the brink of death perform like a soldier.

Lleu stoops over the lower cabinets, and I reach out for the sole
prefilled epinephrine injector and shove it in my pocket.

"Ahh, here we go!" Lleu plucks a bottle of sublingual tablets out of the case and hands it to me. "These should do the trick. Though, now that I look at you, I think you may need a bit more than nausea pills." She motions to my rows of bruises on my arms, the visible ones anyway. A frown replaces her smile, sadness filling her eyes.

"I barely noticed them until after we took off." I hug my arms to my chest. "They'll heal."

"But they could heal faster." She finds another kit and pulls out a cream, preparing it in her hands. "Give me your left arm."

A hiss forms in my mouth, but I suppress it, biting down on my inner lip instead as she massages the cream onto my skin.

"How is Alarik doing after . . . everything?" *After Knox tormented you in your sleep without Alarik knowing*, is what I want to say.

Lleu frowns, not meeting my eye, while she concentrates on the cream. "I think he blames himself."

"He has to know that Knox manipulated him. It's not his fault."

"I've tried telling him that, but he won't listen. He thinks he's a failure."

Knox has hurt a lot of people, even me. But there's something about him hurting Lleu that turns my simmering anger to a boil. Unlike me, she never chose to risk her life among proditors. Him playing with her gentle soul to satiate his sick cravings is unforgivable. It just goes to show that, when it comes down to it, Knox never needs a good reason to do what he does.

And yes, the crows in me are sick too, and though it's hard, I do everything in my power to resist them day by day. He does not. He embraces it. Lusts after pain like an addictive wine dripping down his throat.

Gods, I want to see his face turn blue. For life itself to drain from his eyes while he begs me for mercy.

My crows coo at me, saying the word, '*her*' over and over. They motion their invisible wings toward Lleu's neck.

I bite down on the side of my cheek. *No*, I tell them. *Back off. I would never hurt her.*

But they are persistent, bringing an ache to my chest, to the point of no longer feeling the sting of my arms.

I imagine a door slamming shut between them and me, then placing all my weight against it, keeping them out. But it doesn't matter how hard I resist. That overwhelming guilt for even the mere temptation to hurt Lleu is all-consuming.

To my surprise, they finally back off, accompanied by a flash of fatigue from the exertion and additional pain to all my injuries. It's the last thing I need.

Lleu reaches for my tank and tries to raise the hem to inspect beneath.

I cover my abdomen and scoot back. "What are you doing?"

"You expect me to believe that Knox and Crux only punched at your forearms?"

She's got a point, but I can't let her see this wound. At least, not until we land. "I already looked. There's nothing to treat under there."

Before she can protest, footsteps interrupt her words.

Milo Arris stands in the doorway. His dark, armored royal attire frames his body. Arbitor Monicas's blood still speckles his face and black hair.

My stomach flips at the memory of the arbitors' bodies strewn around the room while Knox's knives dripped with their blood. Another wave of nausea rises up into my throat, but I suppress it.

"Lleu, could you give Margot and me a minute?" the now-former Colum asks.

Lleu nods at him, then reaches for my wrist. "Are you sure you're okay?"

"I promise," I assure her. Whatever is going on will soon pass. My body just needs some time and medicine to heal.

Lleu shuffles past Milo into the hallway, leaving the two of us alone.

I swallow. A lot has happened since . . . Well, if you don't count Knox's coup, I haven't seen Milo since we slept together.

It was a mistake. We were caught up in our emotions, and having sex was a way to get it out of our systems. That was all it was. As far as I'm concerned, we're reluctant allies fighting against the same foe to protect our planets. Once Knox is taken care of, we'll go back to who we truly are—rebel and ruler. This is nothing but a temporary ceasefire.

The only way to fix things is if we work together—you and me," Milo had said as we escaped the Imnicus.

But how much do I want to fix? A year ago, I would've celebrated a coup against Milo and the arbitors, a victory for the instability of the Arris Reign. But now? Well, all I know is Knox will bleed the planets dry even more than Balistar or Milo ever did.

More than that, what does stopping him mean for Milo or the rebellion? For Lavenai and Ashtanabo? Or myself? The future of the entire solar system is balanced on a knife's edge and I don't even know which direction I'd like it to fall.

Milo clears his throat. "Are you doing all right?"

I motion to my arms. "Just a little battered is all."

He leans against the door frame, as if he'd rather let Alarik and Lleu overhear our conversation than risk being alone in a room with me with a locked door ever again. "We need to talk about what we're going to do once we land."

"If you're once again suggesting we go to the rebellion, it's out of the question."

"Once word gets to Lavenai, all soldiers will see me as a fugitive on the loose. We have no manpower. No army, Margot. How else will the four of us stop Knox?"

I hop off the counter, holding back a grimace from the jolt of pain in my abdomen. "Last I saw them was during a mass funeral procession, grieving the lives of rebels *you* commanded to be killed with Gallow Machines. Do you think they'll let you live for a single second once you're within their grasp?"

Milo frowns. "I think, if they let me explain, they'd see I'm an asset more valuable alive."

I stay quiet, replaying his words over and over in my head. He truly wants to be useful to an organization that has wanted him dead his entire reign?

Alarik's voice interrupts, static and interference from the small speakers in the ceiling. *"Colum, Margot, we're approaching the atmosphere."*

"We better get back." Milo motions at me to go first.

"You go on ahead. I have to finish taking this medicine." I hold up the bottle of nausea pills.

Milo scans my body, a wave of suspicion passing over his face, before he shakes his head and disappears into the hallway.

The second Milo is out of sight, I grab the hidden epinephrine and plunge it into my thigh. For now, it will have to do. Milo's ship only stocks one, probably for rare allergic reactions, and who knows the next time I'll find more on a planet like Lavenai. If I have anything going on internally, this should slow its progression temporarily.

Within seconds, my pulse bounds and my chest tightens. My adrenaline spikes, the pain quickly dissipating and nausea disappearing.

The large cockpit is quiet when I enter. Once upon a time, Milo and I shared a kiss here that brought weakness to my knees. A kiss that changed the trajectory of my feelings forever, and, of course, complicated them. But now it's a place of solemnity where we can all read each other's minds with just a passing glance.

Milo and Lleu sit in the passenger seats, buckling their seat belts. Alarik steers the ship at the control panel, stripped down to his undershirt. His mask sits on the dash. His shoulders are tense, and even with everything we're up against, I know he's mostly worried for Lleu's safety.

I plop down in the copilot seat next to Alarik. "How long before we land?"

"About an hour." Alarik presses a few buttons. "I'm doing my best to hide our signal, a perk of flying the Colum's personal ship. The last thing we need is to be denied landing clearance."

I swallow. "What are the odds of that?"

"Before Knox's coup? Zero. Now? It's very possible." I catch him staring at Lleu in the corner of his eye protectively.

"Do you think Dune repaired the communication tower? Or at least made it off the Imnicus?"

"Only landing will tell. But if Knox found out Dune helped Milo escape . . . Well, then I pray to the gods he's not stuck there."

Stuck. I swallow, thinking about Dimitri, Oliver, and Anali stranded on Ashtanabo during this transition of power, probably still risking their lives to destroy temple points. That is, if they weren't captured shortly after I was. But my cousin is strong. He will find a way off the planet. The last thing I need is to worry about the three of them, but how can I not?

"Is there no way to stop Knox's ravens?" I ask.

Alarik frowns. "Perhaps there is, but it's hard to say when he's the only living proditor who knows how to use them. Back in Eskdale, the Vicars declared all alternative magic forbidden and kept the birds' power locked away in the Akumu forest. Balistar unlocked it anyway. Some say it drove him mad and he was just great at hiding it."

"And then he taught Knox all of them?"

"Three of them. Owls, to cause long-term sleep deprivation. Finches, to transport muscle memory from one to another. And of course, ravens."

"There's more?"

"Doves. They tame crows who have lost their way."

"That doesn't sound like dark magic."

"It's because they're not supposed to be needed to begin with, or at least that's the Vicars' opinion."

Though my crows are being tame right now, I can't help but crave the doves. For a second, I almost understand Balistar. If the only reason he initially entered the forest was to help Knox, I can't blame him. Sick crows are unbearable in the same way leeches are. But is it worth being corrupted by other birds? Lavenai's purple hue, as a result of pollution from Balistar's reign, reminds me otherwise.

Alarik continues, "After living with Knox for so many years, I'm inclined to disagree with the Vicars on doves. Before Balistar died, Knox was pleasant enough."

"I'm not following."

"Balistar bestowed doves on Knox to help his sickness, but didn't teach him how to use them. So when he died . . . "

I finish his sentence, somewhat numb by the realization. "The doves went with him."

Alarik nods. "I didn't notice Knox's sickness increasing at first. He was nineteen, so he had the sense to hide it, especially from Milo. But as time wore on, it became harder and harder for him to keep it secret."

"Why would Balistar teach him dark magic without the one thing he needed to tame it?"

Alarik's gaze grows distant and dark. A look of knowing shoots between both of us.

Control. Pretending to be Knox's savior helped keep Balistar's most powerful proditor loyal and awe-struck by him. Knox Arris is another victim of Balistar's charm.

Yet I cannot pity Knox in the slightest.

Chapter 2

Margot

The lights of a lone warehouse guide our descent onto Lavetnai's surface in the deadened outskirts of Merth. The area is fenced in with a small landing bay, and I can tell this location doesn't get ships often, which I suspect is why Milo chose it. There aren't slews of guards or spotlights scanning the surrounding desert-like area. It almost seems to be some kind of military-run logistics center.

Once the ship lands, Milo stands and wipes the remainder of arbitor blood from his face. "Get cleaned up, quickly."

"What is this place?" I ask while Lleu hands me a respirator and Alarik heads to the back of the ship to redress.

"It's a processing center for local trade before goods make it into the city. Mundane things—clothing, food, medical supplies. Also, things we'll need to get into the city undetected. A facility like this will be the last to hear about Knox's takeover, with the way orders trickle down."

Milo inspects me like he would one of his soldiers. Then his eyes land on my bruised arms. I'm still in my clothing from the recreation center, so I don't have anything to cover them with.

My heart thumps as Milo unclasps his cape and throws it around my shoulders. I don't move while he secures it above my collarbone, overly aware of his scent and body heat lingering on the fabric.

"I can find something else." I motion to take it off, but Milo places a hand on my covered arm to stop me.

"You can't have those bruises showing. It will only increase their suspicions."

I shrug off his touch. "What? Don't want them to think *you* did it?"

Milo narrows his eyes.

Alarik returns donned in his proditor armor. "Ready to lower the ramp?"

Milo nods. "Margot, help Lleu with her respirator."

I step over to Lleu, who has hers on crooked. It's her first time on Lavenai and I doubt she's ever had any need for one in her life. Breathing through one whenever she's outdoors is going to be an adjustment. When I was on Ashtanabo, it felt like breathing in the heavens. I'm just thankful these respirators are newer and probably more airtight than what most Lavens receive. Even the ones at the rebellion weren't the best models and have probably shaved a number of years off my life.

The ship ramp lowers and the warm night breeze trails into the ship. The warehouse workers seem to have already noticed our arrival, so lights ignite our path. Outside of the single green warehouse, there's nothing as far as the eye can see.

Lleu coughs while we walk on the dirt path, suppressing a gag at every breath.

"Hang in there," I say. "Your lungs will adjust."

"It's like inhaling gasoline fumes." Lleu holds onto her throat.

Considering the factories and minimal flora on Lavenai, we're lucky the planet is livable at all. Some people who can't afford respirators, even expired ones, bear the air raw. Unfortunately for them, it cuts their lifespan in half.

When we enter the warehouse, three guards are waiting for us, presumably the night watch. Had we come during the day, there would have been daytime workers to deal with too. I can tell by the nervous stances of two of them that they don't get visitors often, much less the Colum himself.

Strangely enough, none of them bow their heads. It's typical protocol when Milo is around. Even I know that. I study them carefully. Yes, they wear standard-issued light gray uniforms, but one has a top button popped, and another has folded up the cuffs of his pants. It reminds me of the mismanaged base the rebellion targeted not too long ago.

The third guard is a woman with a tight brown bun and an impeccable uniform. She isn't nervous in the slightest as she makes eye contact with me. I internally shrink back. Truthfully, I've always been more frightened of female soldiers. Since Ashtanaban women aren't drafted, it means their support of the Arris Reign is so fervent that they joined willingly.

"Colum Arris," she says. "Your visit is . . . unexpected."

"It shouldn't be." Milo motions to the uniforms of the men. "All bases and warehouses are subject to impromptu visits."

The men stiffen and quickly fix their uniforms. Even for Ashtanaban soldiers, they are a bit stronger and taller than I'm used to. Wouldn't someone with their statures be of better use beyond basic night watch?

"So sorry, Colum," the one with a buzz cut says. "It won't happen again."

The bald one does a double take at me after he stands at attention. Something about it feels strange.

The woman puts on a smile and tries her best to make Milo happy. "Then I assume you're here for an inspection?"

"No. My business here is confidential." Milo eyes her uniform, like he's trying to find something wrong with it to get a leg up on her. He doesn't. "I am in need of supplies and a vehicle."

"Affirmative. Would you like me to call someone to transport you around Lavenai?" She reaches for her communicator.

"Absolutely not," Milo bites. "What do you not understand about the word confidential?"

I shoot a glance at Milo, wishing I could tell him to ease up.

She pinches her lips together while somehow managing to keep her face positive. "Anywhere in particular I can direct you to?"

"Clothing, food, and medical supplies."

"Of course. Right this way."

We follow her past rows of industrial shelves filled with boxes. They're palettes in limbo, waiting for the morning shift to arrive to process them. I peek my head around one crate while we pass it and see the label, *X6-18*.

Weapons? Why would a processing warehouse for civilian products have contraband? Unless they stock military items here too.

The female guard stops with the two men behind her. She motions with three fingers to the right. "Over there, you'll find food." Then she moves her hand to the left. "And there, you'll find clothing."

"And medical?" I ask.

"Next to the clothing. Please let me know if you need anything. We will stay out of your way."

Milo dismisses them without a "thank you" and turns to us. "Alarik, gather basic supplies—flashlights and whatnot. Maybe anything we can use as weapons, but remember, we need to pack light. Lleu, pick out civilian clothing for all of us."

Did Milo not see the weapons crate when we entered? Or does that model contain some kind of tracker?

"And Margot—"

"I'll gather first-aid supplies," I say quickly.

Milo frowns. "I was going to say food."

"We'll need both. There aren't many places to get treated on Lavenai if something were to happen."

"Margot's right," Lleu says. "And she'll need medicine and ice packs for her arms."

"Fine." He furrows his brows. "I'll pack the food and pick out the vehicle."

I move to the shelves of medical supplies and grab a bag, stuffing it with medications and wound care items. Everything from fever reducers, expensive antibiotics, and cough syrup, among other things. I make a mental note of this base for later, in case Lucinda wants to target it.

After I find the ice packs, I break one open and slip it beneath the cape and over my wound. It stings like hell, but I keep my jaw level to hide the discomfort.

I sort through a few more shelves and then sigh in relief once I find what I'm looking for. *Thank goodness.*

There are over a dozen prefilled epinephrine syringes in a bin. This is a goldmine compared to the single one on Milo's ship.

After checking over my shoulders, I stuff a handful inside the bag.

"Do you have some allergy I should know about?" I turn to see Milo standing behind me with bags of freeze-dried foods.

"Emergencies happen," I say. "Who knows, maybe Alarik is allergic to shellfish."

"I assure you, he's not." He gives me that same suspicious look from earlier, but it quickly subsides. "We'll stay at a hotel tonight. I've transferred all the geeds on my communicator to an untraceable device."

I nod, but a knot forms in my stomach as he quickly breaks eye contact. Alarik and Lleu may be there too, but sleeping near Milo is . . . It's not a good idea. Yet we don't have a choice. The worst part is, after last time, I'm not sure how strong my will is to resist him.

I can already imagine feeling his hand on my shoulder in the dead of night, his signal to meet him in a stairwell or the bathroom, and holding back groans so as not to wake Alarik or Lleu.

Lleu hands the two of us Laven-style clothing, interrupting my thoughts. "These should fit you both. I kept the colors on the darker side to help us blend in."

"You got my size right." Alarik holds the long-sleeved shirt up to his chest.

"Are you surprised?" Lleu pokes his shoulder.

Milo inspects his clothes and refuses to admit out loud that she got his size right too.

Before the guards come back, all of us take turns changing behind one of the shelves. When Milo emerges in Laven clothing—neutral pants, a long-sleeve shirt, and an olive poncho—I can't help but laugh to myself. It's like watching a noble dress like a pauper for the fun of it.

When the guards return, they say nothing about our change of clothes, but their eyes speak volumes. I know they're itching for Milo to tell them what's going on and why the Colum himself is going undercover.

"I see you found everything all right, Colum," the female guard says.

"Almost everything." Milo motions to a green vehicle. "I'll need the keys."

"A civilian vehicle? Wouldn't you like something a bit more militarized?"

"This is exactly what is needed for this mission."

She bites back her next words. "Of course. My apologies. I'll grab the keys now." As everyone familiar with Milo's temperament knows, once he makes up his mind, it cannot be changed.

We load up the vehicle and pile inside. The guards stand nearby in a line and bow while Milo puts the keys in the ignition to start the engine. I take another look around the warehouse and see the weapons crate off to the side again. Why aren't we taking those? Milo must know they're here.

The guard with the buzz-cut checks his communicator and goes stiff. "Wait, hold it."

Oh gods.

Milo seems to hold his breath too as Alarik lowers the window. It's four against three. And even though we have a proditor, they have guns. Why didn't we take any guns?

The guard approaches the window and studies the four of us. Lleu hides her shaking hands under her legs.

"I just received a notification that the road up ahead is closed for repairs. You'll want to take the detour north."

My nerves settle, and I feel the invisible collective sigh of relief between us all.

"Thank you," Alarik says. "We'll look out for it."

After we pull away from the warehouse, I feel the countdown to successfully hiding from Knox beginning.

Had the guards actually received word from their communicators about our fugitive status, they would have been difficult to fight off. The woman would have probably been overjoyed to deliver Milo to Knox as a show of allegiance with the transition of power. Unlike the men, who looked as though they lift palettes for fun in their spare time. Still, I don't understand what they were doing stationed at that warehouse.

Once we get closer to Merth, Lavenai's capital city, Alarik removes his proditor mask and ruffles his hair.

Lleu stares out the window at the half-dead mushroom fields. "My gods."

I lean over her shoulder to watch the landscape with her—wilted fields, rotted trees, and pale dirt. It looks worse in the daylight. Over the years, I've come to appreciate the beautiful darkness of Lavenai. The way the purple overcast looms over the fields makes it feel like living on the edge of tranquility and despair. It's the Lavenai I've always known, but one I wouldn't mind putting behind me if it came down to it.

As we enter the city itself, the tall, colorful buildings come into view. One or two people walking the sidewalks turn into tens and then hundreds. People are headed to night shifts, most of them factory workers. There's a guard here and there perched up on balconies, scanning the crowds for any sign of insubordination.

A drunk stumbles out of a bar and starts shouting at a nearby guard. He is promptly tased. Lleu visibly grimaces at the sight.

I take note of the cameras on the corners of buildings, and those are just the ones that are visible. I sure hope Milo never had a formal facial scan done. If Knox decides to upload his face to Lavenai's database, we'll be done for, even with respirators.

Alarik watches Lleu's discomfort in the rearview mirror. "Look, Lleu."

A worn-down theater with a sign made of flickering purple bulbs stands on a street corner. Lleu's eyes somewhat light up at it. "Do they still host plays there?"

I nod. "I haven't been to one, but the theater is the one place Lavens can watch stories unfold without censorship."

Milo tenses at my words, and I don't apologize for them. He turns his head away from the theater.

As much as I want to dig the injustices of his rule into him more, the future of Lavenai depends on his next moves. And if, in the end, he decides to side with Ashtanabo once more and leave Lavenai to rot, I'll be the first one to stop him.

Chapter 3

Margot

It takes hours for us to settle on a hotel and we circle the city multiple times while doing so. In my opinion, I don't think we should stay at one at all in favor of setting up camp somewhere on Merth's outskirts. Milo thinks that will draw too much attention. I just don't think he likes the idea of sleeping in a cramped van.

After we finally agree on a hotel called The Equinox, at Milo's insistence, we arrive in an underground parking garage beneath it. I hop out and stretch my legs. Ever since my injection, my wound has felt better. Significantly better. And the nausea has subsided completely. Hopefully I'm through the worst of it.

The garage smells of must, gasoline, and dried alcohol—a scent that has Milo's face scrunching as he steps out of the car.

Of course, Milo forces me to be the honorary tour guide and doesn't move from his spot until I grumble and lead them inside. It's not like I've ever stayed at this hotel before.

At the front desk, Milo pays with his untraceable, probably infinite, geeds. He books the largest two-bedroom suite in the hotel—which is to say the least gross room in the establishment.

It's only when we enter the elevator that Milo has a look of realization. Mold speckles through the ceiling paint and the floor doesn't look like it's been cleaned since before he was Colum. The lights flicker from Alarik's crows, meaning these bulbs haven't been replaced in nearly two decades.

I fold my arms as the elevator ascends. "You know, you could have chosen any hotel . . ."

"I've never been to a Laven-owned hotel before. I heard a while back that this was the nicest one."

"It likely is." I pat his shoulder then exit the elevator as the doors slide open.

Alarik and Lleu look at each other and follow after me, holding back laughs. I can hear Milo huffing from behind.

We reach the room's door inside the musty hallway. Milo unlocks it slowly, dreading what's on the other side.

There aren't any bed bugs, and the mismatched furniture isn't stained. The first thing Milo's eyes dip to is a suspicious stain on the carpet. Lleu shivers like her skin is crawling from the sight. Alarik tries his best to stay polite, but even his face is breaking.

I toss my bag down. "Looks good to me."

"It's . . . quaint." Lleu forces a smile.

Alarik moves to the kitchen cupboards, opening every one of them, before moving into the bedrooms to inspect those. I imagine it's his typical job when accompanying Milo to any hotel as one of his proditors.

"There's no need, Alarik." Milo sets his bags on a mostly clean part of the counter.

Lleu hugs her arms to her chest, warding off the chill in the air. She moves to one of the chairs to sit, but immediately decides against it and sits on the windowsill instead.

Alarik points to one of the doors. "Lleu and I will take the smaller bedroom. Unless you girls want to share."

I shake my head. "No need. I'll take the couch, and our *esteemed Colum* can have the larger bedroom."

I turn to Milo for confirmation, or an annoyed comeback, but he's not looking at me at all.

His eyes are narrowed at Alarik. "She isn't in danger of Knox here, Proditor. I don't see why you'd need to share a bedroom with Lleu."

Ah, so he is that dense.

I step next to Milo and elbow him in the side. "I have a few things to speak to Milo about. You two should get some rest. It's been a long day."

"Thank you, Margot." Alarik takes Lleu's hand. He guides her into the bedroom and slides the electronic door shut behind him.

Milo scoffs. "What the hell was that about?"

I pinch the bridge of my nose. "Please don't tell me you need me to piece the puzzle together for you."

"Everyone knows Alarik hates his position, yet he chooses now to take Proditor Code so seriously when it comes to her."

Milo Arris is a strong, capable leader. An intelligent one. But when it comes to matters of the heart, it's as if all his brain cells dive right off a skyscraper. "Lleu and Alarik are together."

"What?"

"Milo. They're sleeping together. In fact, I'd say they're in love with each other. Does that get it through your thick skull?"

Milo leans onto the counter with his forearms, his entire body going still, like a switch has been flipped in his brain. He laces his fingers under his chin, a thousand thoughts behind his eyes. "How long?"

"I don't know. I'm assuming after you assigned him to her."

"Proditors don't date. They can't. There's no time."

"And once upon a time, that mattered. Now, nothing is certain. Not his role as an Imnicus proditor. Hell, not even your position as Colum. Regardless, I don't think Alarik will listen to you in any matter regarding Lleu."

Milo pushes up from the counter and stares off at the floor, like he's offended at himself for missing something that was obvious to everyone else. "I won't interfere."

"Good." He's accepting enough about it. So much so that I almost want to tell him about the letter just to rub in his face how disloyal Alarik truly is to him. But that's the sleep deprivation talking. Things are always changing, and for all I know, Milo could regain his throne tomorrow and have Alarik disciplined. If Milo finds out about Alarik helping me escape the Imnicus, it's not going to be by my lips. I'll let Alarik decide if Milo should know.

We stand there in silence, and I don't know what to do or say. Now that the conversation about Lleu and Alarik is over, I am overly aware that we're alone together. And gods know we can't handle that.

"So . . . uh." Milo clears his throat. "Are you hungry?"

I shrug. Hypothetically, I should be starving. I can't even remember the last time I ate. But this entire day has stolen my appetite.

Milo avoids looking me directly in the eye, and I can't help but be thankful that the counter is covering his lower half. But I also take note of how he's reluctant to move away from behind it.

"Listen," Milo starts. "About what happened—"

"There's nothing to be said," I say quickly. "It was a moment of weakness for us both."

"We were drunk."

"Yes. Drunk." I don't mention how I only drank a small amount during the toast. Even standing here alone with him messes with my senses. A warmth crawls across my body.

Milo's eyes travel down my neck, to my breasts, then to my hips and thighs. Heat nips along my shoulders and abdomen. I should excuse myself to the bathroom and stop his train of thought. We can't be trusted together, even now.

I need to think of something to stop us. "Why didn't we take any weapons?"

Milo clears his throat. "What?"

"At the warehouse. There was at least one crate of them, yet we only took food, medicine, and clothes."

To my surprise, his eyes narrow. "Margot, that's a processing warehouse. There aren't any weapons in it."

"I know what I saw."

"What did the crate say exactly?"

"Firearms. X6-18 models."

"Shit." Milo places a hand on the back of his head. "You're telling me that warehouse was holding contraband? That model specifically is notorious for it."

My face pales as I recall the two male guards. There was something off about them, and at the time I didn't know it. But their statures make more sense now. Honestly, nothing about that warehouse added up. "Well, it means nothing right now, correct? I mean, contraband is the least of your concerns until you're Colum again."

"If an entire warehouse is in on a contraband scheme, who is to tell where their allegiances lie?"

If they aren't with Ashtanabo or the rebellion, then who would be able to sway an entire warehouse in their favor? Who would be powerful enough to staff their own men?

The realization hits me like lightning, as does a high-pitched noise just outside of our door. It sort of sounds like a—

"Margot, get down!" Milo dives at me.

A boom pierces through my ears, sending the door into shrapnels. Milo covers me with his body, blocking the debris. His weight presses down on my abdominal wound, sending a new shock wave through me. It's excruciating, but I can't find a way to tell him I'm hurting, my ears ringing from the explosion.

Oh gods, has Knox already found us? Was all this preparation and hiding out for nothing?

"Milo!" Alarik's door flies open as Milo finally rolls off of me.

A smoky fog fills the room, as does a strange medicinal scent. Alarik stumbles and drops to his knees.

The same fatigue takes over me, my limbs turning to jelly. I rest the side of my face against the gross cold floor.

"Margot?" Milo grabs my arm.

We need our respirators . . . We need to fight.

Milo's hold on me weakens as the sleeper bomb's smoke takes over him too. His eyes close while I stay stubborn, refusing to let unconsciousness take over.

At the fog-covered doorway, figures rush into the room with gas masks. But they aren't Ashtanaban soldiers nor proditors.

Joriel's goons. *No.*

And as I should have expected, I recognize two of them as the guards from the processing warehouse.

Another figure emerges, walking between the two lines of men.

His cane clicks against the ground, a tailored overcoat hugging his lean build. He stops mere feet in front of me and tilts his head down, face protected by a gas mask.

"Tavish." Joriel leans forward, resting his forearms on his cane. "I've been looking for you."

I black out.

Chapter 4

Milo

Tobacco tickles my nostrils as I slowly regain consciousness. I shake raven strands of my hair off my face, my mind still begging for a few more minutes of sleep. The splinters digging into my biceps ensure I don't. My wrists are tied behind my back to a wooden chair.

Everything floods back at once, including a headache from the sleeping gas wearing off. As I raise my head, the surrounding area comes into focus.

Vanities fill the brick room, each of them filled with make-up and hair supplies. There are racks of women's clothes off to the side—performance clothes. If they weren't so scantily clad, I would have thought we were in the underground of that theater Lleu was gawking about. Wherever we are, it's some kind of base-ment.

Feet away, Margot is slumped unconscious in a chair, her wrists and ankles bound just like mine. The sight of her knocked out on drugged gas tightens my jaw, protectiveness washing over me. A feeling that has been growing on me daily.

Margot still doesn't know that she's still my wife by law. It's not like I had a choice to make our marriage official on paper when I first kidnapped her. If I hadn't, the arbitors could have found out our union was a sham if they ever looked into public records.

Tavish. That was one of the last words I heard before I blacked out completely. If these perpetrators know Margot's real last name, it means that this isn't related to Knox nor is it some random kidnapping. No. This is personal.

I can only assume they got Lleu and Alarik too. And by process of elimination, they must know he was the proditor with us at the warehouse. They'll be keeping him under lock and key like some animal.

"Margot," I whisper sharply. "Wake up."

She doesn't stir. At least she's still breathing, though a bit rapidly for someone who is out cold. Her skin is pale too. I reach out my crows and sense her high heart rate. Whatever they used to drug us must have been hard on her system.

Margot groans and her eyes squint.

"Margot," I say again.

Finally she comes to, rolling her head back until her neck cracks. She blinks a few times as she examines her environment with a stark recognition, and then me tied up next to her.

"I take it you know where we are?" I ask her.

"It's just some unsettled business. I'll sort everything out, I promise. He likes to be dramatic."

"Who's *he*? And what do you mean dramatic? We're tied to chairs in a musty basement."

Margot narrows her eyes. "Just trust me."

The basement door opens and my wrists strain against my bindings. Margot takes a deep breath, as if psyching herself up. What could she have possibly gotten herself into? Some kind of back alley mission for the rebellion?

A few larger men descend the stairs, six of them total. I grimace at the guards from the warehouse. Calling them traitors wouldn't be correct. They're not even Ashtanaban. Them using my planets' warehouses as a way to transport contraband is almost humiliating.

Dress shoes tap against the top of the steps, a cane clicking as the last person makes their way down the stairs.

"My, my, we have quite a bit of catching up to do, Tavish. Don't we?"

My jaw tenses. This has got to be some kind of practical joke. *Him?*

I narrow my eyes at Joriel Sinclair, and he promptly smirks at me.

"Ah, Colum. I must say I was more than surprised to find you holed up in a hotel with Miss Tavish with no guards or Ashtanaban defenses. Were you not at my doorstep looking to apprehend her not so long ago?"

Of course the person who decides to kidnap Margot happens to be someone I encountered recently. Being recognized means things could get dicey, whether he reports us to Knox or if he thinks he can get some kind of reward for holding me hostage. He'll be disappointed if he tries the latter. Anyone willing to pay for me is being cleaned up from an Imnicus conference room floor.

"I should have had my men apprehend you when I had the chance. I knew you were lying about Margot," I bite.

"Guilty. Though what I did for her did not come without a price." Joriel looks between Margot and me. "It seems all three of us have lied in some regard."

"This is between you and me, Joriel. Leave Milo out of it," Margot says in a coarse tone.

"Milo?" Joriel chuckles. "Is it not informal to use the first name of our Colum? Hmm, strange indeed." He suspiciously eyes me. "I recall you telling me that a mission got you quite close with Colum."

"For all you know, I'm still on my mission and you just blew my cover."

"Oh really?" Joriel paces around Margot's chair like a lion stalking its prey. "Then you'll have no issue discussing our deal in front of him. Or perhaps even paying up right here and now?"

He drags his cane up the side of her calf. Margot's eyes widen. She tries to move her leg away.

What is he . . .

"Let's refresh your memory, Tavish, shall we? You and I made a deal: You get to Ashtanabo and back safely with my help, and upon your return—" He moves the tip of the cane slowly up Margot's arm.

Oh . . .

I'll fucking kill him.

What the hell was she thinking promising something like *that* to a crime lord? I pull against my bindings enough for Joriel to gaze in my direction and smirk. But he says nothing, turning his focus back to Margot.

He's clever, I'll give him that. If I try to knock him down a few pegs, it will only confirm what he suspects. It doesn't appear he knows that Margot was temporarily the Columess, as her face was not revealed to the Laven or Ashtanaban general public. But he has enough pieces of the puzzle to figure it out if he tried. If I try to protect her from whatever deal she made, he'll have more to use against us.

But if he tries anything . . .

Keep it contained, I tell myself. But how could I if it came down to it? *That's my wife.*

Joriel stands behind her and rests his cane on the back of the chair. His fingers run along her scalp, moving her hair out of her face. "You know, the day we made our deal was . . . interesting to say the least. It was the first time I've done business while being straddled."

My teeth clench so tightly it sends a nervy pain straight to my skull, my thoughts becoming as sadistic as Knox's.

"And when you nuzzled that sweet face into my neck while wearing that tight dress," he says in a brazen whisper, "I nearly came undone."

Joriel may be looking at Margot, but his attention is on me, soaking in my every reaction. It's like he's trying to get revenge for the way I humiliated him in front of his patrons. I pull against my bindings, not wanting to be bound to this chair any longer.

"It took everything in me to control myself, Tavish. But like you once said, *I respect those who keep their deals.*"

Margot visibly seethes. "Joriel. Can we talk about this in private?"

"Why should he mind? He's nothing to you but a mission, right?" Joriel can barely suppress his smile. He moves in front of Margot and holds her chin gently, tracing her jawline. "So let's talk about that repayment plan, shall we?"

I fantasize about wrapping my hand around his throat and squeezing his neck until it pops like a grape. Before I can attempt to break free and bury my fist in Joriel Sinclair's face, Margot speaks.

"Your empire is in danger, Joriel, and if you don't free us, I will leave you in the dark about it."

Joriel scoffs. "Do you think I'm a fool?"

"Don't you think it's strange that I've spent my entire life trying to overthrow Ashtanabo, yet you found me with a proditor and the Colum himself? Did you not even stop to ask yourself why?"

His lips form into a straight line. "I'm listening. But if you want me to let you go, it better be something good."

"All your success has come from gaps in the Ashtanaban military, bribing soldiers to give you top-level clearance, and we saw that you've even taken over warehouses with your own men to keep your contraband investments alive."

She lists off some more of Joriel's ventures that I certainly wasn't aware of, but at the moment, there isn't room for more anger. I'm just disappointed in myself and the leaders I've stationed below me. Both planets are so large that it really is impossible for me to keep track of every little thing on my own. But to know a crime lord has been controlling parts of my own military without me knowing? Well, I'm glad it appears he's only after money and not power itself.

"This Colum right here, and the current structure of the Ashtanaban government, is the reason you've been able to get away with all this. Things right now are predictable, and therefore, exploitable."

I grimace.

"Your point?" Joriel asks.

"Milo has been kicked off his throne by another Arris. A full-blooded proditor. And as I'm sure your late father could attest to, things were much harder for your family business under the rule of the last one. Not to mention, this new one is more unpredictable than anyone I've ever met."

Joriel's brows furrow.

"If you think Lavenai is bad now, just wait and see," Margot adds. "And if you keep us trapped here, we won't be able to get the upper hand before his rule is sealed."

Joriel stands there, contemplating, then faces me. "Firstly, I will have to verify this with my Ashtanaban contacts. But I cannot let your proditor go. He's too dangerous."

"On my word, he will not touch you or my men without my orders," I say, but if Joriel tries to touch Margot again, I can't promise I won't sic Alarik on each and every one of them.

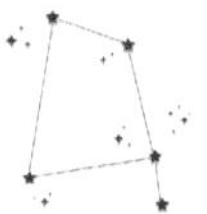

After they undo our binds, Joriel's men lead us up the basement stairs and into the club of debauchery. It must be sometime in the late morning or afternoon, because there's nobody except a bartender washing glasses and an old man mopping the floors.

While we follow Joriel through the club, Margot doesn't spare me a single glance. More than anyone, I know the lengths she's willing to go to complete missions and protect information. But selling her body? I have to control the fury trying to find its way into my face. Something about her deal with Joriel shocks me more than her surviving proditor torture at my own orders. Maybe I don't know her as well as I thought I did.

A table comes into view with a spread of luxurious foods and drinks. Alarik is secured to one of the seats with chains instead of rope. Even his neck is wrapped in a metal ring and strapped to the chair. I hold back a chuckle. The ring might keep him, but he and I both know that he could break through the wooden chair in a few swift movements, but I won't tell Joriel that. I'm just happy to be unbound myself.

"Margot!" Lleu shrieks and rushes out of a booth to hug her. "They won't let Alarik go."

Joriel stops and turns to face me. "On your orders, he will be free."

I fold my arms and speak to Alarik. "We're on neutral ground now, Proditor. When they untie you, stand down."

"Yes, Colum." It must be strange for him to have everyone in the room seeing his maskless face, knowing full well what he is. But if breaking code bothers him, he doesn't show it.

The men who free Alarik wear long sleeves, turtlenecks, and gloves, exposing as little skin as possible in case Alarik changes his mind. But my proditors are fast. He could grab their faces in mere milliseconds. It's humorous to watch, nonetheless.

After Alarik is free, and Lleu tearfully embraces him, which I'm still getting used to, Joriel claps his hands into folded ones. "Shall the five of us enjoy a meal together? It's not everyday I get to host royalty. Or former royalty, I should say."

I narrow my eyes.

"I suppose we could use something to eat," Lleu answers for us all. She's not wrong. Now that we're no longer prisoners, I'm ravenous.

As we take our seats, Margot intentionally sits as far from me as possible next to Lleu on the C-shaped booth, even though the chair on my left is more preferable.

We're all quiet as the meal starts and I can't believe how hungry I am. Or how much this food tastes just like what I eat on the Imnicus. In this moment, I can't help but be thankful for Joriel having access to all this—for now. It beats eating the freeze-dried stuff we got from the warehouse.

One of Joriel's men stops by and whispers something to him. Joriel listens intently before sighing and cutting into another piece of chicken. "Well that's quite unfortunate indeed."

"What?" Margot sets down her water glass.

"You were right about the new Colum. Part of me was hoping it would all be a lie and we could go back to our previous arrangement. It seems we'll have to pause our deal . . . for now."

"Did you hear anything else?" she asks.

"Only that Ashtanabo as a whole is now aware of the change of power."

I look down at the vegetables on my plate. If Ashtanabo knows, it means the leaders of each region are probably paralyzed, unsure of where to go from here. And the people are probably riddled with uncertainty.

Joriel continues, "But for making me aware of this risk early on, and allowing me extra time to move geeds around, you are more than welcome to stay here in hiding."

"Staying is a risk," Margot says. "Knox might remember that Milo sought me out here."

"I have more secret rooms and hiding places than anyone on Lavenai," Joriel adds. "You're safest here. In fact, the bedroom next to mine has a high-level security system built in. It's smaller, but I'm happy to let you use it, Tavish."

I furrow my brows. "Really, is that the reason?"

"Milo," Margot bites.

"Is something the matter, Colum?" Joriel reaches across the gap of the booth and grabs Margot's waist, sliding her into his side. "Or should we stick to Mr. Arris until the cards are sorted?"

"Don't start with that. You know exactly what you're doing."

"Reminding her that she'll one day have to make good on her deal?" Joriel smirks and eyes my body. "Unless you're willing to take her place."

I can't take it anymore. He's dead.

I fly around the table. Lleu screams.

"Don't, Milo." Alarik quickly grabs my arm before I can lunge.

Joriel hops up from his seat and raises his cane like a sword.

Before I can make my next move, Margot tries to stand and shout something. The words don't make it out of her mouth as she falls to her knees, grabbing her head.

"Margot!" Lleu rushes toward her. "What's going on?"

Margot grabs her abdomen, sweat coating her neck. She raises a hand. "It's nothing. I'm fine. I just need some medicine from our bags."

I've already forgotten about Joriel, and it seems he has abandoned our fight too. His eyes narrow at Margot suspiciously.

"You don't look fine," Alarik chimes in.

"What did you do to her?" I say to Joriel.

Joriel puts his hands up defensively. "No more than I did to any of you! My sleeping gas doesn't have many side effects, and certainly not this."

Lleu places her hand against Margot's forehead. "Heavens, you're burning up! Why didn't you say something?"

Margot's skin is going shades paler by the second. I don't know what's going on, or what possibly could have happened in the last twenty-four hours to cause such a decline, but something is seriously wrong.

"What aren't you telling us?" I ask.

"I just need to lie down." She forces herself to stand, then goes cross-eyed as if she's seeing four of me.

She's going to fall.

I quickly rush forward and catch her as her legs go weak. Lleu catches her other arm. Margot's skin is like ice. I need to assess her.

I inject my crows into her, assessing her vitals more deeply than before. Her pulse was high earlier but now it's through the roof. And her blood pressure is dangerously low. My crows assess her blood flow, and when they get to her abdomen—"Shit."

I lay her on the booth and yank the hem of her shirt up, exposing her abdomen and lower ribs. Her skin is covered in bruises, so purple that they're almost black.

Now I'm the one who's pale.

I think back to her strange behavior at the warehouse. Epinephrine. She must have injected it when she realized something was wrong and it hid the signs from me. It explains how off she looked when she first awoke in Joriel's basement.

"Call for a medic. Now!" I shout.

Joriel pulls out his communicator and shouts into it. His men scramble at the additional orders he barks.

I look down at her as she fades, wiping her sweat-coated hair out of her porcelain face. "Hang on, Margot. We're going to get you help."

Chapter 5

Milo

Two medics frantically rush around one of Joriel's lavish bedrooms, assessing Margot with handheld scanners and administering medications and fluids into her veins. She's still out cold, her body clammy and her skin paper white.

And I'm left to do nothing except watch her cling on to life from the sidelines while Alarik holds Lleu tightly in his arms.

"She wouldn't let me see her stomach," Lleu cries. "I should have insisted."

"There's no way you could have known." Alarik smooths his hand over the back of her scalp. "They'll figure it out. She'll be okay."

"I just don't understand . . . Why would she hide something so severe from us? She's bleeding internally!" I say.

Joriel chimes in from his velvet chair in the corner, his eyes locked on Margot. "I've known Tavish most of my life, and if I had to guess, she probably downplayed it to herself. *The mission comes first*, has always been her philosophy. Now look where that's gotten her."

As much as he tries to remain nonchalant, concern flickers in his eyes while he nervously twiddles his thumbs. If I wasn't so worried for Margot, I'd ask him about their real history. At the very least, I know she's never slept with him.

And to think, if he hadn't kidnapped us, she may already be long past saving. He's one of the few Lavens who can get access to top medics in less than an hour. Somehow, it only makes me more angry at myself.

I reach out to her across the room with my crows. Her vitals have slightly improved, but . . . it isn't enough. She's fading quickly. It's the same feeling I've gotten from interrogation subjects hours before life finally leaves their eyes.

I excuse myself from the others and walk up to the medic scanning Margot's abdomen again.

"How is she doing?" I ask.

The woman sighs. "I won't sugarcoat it. It's not looking good. If the internal bleeding would have been caught early, we would have been able to treat it adequately. She needs equipment and treatments that we just don't have. Possibly surgery."

My entire body goes numb. "What's the survival rate if she stays here?"

"It's hard to say without more in-depth scans, but . . . " The medic pauses. "Less than five percent."

I nod, but inside something shatters. A stark realization of my present reality.

Keep it together, I hear my voice and my own father's overlapping. My throat bobs as I suppress any outward signs of fear and horror taking over me.

In an attempt to distract myself, I try to focus back on Knox. The possibilities of his rule and how Margot's condition has put us in perilous danger. I try to be angry at her for hiding her injury. I even attempt to reignite the rage I felt when I learned of her deal with Joriel, but it doesn't work.

No, I can't lose her. I can't.

"I just need to step out for a second." I brush past everyone, trying to make it to the door.

"Milo? Are you all right?" Alarik uncurls his arms from around Lleu.

"I said I'll be right back, Proditor! Got it?"

Alarik slowly nods. Lleu visibly shudders and steps closer to his side.

I bolt out of there, not stopping until I stumble upon an empty room filled with bookshelves and framed paintings. With my fingers laced behind my neck, I pace back and forth.

We could try to find a hospital. Yes, I'll carry her on my back all the way there if I have to.

But I know better than anyone how inept Laven hospitals are. They can barely keep a fish alive with their old equipment and dirty supplies.

All at once, the magnitude of my failure as a leader hits me. Not because I abandoned my father's laws, but because I upheld them.

One of the paintings on the wall grabs my attention and a new kind of pain grips my chest. Whoever painted it must have been Ashtanaban. I'd recognize the Ralia mountains anywhere. It depicts an Ashtanaban utopia with children prancing in the fields and gold overflowing from lakes and rivers.

I look down at Margot's old ring that I still wear snug around my pinky finger. *She's going to die.*

Because of you.

I charge my fist back to launch it into the painting.

"Please refrain. It cost a fortune."

I stop mid punch, swinging back to face Joriel. He rests against the wall with one ankle crossed behind the other, cane nowhere in sight. I tell him, "I thought I said I wanted to be alone."

"Yes, but as it turned out, I needed to protect my assets from an angry royal's fist."

I run a hand down my face and steady my breath.

Joriel scoffs. "You really are in love with her, aren't you?"

I turn my head away, but it's an admission in itself.

"I won't even begin to ask questions, but as it turns out, I am fond of Tavish myself. If it wasn't clear to begin with."

"To me, it seems you just want to bed her."

Joriel sighs. "Unrequited love presents itself in many ways, as I'm sure you know very well."

"There has to be something you can do to help her. I have millions of geeds at my fingertips. I can pay you anything you want."

"As it turns out, Colum, I *also* have millions of geeds." He releases a frustrated sigh. "The funny thing about money is, the more of it you have, the less it truly matters. If I could save her, I would."

"So you're just going to let her die?" I say harshly.

"There is only one thing that can save her now. It's the only place I know that has advanced medical equipment."

"And that is?"

Joriel looks me dead in the eyes. "The rebellion."

The rebellion? "How on earth would we contact them?"

"The real question is, are you willing to hand her to them to save her life?"

I think about it, but it doesn't take me long to answer. "I am."

"You know what that means, don't you?"

Yes, if I find a way to enter the rebellion, my life would be over. They'd kill me on sight. "Yes. But how would I go about entering? It's been an impossibility my entire reign."

He curses and rubs the side of his neck. "You could enter through my entrance."

"*Your* entrance?" I knew the rebellion had many entrances around the city, but this location wasn't mentioned anywhere. "You're associated with them?"

"Open your eyes. Of course I am! But my face isn't in their security database. It won't open without an authorized rebellion member."

"If we took Margot to the entrance, would it scan her face and let us inside?" I used her face once before without her realizing it to get her into the base and steal the identity of rebel's faces, and I'm willing to do it again.

"Leave it to me."

Inside Joriel's basement, I hold Margot's unconscious body close to my chest. Lleu dabs sweat off Margot's forehead. If there's an entrance down here, it's well hidden. All that's in this section of the basement are vanities, racks of dance outfits, and lacy lingerie.

Margot shivers in her sleep, and I instinctively tighten my hold on her. *Hold on. Please don't give up.*

Joriel's men secure the basement door while he directs our attention to a blank brick wall. With the tip of his cane, he scratches a path along the mortar. He stops at a particular brick in the middle of the wall with no discernible marking upon it. He hesitates, his eyes meeting mine, and I nod.

Joriel presses in, and the brick slides into the wall with a soft click.

A flicker appears from the ceiling, as a laser searches the room, scanning each of our faces. It hesitates on Margot, and I prop her up, so it can get a better reading.

"Unauthorized parties noted," says the automated voice. *"Override required."*

I open my mouth to object, but Joriel is already stepping forward.

"Intrus beta protocol," he says, almost proudly.

There's a groan in the wall, and Alarik takes a step back. The bricks vibrate before stacking in on one another, splitting the wall in two. It slowly opens.

All that time and all that work, yet another secret entrance remained here under my nose. And right now, I couldn't care less.

"Make sure that Margot doesn't enter first, otherwise the door will shut and lock before the rest of you can enter. Learned that the hard way a little while back." Joriel's eyebrows furrow.

"Won't this shatter your relationship with the rebellion?" Alarik asks him.

"They and I have always had a strenuous relationship. In this case, I think it's a partnership worth risking." His gaze settles on Margot.

I clutch her closer to my chest. She's so still, the only indication she's still alive is my crows relaying her vitals back to me.

"About her deal," I say to Joriel. "I hope you know I have no intentions of letting her repay you, so you'd be wise to renegotiate the terms with me while I'm still in a forgiving mood."

Joriel chuckles. "Once you regain your throne, pay me a visit and we'll make a deal like gentlemen. Perhaps permanent legal immunity?"

"Don't push it."

Alarik goes first, tapping his toe past the threshold to test it. Once nothing happens, he takes Lleu's hand and guides her inside.

I follow in after them, taking my first few steps into the rebellion.

Chapter 6

Dune

The Imnicus throne room hasn't been used since Balistar's death. Black domed walls slowly fade into glass as it all meets at the highest point of the ceiling, giving a clear view of the stars. Honestly, I wanted to forget this room ever existed, and for good reason. *So much blood. So many screams.*

I stand on the edge of the marble dais in front of hundreds of Imnicus soldiers. Some of them look like they crave a sliver of hope from my words. And perhaps I could have given that to them, had I been the one to write this speech. But what kind of hope can be contained in words outlining the new rules of the Imnicus? Words that effectively make them prisoners? Slaves with military titles?

"All those previously assigned to the Imnicus will stay on board unless granted special permission by Colum Knox Arris. Furthermore—"

There's a terror that looms throughout the room that I could reach out and grasp. A suffocating one that matches the dread upon every face. Most of these men and women were still in diapers last time a full-proditor was Colum. They feared Milo but they're terrified of Knox.

A pair of eyes sears on the back of my neck while I continue reading. *He's* sitting casually on a luxurious silver-feathered throne upon the dais Balistar once used. If I turn around, I'm sure I'd see his lips curl while he watches me do his bidding, as if we weren't equals mere days ago.

It was worse when I gave a speech to the servants and humanoids. Tears were shed, by the humans at least. Knox is already in the process of overriding all the robo-servants' programming.

One girl in particular, a maid who managed the laundry of proditors and higher commanders, marched up to the dais, unfazed by the threat of death. She stuck a finger in my face, demanded to be released back to Ashtanabo, and refused to be kept here by force. She didn't care that Knox was watching her. He even nodded his head as if she was making valid points.

He interrupted her speech and approached her, placing a hand on her back. *"Why don't you join me for lunch to help settle your nerves,"* he had said.

The next day, a new girl was assigned to pressing my uniform, and I never saw my laundry maid again.

Others have disobeyed regardless. To make a more public show of it, Knox threw a male servant out of the airlock with everyone watching. Most have stayed in line ever since.

Proditors may be higher up than the soldiers and workers, but they once respected us. Trusted us with their lives. And now we've imprisoned them within the confines of outer space.

"Are there any questions?" I ask the soldiers. This is the second time I've given them this exact speech, but most of them were still too entranced by ravens at the time to absorb it. Others are new arrivals to the Imnicus.

They keep their heads high, yet their eyes are lowered. During Knox's takeover, many of them survived by giving in to Knox's hallucinogenic ravens. They betrayed their comrades, killing those who sided with Milo. Now that the ravens have worn off, one can taste the shame inhabiting the room as their memories remind them of their wrongdoings. Some rub their fingertips together, as if trying to remove their friends' blood from their hands.

Once they were free of Knox's ravens, some couldn't handle the weight of what they'd done and took their own lives. The loss of Imnicus soldiers was enough that Crux had to have more soldiers sent from land to replenish the numbers. The new soldiers didn't realize until they arrived that they were now highly esteemed prisoners.

"You are dismissed," I command.

After the last soldier leaves, I turn to face Knox.

A white crown fits snugly around his forehead with chains hanging from the sides, resting against his golden curls. A capelet made of black and navy feathers covers his shoulders and fans out around his neck. The rest of his dark attire is well tailored and embellished with silver.

He throws his legs over the throne's armrest and claps his hands slowly. "Well done. I couldn't have addressed our military better myself. They respect you, you know?" He has that look on his face, like he wants me to kneel at his feet, kiss his boots, and treat him like some god.

Respected, I want to say. "I was just fulfilling my duties, Knox." I wince at the blunder. "Forgive me . . . *Colum*."

But Knox is in a jovial mood. He takes the mistake in stride, pondering the word like tasting a new dish.

"Colum," he says, satisfied. "Strange, isn't it? You'll get used to it eventually, and it will roll off your tongue with little effort. It was that way for me when Milo took the throne, remember? It was difficult, addressing my own cousin as Colum." Knox shakes his head and smiles, as if reliving fond old memories as if they haven't been at each other's throats since Milo left the womb.

I can't say Knox always despised him, but I'll never forget the resentment he embodied when Milo was named Balistar's official successor. Knox congratulated Milo, left for his dorm, and I didn't see him the rest of the evening. Consequently, a maid was found not long after mutilated in her room. Sometimes I wonder if that was Knox's first unauthorized kill after Balistar's death.

"There will be more addresses to the soldiers until I'm convinced that they are in true submission. Or until my attackers are caught."

If Knox learned it was Alarik and me who ambushed him to save Milo, what would he do? In that instance, I would have no choice but to escape on a ship to Ashtanabo. But the new security clearance system for reserving ships would make that close to im-possible.

"We will find them," I assure him. "Crux and Onyx are still questioning soldiers."

"Good. I've been so busy announcing the change in power to Ashtanabo that there's been no time to solve that little mystery."

"Ashtanabo is taking the news in stride. Leaders from every region have sent gifts to show their approval of your coronation. The chancellor of Ralia, the emperor of Susuku, and the Prime Minister of Zreath have requested meetings with you. The people are . . . adjusting."

"Tell the leaders I'll meet with them in time. My cousin's apprehension is at the forefront of my mind."

"Last Commander Aisil told me, nowhere in Ashtanabo has reported him. Wherever Milo is, he's well hidden."

"Hmm, can't you use that little bond of yours to track him?"

I take a long, slow inhale. "That's not how it works."

Or rather, that's not how it once worked. Recently, it has strengthened. Enough that I know that Milo is safe.

And that he's on Lavenai.

"If I recall, your family swore an oath to the entire Arris line," Knox adds.

"Direct line," I clarify.

His eyes narrow. "Oh, come on now. I'm sure it can be extended adjacently." He snaps his fingers to call someone in.

One of the side doors opens and a courtesan enters. She's dressed in lacy garments, her long legs on display. She kneels to my right facing the stairs, bowing her head to Knox.

"It's not just a verbal bond, but one that links Milo's and my crows, as well as our fathers'. I serve you as—" I lose my words. The truth of the matter is that I have no reason to serve Knox. I am just as much a prisoner as the rest of the maids and soldiers. "A proditor serving a Colum."

Knox purses his lips and signals to the courtesan. Great. We're having a conversation and he's already distracted by women.

Instead of going to him, she scoots in front of me on her knees. Knox grins.

What the hell does he think he's doing? I keep my composure as her smooth hands caress the leather of my boots and slide up my calves.

"You could bind your crows to me too, couldn't you?" Knox adjusts in his seat, crossing his legs. "Balistar was more than just an uncle, you know. He was a mentor, and more of a father than Callisto ever was to me."

"Eagle magic is long lost."

"Then perhaps we could pay a visit to the Vicars? Visit the Akumu forest and learn forbidden magic as Balistar once did. I hear there are dozens more birds."

"If visiting the Akumu forest was still possible, Balistar would have done it long ago."

The courtesan rubs her palms up my inner thighs and presses her lips to the front of one. My gloves crinkle as I curl my fists and conjure every thought possible to stop the blood from flowing to one place. I won't give Knox the satisfaction. He can't seduce me into breaking my oath.

"Such a shame," Knox says.

"I still serve you," I assure him, but don't fully believe it myself. "Whatever you need me to do, I will. But I cannot extend my oath to you."

As the girl reaches for my belt, I roughly grab her wrist.

"Ah, I see. I suppose that's that." Knox directs his attention to the courtesan. "Come here, Dove."

She pushes to her feet and walks up the dais toward Knox. Only then do I see it. The bruises lining her sides and back. She sits on his lap and presses her mouth to his defined neck, sucking on his skin and leaving marks of her own. If it pleases him, he doesn't show it.

"Do you have anything else to report?" Knox asks as the courtesan unbuttons the top of attire, exposing his chest and abdomen.

I keep my eyes level with his, refusing to break. "I do not."

"Then you are dismissed." He holds the back of the courtesan's neck and moves her up to straddle his lap, kissing her. His lithe fingers snake into her hair, and he groans softly into her mouth.

I turn away to leave as he spins her into the throne, trying to block out the sounds of clothes ruffling, moans, and tongues moving together. It's not as if I haven't seen Knox, or the other proditors, for that matter, bed women without regard to who else was in the room. But with Knox, there's always another element. Sex is only a front for what he really wants from girls, and I don't want to be anywhere near it.

This girl may have enjoyed the marks he left on her for now, but it won't be long before it's too late. That's always his play with women—find the masochists and get them hooked. Push them as far as they're willing until the day he's not playing anymore. He won't stop at love bites. Whatever he did to my laundry maid will be the same fate for this courtesan. She'll be nothing but cold flesh and a stagnant heart when he's finished with her.

I stop halfway down the runner. I should make up some excuse and get her to safety.

As I go to turn around, the throne room doors fly open. Commander Aisil rushes in with a slew of guards behind him.

Knox sighs and gently moves the courtesan off him. He zips his pants up, not bothering to replace his capelet or button his shirt. "This better be good."

"Colum," Aisil says with a look of panic on his face. "It's news from Ashtanabo."

"You found Milo? Good. Where is he?"

"No, it's not that." Aisil looks at me and then Knox again. "It's the temple points."

Knox frowns. "What about them?"

Commander Aisil visibly swallows. "Ralia's eastern point was just destroyed."

Chapter 7

Milo

Water drips onto my forehead from the tunnels, and I do my best to protect Margot's face from the droplets. My pants are soaked up past my ankles. It's so grimy that I'm having trouble believing there's a rebellion hiding down here. Was Joriel lying to us? Was this his way of getting me out of his hair for good? Trapping us underground with no way out?

With my senses heightened, a pulsing red light catches my eye—a well-disguised camera in the corner hiding among sewer scum and shadows.

"Which way?" Lleu whispers, as if we're trying not to be caught.

I use my crows to check for any nearby disturbances in the normal sound waves of the surrounding tunnels. My eardrums ripple with the crows' amplification, frantic footsteps headed in our direction. Quite a few pairs of them.

The rebellion knows we're here.

"Go left," I tell them.

After a few more turns, we stop in front of a door. It automatically scans Margot's face, but it takes longer to gloss over her features than I'd like. What if the rebellion has locked us out? But before I can hold on to the thought, the door opens.

Alarik and Lleu follow behind me as I slowly walk into the base. White-brick hallways surround us and it's a hell of a lot cleaner than the sewers. I take in a deep breath, the air clean and even more purified than Joriel's establishment. Something tells me the rebellion must have sponsors far above that crime lord if they can afford something like this.

Margot unconsciously quivers in my arms, so I press my lips to the top of her scalp. *Hold on, we're almost there.*

Or rather, *they're* almost here. I no longer need my crows to hear boots stomping or guns clicking against uniforms.

No matter what happens next, I can't regret it. Not as I beg them to help Margot, nor as they potentially lodge a bullet into my brain. The rebellion is a place I never thought I'd enter willingly. But that's the thing about fate—it's out of our control.

"They're over here!" someone shouts. "And he has Margot!"

I stop in my tracks as a group of rebels rush around the corner, weapons in hand. By the death glares on their faces, it's safe to say they know who I am.

They point their guns at us, and I don't want to know if I'd already be lying in a pool of my own blood if I weren't holding Margot. Alarik visibly tenses and holds Lleu closer to his side.

"Lie her down, slowly, then get on the ground!" a female rebel yells.

"Alarik—" Lleu chokes.

"Do as they say," he tells her.

I become overly aware of my heartbeat, realizing that each one could be my last. I kneel with Margot in my arms, place her on the ground in front of me, then raise my arms. Lleu and Alarik lay on their stomachs.

"Margot is bleeding internally, and if she doesn't get medical attention quickly, she'll die," I explain firmly.

"I said on your stomach, Colum!" the girl yells again.

Before anyone can act, a figure rounds the corner—a middle-aged woman with white-blonde hair. There is a certain air about her, one filled with all the confidence and political passion someone needs to be a leader. One where her subordinates highly respect her. She's the kind of person who can control rooms with a single glance.

So when she looks at Margot half-dead, and then me with fury, I almost lose my guts.

The woman pulls the firearm off her holster and stomps forward. She grabs my collar and places the barrel right against my forehead. "What did you do to her?"

"Nothing!" I grit. "But if you don't get her help immediately, she won't make it!"

My crows sense Alarik's energy behind me, amping up for a fight. Yet when this many firearms are involved, there's nothing he can do. Crows don't make him bulletproof.

"Send for the medics," she commands the other rebels. "Colum, I don't know what drug you gave her, or how you used her face to get through our entrances, but I'll tell you one thing—you will personally pay for every single one of her injuries."

"Her injuries were not my doing." I bite the inside of my cheek, controlling how much more I want to lash out. This woman looks as though she dreams every night of killing me, and I don't doubt she actually does. "I'm not here as an enemy."

"Ah, then what are you here for? What business does the man who hunts us like rabbits have with the rebellion?"

She won't listen to reason in this state, but I must try to convince her that I'm not here with ill intent. "The game our planets once played is ending and a new one is about to begin. Not even I can stop it."

"Meaning?"

"My cousin besieged my throne, killing the arbitors in his wake."

"And Margot's injury?"

"Caused by him and a group of rogue proditors. Margot must have not realized the extent of her injuries, and by the time we learned of them, she had already collapsed."

"Are you saying she is traveling with you on her own accord?"

I glance over at Margot's unconscious body. "I don't think she likes it anymore than I do. But after she got sick, we didn't know where else to go that had the capabilities of treating her."

The woman lowers her weapon, but I know she isn't convinced. "So nobody from Ashtanabo knows you're here?"

I nod. "Nobody, I swear."

"Good. Then you'll be that much easier to kill." She raises the gun again.

I close my eyes, bracing for the blow. Will these really be my final breaths? I can't say I don't deserve it. Lleu's sobs echo throughout the hallway.

"Lucinda, wait a second!" another feminine voice says.

The woman with icy blonde hair, Lucinda, lowers her gun, and I sigh a breath of relief.

But that breath immediately stops, along with time itself, when the second woman steps into the hallway.

All at once, I'm a young Vicar boy again who spent his evenings standing on a chair, helping his mother cook. Who laid his head on her lap while she read him bedtime stories from handwritten books bound with twine.

Seeing her is like being hit in the face with ice water or being struck by lightning.

My mother stands there, her once raven hair peppered with time. I can't form a word. A thought. She stares at me with widened eyes and labored breaths.

Everything feels numb and my chest constricts. All this time I thought she was on Ashtanabo.

What is she doing here?

My mother doesn't address me. Instead, she redirects her attention to Lucinda. She can barely seem to look at me anymore. "I would like to discuss this before we make any decisions on his fate."

Lucinda holsters her gun. "I'm not sure this is up for negotiation."

"He holds valuable information. Intel more valuable than my network of informants. At the very least, interrogate him first. Then we can come to a decision."

Lucinda pauses. "What could you provide?"

It feels impossible to think after nearly dying. Or after seeing my mother. But I manage to muster up a few things. "Air traffic procedures, supply routes, military protocols. Hell, I can even draw the internal workings of a ship engine if that's something you'd want."

Lucinda considers this, pacing in front of me while everyone waits for her answer with bated breaths. Finally, she stops in place and glares at me. "Take him and the other boy to the cells. Give the girl a locked and guarded room."

Medics finally rush around the corner with a gurney and roll Margot onto it. She's gotten paler since we've arrived.

As the guards drag us away, my mother doesn't spare me another glance, turning her back and going about her way.

Chapter 8

Milo

The rebellion cells are made of glass, yet they're suffocating. Alarik seems to think so too, his eyes closed like the surrounding cell is the last thing he wants to see. I know Lleu being imprisoned elsewhere is driving him crazy.

All of us knew the risks when we decided to go underground. The risk that, even if the opportunity presents itself, I'll never be able to return to my throne after turning myself into the rebellion. But the longer I'm away from it, the less it weighs on me, even given what I've been through since arriving on Lavenai. It makes me wonder if I'd even want it back.

I sit on the ground next to the cot, leaning my head against the glass, letting my breath fog it up. A gun was just held to my head, and hell, I just saw my mother again for the first time since childhood. Yet Margot is all I can think of.

The guards say I'm not entitled to an update on her health, and I wish she were near enough for my crows to reach out to her. Did they have to do surgery? Have her vitals stabilized?

The rebellion leader put up a front, but I know she was worried for her. I remember my father telling me about Lucinda Demille-Watts and his jaded past with her. He often muttered her name in anger under his breath on bad days. He tried to use her and the leader of her former crime organization to take over Lavenai. But she resisted and refused the plans her superior had for her. Her kind face is deceiving and she's as dangerous as they come. Apparently, she and hundreds of others had been injected, against their will, with some experimental drug derived from dark matter. She was the only survivor.

During my reign, I haven't heard any reports of rebels using drugs from the Laven drug wars to succeed in missions. The drug empire fell into oblivion after my father took over, with most of their warehouses destroyed at his command so that Lavenai had no way to fight against his proditors.

I wonder if my father would have made use of such drugs again had he lived longer. He mentioned it once or twice toward the end of his life, but the drugs were one of many threads left unfinished. One of many I abandoned in the chaos of my succession.

The mystery of his death is something no one has come even close to solving. Poison was found on his body, but no evidence of where it came from. There was a maid accused in the aftermath. One who was already rumored to be sleeping with him, but that was debunked quickly. My father truly never took another lover after my mother. That much was certain.

Alarik sits on the ground with his hands folded. "Your mother looks well."

"She wouldn't even look at me."

"Maybe not . . . but she saved your life."

He's right about that. By all accounts, she could have let me die. And considering how long it's been since she's seen me, I wouldn't be surprised if she had. It's not like she loves me to the degree she did when I was three.

I smooth my hair out of my face. "Margot knew the entire time that my mother was here and never told me."

"I don't think she thought you had a right to know."

"Yes, but she could have used it against me."

"And I suppose that shows the kind of person she is. And the kind you are."

I shoot a confused glance at him. He's being a bit . . . demeaning. "You're a lot more bold now that I'm not in power."

"Yeah, well . . . " Alarik scratches his jaw. "I've not always been your most dedicated proditor."

"Because you went behind my back and helped Margot survive her interrogation, right? I don't think having a heart makes you disloyal."

Alarik says nothing and breaks eye contact.

"What?" I ask.

"It's . . . nothing, Milo."

"Don't tell me you considered joining up with Knox too."

He quickly shakes his head. "Nothing like that. Though I can't say I've always agreed with your actions either."

I frown. Now isn't the time for me to pick a fight with Alarik, but I know we're no longer talking as superior and subordinate. "What aren't you telling me?"

Alarik sighs, frustrated. "I'm the one who sent Margot the letter and helped her escape the Imnicus. And I don't regret it."

Realization crashes over me. I don't know what else to do, so I stand and start pacing my cell, unable to look at him for the next minute or so. He says nothing to soften the blow.

How could I have been so blind? Because I wanted him to be loyal to me the way he was when we were teens?

Am I angry? Upset? Part of me wants to yell. To feel anything negative toward Alarik whatsoever. But with everything that has shifted, I feel absolutely nothing but a stark surprise. Maybe a little hurt. Alarik and I used to be close. Yet he's spent most of his adulthood secretly undermining me.

I stop in place and finally look at him. "You're becoming more honest. I'm not sure I like it."

"Well, I'd get used to it. I hated your father, maybe more than a Laven would."

"And I'm assuming you hate me too?"

"No." Alarik rubs his thumb pads together. "Deep down, I knew you weren't him, and if fate had given you a choice, you would have stayed a Vicar."

The prison doors slide open, and Alarik and I immediately end the conversation. Yet the looming thoughts stick. Thoughts of who I could have been if my father weren't Balistar Arris.

Lucinda enters with a group of armed guards, that jaded frown still painting her face. "Milo Arris, per Imory Nolan's request, you will be interrogated before any final decisions are made about your fate. Or your usefulness."

I know Lucinda despises me. Not to mention I killed off many of her rebels over the last six months. I'd be insane to think I deserve anything less than a painful death by her hand.

I stand and raise my hands above my head as the guards unlock the cell door. "I won't fight you."

By the grimace on her face, I can tell my cooperation bothers her. She wants me to be as horrible as my father was. She wants to look into my eyes and see him. It would make ending my life that much easier.

Alarik watches while they pull me from the cell and cuff my wrists. At this point, if my mother recognized Alarik, they wouldn't touch him, knowing he's a proditor. Not unless his hands and every inch of his skin are covered.

They lead me down the hall and into a rectangular room with concrete walls. Dust covers the table and two chairs, and a single bulb hangs from the ceiling.

The guards connect my cuffs to metal rings on the table, and once I'm secured, the guards exit, leaving me all alone with Lucinda.

She doesn't take a seat. Instead, she folds her arms and leans her upper back against the far wall. "Should we start with how you managed to trespass? Or should I ask about how you beat my star rebel half to death?"

"Please tell me she's all right."

She's silent for a second. "Yes. It took some work, but she's stable now."

I breathe an audible sigh of relief. "Thank the gods."

Lucinda raises an eyebrow. "Suffice to say, I'm having trouble believing your version of the story—that your cousin besieged the Imnicus, beat her, then you both escaped and sought the rebellion out for treatment. In what world would she trust you? And why would you have any desire to save her?"

There's a lot Lucinda doesn't seem to know, namely my complicated relationship with Margot. I won't readily admit to the romantic part of things. At the moment, Margot and I aren't anything. We just slipped up once.

Rather recently.

I word my answer carefully. "My cousin decided I wasn't worthy of ruling. He claimed I no longer aligned with my father's ideals, and in turn, he slaughtered the arbitors to put himself next in line. The arbitors had already sentenced me to be nymbed, but when Knox realized Monicas would be taking my place, he was furious."

There's a flicker in Lucinda's eyes indicating that she might believe me. "It was the crime lord I once served, Donovan Mac-Manus, that invented nymbing." She looks around the cell. "In this very underground that once served as his headquarters."

"I was told that you murdered Mr. MacManus."

Lucinda's eyes darken. "He was like a father to me."

But she doesn't deny killing him.

Lucinda finally takes a seat in the metal chair across from me. "Tell me . . . what is the nature of your relationship with Margot?"

"Relationship?"

"Don't play dumb with me. We have cameras everywhere. You kissed her head."

Dammit. I didn't even think twice about it when I did it. I was just worried. "Recently we found a mutual ground and wanted to stop my cousin together, with your help, I will add. It was nothing more than concern."

"There seems to be a crater-sized hole in your story, Colum." Lucinda frowns. "How many times did you sleep with her before she regained her memories? And don't lie. Any more dishonesty during this interrogation will only shorten what little time you have left."

I exhale deeply. "I lost count."

Lucinda rubs her temples and curses under her breath. "And after she regained them?"

"Twice."

"When was the last time?"

I avoid eye contact with her. "A few days ago."

Lucinda scoffs and lets out an insincere laugh. "Unbelievable."

Margot is going to be pissed at what I just admitted. But if I want to gain Lucinda's trust and stay alive, I can't cover things up. "Neither of us planned it, and it was never my intention to bed her.

Know that she's as loyal as they come to the rebellion and would never choose me over her morals."

"I know. It's why I haven't branded her as a compromised agent. Though I won't deny I'm disappointed." Lucinda scratches the back of her neck. "You killed many of her friends very recently, if I recall correctly. Gallow machines? Those haven't been used in two decades."

"I know there's no way you will ever trust me, but believe what my mother said—if you keep me alive, you will have an edge over the Arris Reign that you've never had before. I know more insider secrets than anyone. Passcodes into bases. Weak points. Staffing issues. Secret storage facilities. You name it, I'll get it for you."

"I'll be frank with you, Colum. I want you dead. As soon as possible."

The muscles in my neck tense. Will she really forgo the most valuable source of information the rebellion has ever had just to fulfill her need for revenge?

"But, I highly respect your mother," she adds. "Unless she approves of your execution, I will never go against her wishes. She's been an invaluable resource to us, so I will do her this favor. Just know, you'll remain nothing but a prisoner for the rest of your life. We will use your information and your secrets, and you will receive nothing in return. Not a scrap of payment, no favors, and certainly no forgiveness."

Chapter 9

Dune

Eastern Ralia lies in devastation—thousands of miles of land destroyed and millions of people left without homes, and soon without food. Displayed on the monitors in the command center, crops are taken over by sharp weeds. Many trees have grown five times their natural size, uprooting houses from the foundation.

I always knew Ashtanabo would be unrecognizable if a temple point ever fell, but I never thought it would be this bad again. The only way out of eastern Ralia now is by ship, but most of those have been taken by the floods. Part of me wonders if the rebellion ever considered the level of catastrophe that would occur by destroying a temple point.

Knox sits at one of the commanders' large desks, unblinking as he watches the footage of cities reverting back into their pre-Balistar state within the span of hours. I can't decipher his expression, nor what's going on in his head. But whatever he's thinking, it isn't good.

Commander Aisil clears his throat. "A ship can be prepared to leave for western Ralia within the hour. We must speak with Chancellor Ekon about relief efforts."

"Now isn't the time for relief," Knox says. "We have fugitives to apprehend."

"But, the Ralians . . . without help . . . "

"Do you suggest the Colum himself holds Chancellor Ekon's hand? He has advisors. An army. Proditors. I cannot be everywhere at once, and he was assigned by my uncle to manage situations like this."

I'd understand Knox's argument if forty million people weren't affected. He at least owes the chancellor electronic correspondence or some kind of mass statement of condolence. Knox doesn't have the luxury of arbitors to do the dirty work on land until he assigns his own council, and there's no time for that any time soon. The cards he's being dealt are changing too quickly.

Knox scoots back and kicks his feet onto the desk. "Margot and her rebellion friends were already in pursuit of the temple points, so it's easy to deduce who did this. Do we have a read on their faces?"

Commander Aisil frowns. "Their faces were covered, unfortunately."

Aisil damn well knows we have their faces, and I could expose his lie if I desired to. I was the only one with him when we saw them on surveillance. A part of me thought he would reveal that information, maybe just to quell the rumors that he is a coward. From the stories I heard, there was a time before when he was not so passive. The times before he met Balistar. Some say Balistar never would have overtaken Ashtanabo without Aisil's help.

"My cousin encountered them by the Susukan temple point, didn't he? You're telling me there is not a single record of their confirmed faces?" Knox spits.

Aisil nods. "It was back before Milo ordered heavy guarding and surveillance of the temple points. Before Matsumoto's prison escape, nothing could take those points down."

Perhaps I underestimated the commander after all. I know he worked very closely with Milo and me to apprehend Margot on Ashtanabo. For years, Aisil has been the passive commander, who won his title by aiding Balistar, and then coasted through his quiet life on the Imnicus. But with Knox threatening it, well, it seems the man has more of a backbone than I realized. He's wise to keep his undermining subtle enough that nobody notices. I'm sure as hell not going to expose his plans.

An officer clears his throat. "Colum Arris, I have intel that may help." He stands at attention in his tidy dark green uniform, not a hair or thread out of place.

Knox reclines further. "Let us hear it."

The officer keeps his head held high, but doesn't make direct eye contact with Knox. "It was a top secret endeavor, but soldiers on Ashtanabo did catch wind of the rebellion fugitives. I was the one who received the message. They were ready to apprehend them at the order of the Colum, but then he . . . " The officer takes a deep breath. "He said that it wasn't them. In short, Milo was without a doubt lying, but I don't have the faintest idea why. After all, he was the one who gave us the assignment in the first place."

"And you were the only one on the Imnicus who saw the footage beside Milo? Why didn't you say anything?"

"I got the transmission shortly before, well . . . you know. It took a backseat in my mind until now."

Knox's lips curl, and I fight the urge to close my eyes in disappointment. If Knox gets his hands on Margot's friends, he'll do more than simply execute them.

"Show us the footage." Knox motions to the surrounding screens.

The officer nods and moves to a station, searches the archives, and brings up a video of Anali Matsumoto and Margot Tavish's rebellion friends sneaking through a city in Zreath.

Knox watches closely, studying their faces intently. And he never forgets a face.

"What's your name?" Knox asks.

"Fredrick Bellis."

"Well, today, Fredrick, I am promoting you to commander. We're down a few, so the promotion is immediate. Does that sound favorable to you?"

Officer Bellis's face lights up, while everyone else in the room becomes further on edge. Becoming a commander takes years of hard work and dedication, and it's something many young men dream of but rarely accomplish. Yet Knox is just handing out the title like candy.

"Y-yes! I accept, Colum. Thank you," the officer says.

"Then I put you in charge of apprehending them once again."

"Of course."

"And bring them in *alive*. We can't have others following in their footsteps." Knox hones in on Aisil. "The rebellion cannot go unpunished. Drastic measures must be taken."

"What do you suggest, Colum?" Aisil asks.

"I have something in mind. Something that might supersede how far my uncle was willing to go to stop them."

His words send chills down my spine. Something worse than what Balistar would do?

After I shower in the proditor quarters, there's a knock on my door. I tighten the towel sitting low on my hips and check the video intercom.

Crux and Onyx stand there waiting, fully masked in their proditor armor. But why at this hour? I imagine myself opening the door, listening to those impending, yet unsurprising words, *"Dune Catawnee, you're under arrest for conspiring against the Arris Reign."* After all, they wouldn't send guards to arrest me.

I open the door. "Yes?"

Onyx leans against my door frame and crosses his arms. "Get dressed, we're going to the Jupiter."

"Now?" There are still droplets of water on my skin. My relief immediately turns to annoyance.

"Come on, Dune. We've done nothing but work recently. Trust me, it will be fun."

Crux rolls his eyes at Onyx. It seems I'm not the only one being roped into having a night out. Right now, they're the last two I want to be trapped in a nightclub with. Crux mostly. To think we grew up together. Broke bread. Experienced so many firsts as near-brothers. First girl. First drink.

First kill.

But if I don't go, they may sense something is off. Normally when I'm on the Imnicus, I never decline their invitations, as I'm planet-side more often than not.

"Give me ten minutes," I say.

After I get dressed and dry my hair, the three of us are off to the Jupiter. I can't help but wonder why they'd still want to club during times like these. Of course, I've never been much for nights out.

Still, everything is so up in the air. Maybe it's easy for them to relax when Knox isn't testing their loyalty at every turn.

Once we arrive at the Jupiter, it seems everyone is coping with Knox's transition by finding the bottom of a bottle. Soldiers and servants fill the club, dancing, drinking, and doing anything to keep their minds off their present reality. A reality where their dream job has now left them imprisoned in space.

We take our regular leather booth in the VIP area. Robo-servants deliver our usual drinks instead of a human or humanoid, which I try not to let bother me. I take my lemon seltzer water off the tray. I'm not too fond of alcohol and drink it maybe once a year. It's not within Nonakan culture to overindulge. I suppose it's why my family meshed so well with the Vicars.

The server closes the curtain and we remove our masks.

"Oh, come on Dune. Are you really going to drink that crap again?" Onyx takes a large swig of his liquor and sets it down firmly enough for some to spill over the sides.

"The crows don't like alcohol."

Crux scoffs. "Try telling Knox that."

"Is he the best example?" I counter.

Crux runs his thumb along the handle of his glass mug. "Tell us, Dune, how are you adjusting to Knox's reign?"

It's a trick question. Any honesty will be used against me, and both of them know me well enough that I can't completely lie through my teeth either. "I'll admit that it took me off guard. He conspired with you both and made no plans to consult Alarik or me."

"And now?" Onyx asks.

"I'm a proditor. It wouldn't be hard to sneak out on a ship if I didn't want to be here."

Crux nods in approval, my answer acceptable enough. However, I see the true purpose of this outing now. To get me drunk, test my allegiance, then report back to Knox.

"There is one thing you have wrong, though," Crux says. "Knox only let me in on his plans, not Onyx."

I make eye contact with Onyx. He had no idea what Knox was going to do, and yet he's one of Knox's closest confidants right now. Before all this, he was almost as loyal to Milo as I was. Sure, he liked to defy him when it came to drinking and girls, but never once had he challenged him about his ruling.

Onyx shrugs. "When Knox told me to join him, I agreed."

Although he's not saying it, Onyx must be thinking of his father. He means, *"If I didn't side with Knox, whose ideals resemble Balistar's more than Milo's, what would Kyouya Tanaka think?"*

I focus in on Crux. "And you?"

Crux folds his arms. "I'm on the side of anyone who will end Margot."

"Margot? Why her?" Of course, stopping her and the rebellion has been our plan all along. But I didn't expect Crux to be so . . . personally invested?

"It's none of your damn business." Crux finishes off his drink, replaces his mask, and leaves from behind the curtain to go out into the more public booths.

I sit there, more confused than when we first arrived. What business does Crux have with Margot that the rest of us don't?

"Well, it looks like it's time for the night to start." Onyx stands and stretches.

"Wait." I grab hold of his forearm and pull him back down. "What does Crux want with Margot?"

Onyx looks away and takes a deep breath. "He'll kill me if I tell you."

"He'll already do that for even smaller infractions."

Onyx scratches his white-blonde hair. "Do you remember Lorali from the Vicar temple?"

The name comes back to me vaguely. Mostly because I was enrolled in the school, not the temple. "She was in her early thirties, right? Unmarried?"

He nods. "She was one of Crux's mentors."

I know anything about the temple is a sore spot for Crux. As an orphan, he was the only one of the five of us proditors who had to go there. The only one who watched his father take his mother's life and then his own right inside their hut's kitchen. His sister was quickly adopted afterwards, but him? Nobody wanted to take in the son of a madman.

"What does that have to do with Margot?" I ask.

"Lorali was beautiful. Blonde. Curly. Similar complexion."

Now I remember Lorali's face as clear as day. She never took a husband or lover, even though she was the most sought-after woman in all of Eskdale.

Onyx continues, "There were always rumors about the temple students and the ways they were treated. Once when Crux was drunk, he accidentally told me the story and—well, I'll just leave that between him and me."

I don't let my mind theorize what Lorali did. All I need is Crux's bitter rage to confirm that Onyx's words are true. "He knows that punishing Margot won't erase what she did to him, right?"

"Eskdale is sealed off for probably the rest of eternity, and he'll never be able to get his rage out on Lorali herself. So he's going for the next best thing."

I can't pretend to understand Crux. He's violent. Angry. And I only ever see him smile when everyone else is frowning.

"Can we go out there now?" Onyx asks like a child wanting to play outside.

I nod, replacing my mask.

When we emerge from behind the curtain, Crux is already in another booth with his arms around two off-duty maids.

They run their hands across his chest and along his thighs. He doesn't even look at them, watching the dance floor from across the room. It seems he'll need at least two more drinks before the barely tolerable version of himself awakens.

Eyes are already on us. Most from terrified Imnicus employees who once didn't fear our presence. All of us proditors could let off steam at the Jupiter without constant sets of eyes. But after Knox's siege, those days are mostly over. Somehow, there are still a few women who can turn a blind eye to the slaughter Crux and Onyx performed in the command center.

This is why I prefer our time off, when we take off our disguises and go to Ashtanaban clubs on land, nobody the wiser of who we really are.

The rest of the night goes how it normally does. We drink, and women approach us. Onyx tries dancing before he realizes the energy is completely off. I can't ignore the hint of pain in his eyes. Out of all of us, Imnicus personnel liked him the most.

It's not until a few hours later, when Onyx and Crux are drunk off their asses flirting with the same woman, that I posture to leave.

"Wait . . . we'll come with you," Onyx says, inebriated.

They slide out of the booth and follow behind me. It isn't until we're a few hallways down that I hear a giggle and look over my shoulder. A girl walks between Crux and Onyx, her arms linked with theirs. Ah, so it's going to be that kind of evening.

When we get back to the proditor quarters, Onyx has gotten more handsy with the maid and Crux is fumbling to unlock Onyx's door. It's far from the first time they've shared a girl.

"Well, goodnight." I open my door.

"You're not joining?" Onyx asks. "Becs is more than happy."

I eye the girl. Even after the siege, she looks more than happy to have proditors all over her. Somehow, it makes her just as terrifying as the two of them.

"I think I'm good," I say.

"Suit yourself." Onyx playfully pushes her into the room. Within seconds he has her blindfolded and kissing noises ensue.

Crux watches me carefully as he steps into Onyx's room. "Goodnight, Dune."

My jaw twitches. "Goodnight."

Chapter 10

Margot

I claw my way through a dense labyrinth of fog. Each turn looks different from the last, and just when I think I'm close to escaping it, I'm back at the beginning of the maze.

Crows land at my feet, and another perches on my shoulder. A ripple of their magic rushes through my veins, pumping through my heart like blood. Promising me things no human or even proditor can.

Your purpose isn't complete, they tell me.

A crow with white streaks on its wings takes off in flight ahead of me. I follow it.

Every turn of a corner gets me further through the maze than my last attempt. The other crows follow alongside me, and though I'm making the choice that any human would in letting them guide me out of here, my thoughts don't let me take comfort in it.

Should I be trying to escape this? Is the other side of peace really so much worse than the other side of life?

Still, a soft light glows in the distance. The white-streaked crow perches itself upon a gate near it.

When I enter through the gate, a painful pressure hits my chest and claws grip my ankles, pulling me beneath a surface. I don't thrash. I don't scream. Not even as I fall deeper and deeper . . .

"Margot? Are you awake?"

I slowly blink my eyes open. A flood of light beams from the ceiling. Machines surround me, some monitoring my vitals, others pumping fluids into my veins. My other senses start to return. Medical machines beep around me at a steadily rising rhythm. Faint stale notes of blood stick to the back of my tongue.

When I see who is standing at the end of my bed, I figure I must be dreaming.

"Lucinda?" I try to sit up, but a sharp pain shoots across my abdomen. Nope. Not dreaming.

"Easy." Lucinda elevates the bed for me. "You're not in any condition to be moving around yet."

I sit back and place my hands on my stomach. "I don't under-stand . . . Am I dead?"

"You nearly were." She takes a seat on a chair next to my bed. "You're back at the rebellion."

Nothing after I collapsed at Joriel's brothel comes back to me, which means I haven't been conscious in any capacity since then.

Wait, but Milo was with me. Alarik and Lleu too. "Did Joriel bring me here?"

Lucinda smiles weakly, and I don't know how to read her ex-pression. It's disconcerting. Maybe it's because she hates hospitals and all things medical, given her past with them. "Let's make this a debriefing. Then we can rehash what happened to you."

"Okay." I don't like this at all. The Lucinda I know would usually ease into things like that. Ask me how I'm feeling, maybe even scold me in love. But I can sense the wall she's put up, and I promptly put up one of my own.

Lucinda folds her hands together. "Where are Oliver and Dimitri?"

It takes a second for me to fight through my grogginess and recall the information, but eventually I find the answer. "They're still on Ashtanabo. I had a run in with a proditor and we got separated."

"Do you know if they're still alive?"

"I hope."

"And the status of the temple points?"

"All intact." I feel somewhat disappointed. All this chaos has happened, yet we have nothing to show for it. "We got close once in Susuku but it was saved by a proditor before it could fully be destabilized."

"Then I assume you found Matsumoto?"

"Yes. She's as powerful as Imory said."

"And how did you get back to Lavenai?"

The surrounding air is stiff and I become uncomfortable in my own skin. I can't admit to her that I escaped the Imnicus with the Colum, a proditor, and an actress-turned-maid Milo once used to deceive me. "It's complicated."

Lucinda's lips form into a straight line. "Is there something you want to tell me?"

Of course, how could I forget? "Knox Arris has taken control of the throne. The arbitors are dead. I'm not sure how much time is left before it's announced to Lavenai."

Her eyes drop in disappointment.

"Lucinda?"

"I never thought you'd be the type to omit the truth from me, Margot. Have I not been like a mother to you?"

My face pales.

"I'll only ask you once. Did you escape the Imnicus alone?"

The weight of a thousand rocks falls onto my stomach. "No." A realization strikes me, threatening to swallow me whole. "He's here, isn't he?"

Lucinda's eyes flash in anger. "The rebellion is now compromised because of your actions. And after everything we've worked toward—"

"Lucinda, I would never let him in!" But how Milo managed to get past Joriel's entrance is beyond me. "Believe me!"

"Maybe that's true about the base . . . but what else have you let him into?"

My hands shake and I can hear my heartbeat increasing on the monitor. "I don't know what you're talking about."

"Stop lying." Lucinda raises her voice. Her eyes dip to the black diamond ring on my thumb, as if she realizes whose it truly is. That it wasn't just a souvenir. "Why won't you tell me the truth?"

"Because how could I? You'd never forgive me!" I bury my face in my hands and then angrily swipe my hair out of my face. "I went against every value. Every rebellion moral. Is that what you want to hear, Lucinda?" My breaths are laden with fury, not at Lucinda, but at myself.

Lucinda laughs sarcastically. "And do you really think he loves you back? That he didn't manipulate you, injure you, and then knock you out to gain access to our base?"

"My loyalty will always be to the rebellion."

"Your comrades don't seem to think so. Rumors are spreading faster than I can control. They were already on edge after you last returned. After the Colum showed up on our doorstep, one asked me if we should scan your brain for some kind of mind-control chip. Others think you're on the brink of betraying us all with those crows you hold."

"I've known many of them our whole lives. They should know I'd never turn them over to the Arris Reign."

"How can they believe you? How can *I*? You told Dimitri and me you never slept with him, but that couldn't be further from the truth. You know I'm not against manipulation tactics when it comes to missions, even more controversial ones, but this . . . I could forgive you for what you did before I restored your memories, lies or not. But days ago, Margot?"

Milo told her? "Him and I are nothing." The words hurt as they leave my lips and I know as well as Lucinda that they're far from true. "Have you interrogated him?"

"Yes. And he's a lot more forthcoming than you've been." I've never seen Lucinda so upset with me, but I can't blame her. Milo was the son of the man who helped destroy her life. Destroy the planets. Her soul has never found rest because of him. So Milo waltzing into the rebellion so easily must be eating away at her.

"What are you going to do with me?" I ask.

"I'm not sure. For all I know, the entire base has been compromised beyond repair. Thanks to Joriel, the Intrus Beta Protocol has now been disabled. It's not hard to deduce how Milo got in."

Is she really considering kicking me out because of this? After everything I've done? After everything my mission has put me through? "You know, I'm not the only one to get involved with someone I wasn't supposed to."

Lucinda's eyes flicker, and for a second, she looks more my age than her own. Perhaps bringing *him* up was a bad move. Two decades have passed since then, and I know it was a low blow.

Her eyes shift back to cold iron, glaring even worse than before. "Which is why I know just how dangerous it can be."

There's a knock and the door slides open. A medic pops her head in. "It's so good to see you awake, Margot. May I, Lucinda?"

Lucinda nods, but I know this conversation is far from over.

The medic goes about her assessments on me, and the entire time, Lucinda stays. If the medic notices any kind of tension between Lucinda and me, she doesn't show it.

After she presses on my tender abdomen a few times, I forget all about our argument. What the woman tells me next could change the entire trajectory of my life. If going untreated caused permanent damage, my career as a spy will be over, regardless of what Lucinda says.

Finally, the medic steps away and types a few things into her tablet.

"Am I going to be okay?" I ask.

"Normally with severe internal bleeding, we'd be looking at everything from organ failure, shock, drains . . . "

I lie there in dreaded anticipation.

"Thankfully, your body responded extremely well to our treatments. In all honesty, most people in the same condition would have died already. What I'm saying is, your recovery shouldn't have been possible."

Lucinda and I exchange a glance.

"Elaborate, please," Lucinda says for me.

"Her lab results are incredible given how bad of shape she was in. I'm stumped. It's as if something else is healing her."

I don't know what she is talking about. Something is keeping me alive?

"We'll do an iron infusion today. Tomorrow, you can be discharged with pain medicine. You'll still have some soreness and headaches, but as far as I'm concerned, you no longer need the medic bay," the woman says.

This is impossible. I had internal bleeding, and now I'm nearly healed? It seems Lucinda is just as shocked as me. But there's this gnawing feeling in my chest that replaces itself with the stroke of a crow's wing.

It can't be . . . unless . . . I need to speak to Milo as soon as possible.

The medic gives me a few more instructions before leaving us alone.

Lucinda takes a deep inhale and stands. "At the end of the day, disciplinary action would be an irresponsible use of our time. If Knox Arris is currently running the show, then we need to be ready for what he'll bring upon Lavenai."

"He was the one who . . ." I motion to my back where the jagged neck-to-sacral scar lives.

"I remember. If that's what he enjoys behind closed doors, then I can't imagine what he'll do in public. I am going to speak with Imory. As you can imagine, she's shaken up about this."

Imory. Oh gods.

Has Milo seen her yet? I can't even imagine what is going through his head right now. Is he angry at me? In shock?

"You rest up then take one of the visitor suites for the time being. I'll spare you your shared room given the rebel tensions of having Milo Arris imprisoned in-house." Lucinda moves toward the door. "Your comrades are not happy."

Chapter 11

Margot

The medic gives me an infusion late in the evening, and I'm discharged in the morning. I thought Lucinda might have another rebel escort me around like some prisoner, or worse, thrown into a cell.

Instead, I am released to roam freely, which is somewhat a relief. She has revoked some of my security access, meaning weapons and intel rooms are off limits. So are the holding cells, which is difficult because I have questions for Milo that need answers.

I at least have to see him, even if it's through a screen.

Other rebels take notice of me, stopping to watch me pass. None of them offer me a word of condolence for barely surviving. Nor do they spare me the most pitiful of smiles.

Many of them narrow their eyes or cross their arms. To them, it doesn't matter if I survived the Imnicus twice or brought our rebellion closer than we've ever come to dismantling the Arris

Reign. The second Milo stepped into the rebellion with me in his arms, they knew I had gotten too close to Ashtanabo's people.

I was already on thin ice the last time I returned with crows inhabiting my mind. They know I'm stronger than them. Dangerous. And they don't even know half of it. My crows sneer and laugh at all of them as I walk past the silent groups of rebels, and for a second, it feels like all of them see my crows as visibly as I do. I'm no better than a proditor to them. And with Knox's crows, I'm worse.

I ignore the rebels until I find the surveillance room that serves the prisons, which typically goes unmanned. Mostly because we've never had prisoners before.

As I step inside the security room, I stop dead in my tracks.

Imory sits in front of the cameras, her hands folded under her chin as she watches the feed—the feed of Milo sitting in the corner of his cell. His forearm rests on his propped-up kneecap and a small five o'clock shadow has formed along his jaw.

I swallow. Because I hid my wounds, I not only forced Milo's hand in being reunited with a lost family member. But hers too. I wish I could have warned her, but getting in contact with the rebellion is difficult for a reason.

Milo saved my life, and because of it, his own is at risk. Lleu and Alarik's too. Part of me feels guilt. I should have been honest with the others about my condition, or at least realized the severity of it. I wasn't thinking straight, but to be honest, I haven't been for a long time now.

Alarik is on another screen, sleeping on a hard cot. I imagine him dreaming of Lleu. Lucinda spared her a cell and placed her in a guarded room instead. She must be terrified.

I clear my throat. "Imory?"'

Imory jumps in her seat and quickly wipes her cheek with her shoulder. "I'm sorry, I didn't hear you come in." When she turns to look at me, her eyes are bloodshot and that normal put-together joy usually radiating from her face is nowhere to be seen. "Are you feeling better?"

"The medic gave me a good prognosis." My eyes dip to her fiddling fingers. "How are you?"

Imory forces a smile, but it doesn't shield the truth. "I'm well. Most of all, I'm happy to see you are all right. Lucinda said you could have died."

"That's one way to put it." I dig the toe of my shoe into the ground. "You know, you could go speak to him if you wanted to."

"I'll see him in my own time," Imory says shortly. "Right now, there are bigger things to be dealt with. Like Knox."

"That and regaining Lucinda's trust."

"She might be upset at you, and rightfully so, but I don't think there's anything you could do to make her not trust you. You're like a daughter to her and her pain will fade. Trust me on that." Imory stands and leaves her keycard on the table with a wink. "If you'll excuse me, I have a virtual meeting with one of my informants."

"Yes, don't let me keep you." I move out of the door frame to let her through.

She gives me a smile and goes about her way.

Imory is a good woman who loves to help everyone she meets. There isn't a world in which she deserved to marry someone who became the most wicked man in the galaxy. When the roles were reversed, and Ashtanabo was the impoverished planet, she moved there willingly to provide relief. It's how she met Balistar. Would she still have gone had she known her own planet would be in danger because of him?

I pick up the keycard and unlock the door into the holding area to step inside.

Alarik is still fast asleep, not so much as twitching as the door whooshes shut behind me. But another set of eyes is locked on me, studying my abdomen, then my face.

"Margot." Milo stands quickly, placing his hands on the glass. His lips are parted, eyes in a state of shock. I can only assume they haven't been giving him updates on my status. "I wasn't sure if you were—"

"Dead?" I place my hand on my abdomen. "It's all right. I'm fine now."

Milo nods and presses his lips together. He seems genuinely worried and it brings a tightness to my chest I don't want to acknowledge. If he and I were still together, would he take me in his arms and never let go?

I push away the warm thoughts. We're just two people working toward the same goal.

Milo lowers his hands by his sides, as if he can read my mind. "My crows felt your vitals. It didn't seem like you'd make it, even with surgery."

"Luckily, I didn't need surgery. Just a few treatments and infusions."

Milo shakes his head. "How is that possible? I was there, Margot. You were dying."

I check over my shoulders. At any moment, someone could step into the surveillance room and see me in here with Milo. "We should talk somewhere private."

He raises an eyebrow. "What if your leader finds out?"

I place my keycard over the cell's lock. "She doesn't have to know."

He reluctantly accepts and arranges his pillow and blanket to look like a lump of himself. It's humorous.

I manage to sneak him into a nearby interrogation room—one I know has a malfunctioned camera.

Milo quietly takes a seat while I secure the door behind us, then I stand on the other side of the table. We stare in silence for what feels like a lifetime, enough that a simmering heat is already forming within me. This isn't a good idea, but what else am I supposed to do?

I break the silence first. "Before I awoke, I dreamt of my crows . . . Well, Knox's crows. I think they are protecting me." More than protecting me, but I keep that part to myself. They haunt me. Turn me into a version of myself I detest. Their possessiveness is all-consuming, and by allowing them to save my life, I feel like I'm helplessly falling into some kind of trap.

Milo folds his hands together and shakes his head. "You have crows as a result of finch magic, meaning your human blood doesn't allow you to have the same healing properties as a real proditor. Margot, it just isn't probable."

"Yet, I've just survived bleeding out internally with little to no long-term consequences. I may as well have had a really bad cold."

Milo sighs. "Sit down."

"What?"

"Just . . . take a seat." Milo places his palms face up on the table.

He wants to use his crows to assess me? This isn't a good idea. Being alone with him is already a risk, and I've shaken Lucinda's trust in me for sleeping with him recently. Touching him might throw us past a point of no return.

Still, I need to know what Knox's crows are up to.

I finally sit across from him with a lump in my throat, but I don't place my hands in his.

Milo raises an eyebrow at me. "I might be able to do some things without contact, but this isn't one of them."

"Fine." I reach forward and slowly lower my hands into Milo's warm ones. A deep breath escapes me.

"Close your eyes," he says.

I obey, trying to relax, but his touch is searing. Not a single tangible thought forms in my head and I hope this is over quickly.

A painless pecking sensation taps against the side of my temples, and my refusal to open my eyes turns into an inability. This isn't a typical proditor technique that could be used for torment. I know, deep down, I could escape it if I tried.

He shifts his hand and elbows, lacing his fingers with mine, and my heart skips a beat.

But that feeling is short-lived. My crows' coos are grating, and I can feel them hopping around our arms and feet. One pecks at my forearm.

Milo sucks in a breath and quickly unhands me, the trance breaking. I open my eyes and he's rubbing his own wrists, his eyes wide.

"You felt that too?" I ask.

"Knox's crows don't like when I intrude."

"So you have a lot of direct experience with them?"

"More than anyone needs in one lifetime." His eyes flicker, recalling a dark memory. "His crows are protective of you . . . but it isn't by his will. Dark magic—finch magic—is a complicated craft, and there isn't a lot of text on it besides what little knowledge my father passed on. All I know is they should not be healing you."

"Then why are they helping me?" Especially when I refuse to give into the same sadistic nature they've coaxed Knox into.

"I don't know. But whatever you do, don't trust them. Crows can be manipulative, even healthy ones. It's why meditation was a huge tenet in Vicar circles."

What Milo says makes some sense. But what do they want with a human who can't use them?

My lips part as Milo laces his hands with mine again. It sends electricity up my forearms, and as much as I should, I don't push him away. I can't seem to. I don't want to.

"About my mother . . . " Milo starts. "You knew she was here?"

My hands go cold with his words and he seems to sense it. His thumb runs over the side of mine. I shouldn't feel guilty, but I do.

"Her involvement in the rebellion was a surprise to me too. I only met her after I escaped the Imnicus."

"What is she like?" he asks with an almost child-like wonder.

My heart drops. It's a side of Milo I haven't seen before. He was only a toddler when she left. It makes sense that he would ask. Nobody remembers much at that age, and even if he did, people change.

"She's one of the kindest people I've ever met," I say. "Maybe one of the hardest working. It seems she's always doing something, whether that be helping our rebellion or cleaning a break room nobody asked her to."

Milo chuckles with a hint of sorrow in his voice. "She hasn't asked to see me."

I don't have any words of condolence to offer him, but I squeeze his hand slightly. Imory wants to see him. But she's also spent years trying to take down the Arris Reign. She's conflicted. Milo has to know that.

"Right now we need to focus on getting Lucinda to trust you," I say. "That's no easy feat. She doesn't even trust me much right now."

"Because we've been sleeping together?"

"*Slept* together." I frown and tear my hands from his. "And you broke into an impenetrable base using my face . . . without my permission, I might add."

"You're alive, aren't you?"

My jaw tenses. "Yes . . . but rebellion protocol states that nobody's life is worth compromising our safety."

"Then maybe your leader should have remembered to disable the override."

That she should have. It's why I know Lucinda is partially angry at herself. It was probably one of the biggest oversights of her rebellion career. "Be honest, did you save me just to get into the rebellion?"

Milo frowns. "You still don't trust me?"

"Milo . . . you have to understand . . ."

"Joriel was the one to suggest it, but I was prepared to risk my life and take you to a Laven hospital, consequences be damned."

"But why? I held a knife to your throat just days ago."

"And I did to yours too," he counters. "How much longer are you going to deny it?"

"Deny what?"

"That this table is in the way."

I scoff but it sounds too forced. Too real. My body begins to ache. "You're still you, and I'm still me. If Knox was forced off the throne and you became Colum again, wouldn't you use the knowledge you now have to destroy the rebellion?"

"I wouldn't." There is a glimmer in his eye, one of truth and conviction. One that was never in the Colum I once knew and feared. It's a look I've seen a thousand times before in the eyes of rebels, both born into the organization or recruited.

I have to stop this before this goes further. My cheeks are too flushed for my comfort. "We should go back."

"Should we?" Milo challenges.

I quickly stand, but Milo does too. He slowly walks around the table, not stopping until he pulls me into his chest.

Milo stares down at me, his lips parted. He traces the side of my jaw with one hand, holding my lower back with the other.

"I know you have no reason to trust me. None of you do. But I don't want to live in a world where you hate me. Or where I'm the subject of nightmares. A million lifetimes won't make up for what I've done, but I want to do it—I want to help the rebellion."

My bottom lip trembles as he moves a curl out of my face.

"I love you, Margot Tavish."

"Milo—"

He interrupts my words by crashing his lips into mine. A fire ignites within me, and I give in completely, wrapping my arms behind his neck to get a better angle. His touch consumes me. Grasping at my hatred for him is like trying to grasp at smoke.

He reaches between us and unzips the top of my jacket, then we let it drop by my feet. Chills rush through my limbs when he interrupts our kiss to pull my top over my head. I can't contain the sharp inhale that escapes when his lips suck the skin below my collarbone while he unclasps my bra. Nor the moan that follows when he takes one of my nipples into his mouth.

I grasp the back of his hair and look down at him, but he's already looking at me, soaking in my reactions. The old me chimes in, trying to convince myself that Milo is manipulating me and that our base will be infiltrated within a day. But I know he's telling the truth. I was there when Knox tried to kill him. When the arbitors were murdered in cold blood. I met his father in a proditor entrancement and know exactly why Milo became the way he did.

Milo runs a finger down my clothed slit, then unbuttons my pants and slides them down my legs with my underwear, leaving me completely bare for him.

"Sit on the table," he whispers.

I do as he says, but before he can lower himself to his knees, I reach out for him and grab the hem of his shirt. He stands there quietly while I pull it over his head, then take in the sight of his body. Sometimes I forget he's a trained fighter with the physique of one. More slickness builds between my thighs.

His mouth is on mine for a time, our tongues desperately moving together, but it's not long before his breath runs down my body. He kneels before me and the table, throwing my legs over his shoulders.

I grip the edge of the table as his lips nearly make their way between my thighs. "Milo—"

"Yes?" He pauses, staring up at me, his eyes dark with need.

That look alone is almost enough to let him keep going. But there is something I have to tell him first. "Give me time . . . to say it back."

"I'll wait an eternity if that's what it takes." Milo lowers his head, placing open-mouthed kisses on my aching heat.

Silk and flames consume me. I move my hips in tandem with his desperate tongue and he groans in approval. There's a part of me that begs myself never to trust him as he licks a line up my slit and my head tips back with pleasure. The part that screams reminders of his wrongdoings as I hear him fumble with his belt buckle, his mouth staying firmly in place, while I lie fully back on the table, breathless.

My body can't take it anymore, arching off the table. My moans echo off the soundproof walls, and I know I already need more of him.

He's one step ahead of me, capturing my mouth again while he slips off his own pants. But as he rests his forearms next to my head and stops to study me, I see the Vicar who never wanted the life he was handed. The one Imory once told me about who loved everyone he met.

So when Milo's body joins with mine, my fingernails scraping down his broad back, I know that the man that's taking me upon this table isn't one I've ever slept with before. He's a new version of himself who wants revolution. Who has abandoned the Arris Reign. Who will take Knox Arris to his grave.

Who will put another nail in his own father's coffin.

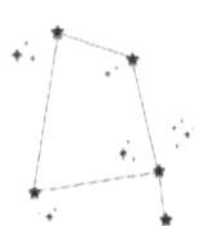

After I secure Milo back in his cell, I take the long way back to my suite.

I slept with Milo. Again.

This time, I don't regret it.

When we had exited the interrogation room, I half expected Lucinda to be standing there, ready to shoot Milo in the head after all. Instead, Alarik was awake in his cell and said nothing as I placed Milo back inside and left without another word.

Sleeping with Milo was a risk. I want to say I can't let it happen again, but when I'm alone with him, we're both forces to be reckoned with. My body betrays itself around him, and I can't help but embrace it fully.

A few hallways from my suite, the lights flicker.

The crows haven't let up much since they saved my life. My thoughts are getting harder to control. More vivid. More addicting. Milo mentioned meditations the Vicars used to do. I regret not asking him more about it.

You can't out-think *us*, one crow relays through the Nexus. *And why get rid of us? Everyone who once was with you is now against you. Without us, you have no protection. No certainty of your own life. We can give you power beyond comprehension. Even more than the Vicars, if you just let us in completely.*

I stop and rub the sides of my head, telling them, *"Be quiet."*

Before I can control it, they inject thoughts in my head that leave me clawing my skull. Thoughts accompanied by *feelings*. Ones that I want to push out of my head, yet never stop thinking about.

"Stop!" When I relay the thought, I imagine a gust of wind capturing them and pushing them as far away from me as possible.

They grumble, but it works. I lower my hands, placing my hand on my sternum to steady my breaths.

Those fantasies they placed in me . . . It's not that I worry about giving in. It's how my brain feels imprinted after. How out of control I am of my own mind. If they keep playing on my emotions, it's only a matter of time before they consume me.

Again, the lights go dim and I widen my stance, expecting a round two from the crows. For them to punish me for pushing them away.

Warning lights ignite the hallway, flashing orange. This time, it isn't my crows' doing.

Something is wrong.

Chapter 12

Milo

While I stared down at Margot while we made love, I knew that if I gained nothing else in this life, seeing her heart, soul, and body laid bare for me was all I needed. No title nor power could ever compare.

She has a way about her that makes me forget who I am and anything I once stood for. It's as painful as it is pleasurable, almost like looking into a warped mirror where I'm forced to confront the misdeeds of my past.

I often dream about Margot strapped to that Imnicus interrogation table, my proditors delivering different modes of torture to get her to talk. At the time, I didn't love her—I didn't even know her. Her life and her pain meant nothing to me.

These nights, I always wake up sweating, unable to cope with what I did to the woman I love. I deserve every nightmare and palpitation. Every ounce of regret that weighs on my chest like a boulder. I've killed, schemed, tortured, and betrayed more people than I can count. But it took only one to wreck my soul.

After we slept together in the rebellion interrogation room, she locked me back in my cell. Alarik and I made eye contact, but he said nothing and I offered him no explanation.

Now I lie in my cot, thinking about her. Wishing I could fall asleep so I could dream of her until the next time we meet. It could be today; or it could be weeks from now. I'm at the mercy of Lucinda and the rebellion from this point forward, and I have to be okay with that.

I'm jolted from my thoughts by rebel guards flooding into the prison ward with guns and handcuffs.

"Milo Arris, come with us," one bites.

I shoot to my feet as they unlock my cell. "What's going on?"

One of them enters my cell, grabs my collar, and shoves me outside. Two of them force me onto my knees, securing my arms behind my back with enough force to dislocate my shoulders. Alarik hasn't been yanked from his cell. They won't risk grabbing a proditor without good reason.

I do my best to endure the pain. "Tell me where you're taking me."

One of them rolls his eyes. "Lucinda sent for you. Right now that's all you need to know."

Did Lucinda find out about what Margot and I just did? Or has my mother changed her mind about sparing my life?

A shin lands in my back, and I grunt, almost toppling over. Then two pairs of arms grab me and hoist me to my feet.

Even though I'm willing to die, I don't feel ready to. After everything, I need to see my father's laws fall while I'm still alive. But there will be no convincing these guys.

They pull me out of the ward and into the halls, my crows and adrenaline surging. Rebels are staring, some in awe and others with a seething anger. One girl even looks antsy, as if she doesn't want to lose this rare opportunity to take out Balistar's son.

I'm led into a crescent-shaped room with tiered seats. Rebels fill most of them. I expect to see a guillotine on the stage, and Lucinda waiting eagerly to chop off my head.

But not a single rebel already seated turns to look at me, their eyes glued onto a large translucent screen. My breath hitches when I see Margot sitting near the front, watching just as attentively, with Lucinda.

My ribs constrict at the sight of my mother. She's standing off to the side, holding a tablet in her hand and frantically scrolling through it.

Once upon a time she was a human in a Vicar world. A home-maker. Her days mostly consisted of taking care of me in our small hut. It's strange seeing her as a woman taking charge with her underground network. She probably knows this planet like the back of her hand.

The screen steals my attention as the guards push me down into a seat in the back row. What's being displayed squashes all thoughts of my mother. It can't be . . .

Ralia's east temple point . . . has been destroyed.

A Laven newscaster voices over the footage of half of Ashtan-abo's Ralia region falling into ruin. The land is flooded, rain and waterfalls are completely out of control. Land splits to create new bodies of water. Ralia was already known as the land of the lakes, but this is more than that. Another clip shows a hurricane forming within the lakes, which I thought was impossible.

Scarcity once filled almost every region of Ashtanabo before we stole from Lavenai. For Ralia, it was the opposite. They had been struck by nature's overabundance, like weeds overrunning a flower garden. Trees were uncontrollably big. Plants grew, but thorns choked out food sources. And just like the Mountains of Eskdale, there was too much damn water.

The newscaster speaks. "Temple points serve as balancing siphons between Lavenai and Ashtanabo, taking the overflow and directing it toward areas of lack. Lavenai's abundance has served to provide crops to countless regions in Ashtanabo, but with the temple point's sudden destruction, all that energy was thrust into the region like a collapsed dam. As a result of all this, the Laven region of Staeziemie has unexpectedly started coming back to life."

The rebels roar with cheers and claps. Some laugh and hug, smiles wide enough to sore a jaw.

Staeziemie was a region once known for its flower fields, dairy industry, and multi-city festivals. The temple points took all of that from them, leaving them with dead tulips and sick animals. Post-takeover, it could only be described as what some may call a nuclear wasteland.

I realize now how complex this situation is, the Colum side of me taking over. Though Staezemie is saved, Ralia has a population of forty million. There will be casualties. Entire sections inaccessible to aid and food. The crop fields have been destroyed, and despite Ralia's abundance, there's no infrastructure to take advantage of it.

I might have been able to gather the resources and the manpower to help the citizens of Ralia, but I have no confidence that Knox has put any attention where it belongs. His eyes are set firmly upon finding me.

"Wait a minute," the reporter says. "We interrupt this broadcast for a message from . . ." He places his fingers against the transmitter in his ear, and his eyes widen. "From Colum . . . Knox Arris."

Margot looks over her shoulder and sees me, fear seizing her face.

So it's begun.

The screen shifts to a prerecorded video.

When my cousin appears on the screen, he stares into the camera with a lethality that sends a visible chill down everyone's spine. My father's old throne room surrounds him—a throne room I swore to never use myself. I never liked the pompousness of ruling. I didn't need the world to worship me. I just needed to carry out my father's wishes. That was all.

But Knox has taken an approach my father would have been proud of. He sits on a throne with a back made of silver feathers. Whereas my outfit was functional, with embellishments highly recommended by Arbitor Monicas, Knox wears an ivory forehead crown with pride, chains hanging from the sides. A capelet made of feathers rests upon his shoulders. At his sides stand my old friends, Onyx and Crux, dressed in over-armored versions of proditor attire. I'm not sure if I should be terrified or relieved that Dune isn't on screen.

"Citizens of Lavenai, the Ashtanaban soldiers stationed there, and proditors alike. It pains me to announce that your former Colum, Milo Arris, has betrayed you." Knox delivers the words with a subtle tsk.

"With his own two hands, he slaughtered the arbitors to give himself more power. I stepped in and saved the remainder of the Imnicus. He fled into hiding, along with the Columess.

"As heartbreaking as it is, I thought the change would be glorious. That, after our planets being enemies for decades, we could go into my rule and turn the chapter on our quarrels. Unfortunately, another card has been played, leaving reunification impossible. The rebellion has been left unchecked for far too long and has now devastated an entire region on Ashtanabo. This cannot go unpunished."

Rebels murmur between one another, and Margot exchanges another look with me. What could Knox possibly do to the rebellion that my father or I haven't already tried?

"Rebellion leaders, I am speaking directly to you now."

A few rebels jump in their seats, as if Knox's presence has truly entered the room.

I rarely addressed the rebellion publicly. Even Monicas, who did most of the talking for me on jumbotrons, would make vague reports on major events regarding them. Our strategy was to keep attention away from the rebellion within the Laven public so that more wouldn't follow alongside them.

"I understand you think that you've flown under the radar over the last two decades. That, as long as you didn't make any rash moves, the Arris Reign would never apprehend you. Today, that ends. I no longer need to come to you directly. What good would it do me? No, I think I'd like to try something different."

He shifts in his seat and crosses his legs as footage appears to the left of the screen.

Inside of a large room sits a group of around twenty people cuffed, gagged, and blindfolded. The Laven symbol is painted on the back wall. Guards with guns surround them.

Rebels lose it. Some shouting, a few crying.

"Quiet!" Lucinda shouts. "Calm down!"

"You have forty-eight hours to turn in a minimum of twenty of your members, and that must include your leader. If you do not, innocent Lavens will pay in your place. Twenty lives lost every-day you keep yourselves hidden. Televised." Knox smiles. "Want a taste?"

Bullets and screams ring out on screen, and Margot grips the armrests of her seat. Bodies fall one after the other and my heels dig into the ground.

One tries to crawl away, covered in blood, but a guard steps forward and ends her with a shot through the head. Blood splatters against the camera lens.

Rebels are petrified, and I can only imagine how Knox shook the souls of everyone watching. Lucinda is frozen.

Knox is crossing lines that the Arris Reign hasn't touched before. I can almost feel everyone's hearts collectively stopping. My own father, as wicked as he could be, never threatened the lives of the innocent to get to the rebellion. He preferred to deal with rebels directly.

The rebellion could do nothing. They should do nothing.

But I know by the franticness in the room that they will act. The rebellion was founded to free the Laven people. Now, Knox is using the entire population as hostages.

Knox speaks, "If the rebellion cooperates and turns themselves in for their crimes, I know that in time, we can create a new solar system together. One where all of us can thrive. Anyone who supplies information that leads to the arrest of a rebel will be given Ashtanaban citizenship and a new abundant life. I hope everyone, citizen or rebel, takes my words into careful consideration." Knox stares into the camera with an intensity that finally gets into my head. "To Arris Reign."

The shock in the room turns to silence, besides a single cry from one of the younger girls. Everyone is dazed and in a world of their own, including me.

The only leverage we have is that Knox doesn't seem to know Margot, Alarik, Lleu, and I are on Lavenai, much less with the rebellion, so he can't threaten Margot or me directly. Yet.

Lucinda finally squares her shoulders and looks over all of us. "The rebellion will not sit quietly and listen to the demands of a crazed lunatic. Nor will we sit back and let innocents be slaughtered."

"But he'll kill everyone!" a rebel shouts. "There's no time to plan. We don't even know where he'll take the next batch to be slaughtered. He already proved that he wasn't bluffing!"

"I know." Lucinda closes her eyes. "This is obviously a predicament we've never been in before."

Though Lucinda doesn't seem like the kind of woman who often shows fear, there's a doubt that showers over her. I can feel hopelessness blanketing the rebellion. A caving in, which is exactly what Knox wanted. But, realistically, what can she do?

This could be my chance to gain Lucinda's trust.

I clear my throat, speaking over the rows of the auditorium. "With me on your side, there are more options at play."

Lucinda takes a stance, as if she is going to tell me to keep my mouth shut unless spoken to. But my words seem to cast a dark comfort over the room.

I don't wait for her permission to continue. "Get the people to rise up with you. Ashtanaban soldiers and proditors outnumber your organization by a landslide. On your own, there's not much that can be done. But Knox killing innocents will already spark anger in them."

"How?"

"Ride the flame. Knox has always idolized my father. He thinks that wrath and an iron fist will quench all fires, but he's clearly wrong. My father's anger toward Lavenai resulted in you rising up. As for Knox's, we'll fan the flame into an inferno. Hack into the jumbotrons. Make an announcement. Tell them what they've been waiting for: that strength comes in numbers. It was what my father always feared, and Knox overstepped far more than my father ever did. The minute he pulled innocent lives into the crossfire, he sentenced his reign to death. The fear of an uprising is gone when the reality of death already exists. Pull them across that line and you'll have yourselves an army."

Margot studies Lucinda's face carefully, holding her breath. Lucinda can't let her pride get in the way. It's the only way to save the Lavens without turning themselves in. Even then, that may not be enough, but the rebels have to try.

"We've never been able to breach the firewall on those monitors. Your father knew the most important line to a submissive populace is the spread of information." Lucinda says.

"I know every code and every override. Conceal my voice, and I'll even deliver the announcement myself. I will speak the same words I once feared you'd deliver."

Rebels murmur to each other, their voices no longer filled with despair but with hope. Lucinda's eyes sweep the room, taking in the sight. She has to know there is no other option if her own rebels are curious about my plan.

I continue, "Let me help you, and I can make the rebellion unstoppable."

Lucinda's lips form into a straight line before speaking. "We'll try your plan."

Thank the gods.

She adds, "But I'm sending Proditor Alarik with my team. If I'm risking men, so are you."

My tongue tastes bitter, but I manage to nod.

Chapter 13

Dune

Back in Nonaka, I remember the day my father discovered that half the tribe had crow magic during a ritualistic ceremony. The ceremony started out like every other one we'd had. The entire tribe was dancing and eating. I still remember flecks of ash brushing my face and the pulsing light of the bonfire. I remember lying in my mother's lap as the evening wore on.

My father threw herbs into the fire, as was common in this particular cleansing ritual. I wasn't paying much attention at first, nearly asleep, dreaming of the games I'd play the next day. There was a gasp from the tribe, loud enough for me to climb out of my mother's lap and stare at the flames changing shape. Crows made of fire darted out of the split wood, burning so hot, everyone stepped away.

The flames grew three times their height in an instant, morphing into a sweeping crow's wing.

Everything went dark as the fire quenched itself, the wood no more than ashes.

That marked the beginning of our Nonakan Tribe truly discovering our powers. It was only a matter of time before we found the Vicars, who taught us to fear what we were given.

My mother still says that Ashtanabo's demise was inevitable. That our gods are punishing us. In Nonaka, we believe nature demands to be seen, and when we refuse to look, it takes drastic measures to make itself known.

While I think about calling my mother, Officer, or rather, Commander Bellis delivers news within the Imnicus command center. "Colum, we've apprehended one of the rebel terrorists."

Knox looks all too pleased from where he overlooks all the stations, his capelet moving with him while he paces. "Well done."

I've spent the majority of my life under the rule of an Arris, but sometimes I look back to my short years in the Nonakan tribe and ponder if Ashtanabo is trying to escape the will of the gods. How much longer will we take and destroy before we accept nature's punishment? Because if the gods want us destroyed, who will stand in their way?

But now, this one rebel will pay for all of it.

Maybe I should be relieved that one was caught. After all, every time a temple point is destroyed, my own family's lives are in danger. But every day since Knox announced he'd kill thousands to stop the rebellion once and for all, I lose a shred of my own convictions.

Knox motions to Onyx. "Notify the hangar to ready my ship."

"You're going yourself, Colum?" Commander Aisil stutters. "I'm sure justice can be enacted by proditors on land."

Knox's lips curl at that. "This is an interplanetary threat and requires my personal attention. Besides, it's not everyday we apprehend a member of the rebellion. Dune will accompany me."

My gloves crinkle where they meet behind my back. "Me?"

"Of course, you. You are the Imnicus' primary diplomat, right?"

"Yes."

"While we're there, I'm sure you can do a few inspections or whatever it is Milo had you do."

"Yes, Colum." He's not wrong. I am off the Imnicus more often than not completing missions and inspections for the Arris Reign.

But out of everyone I tortured, the only ones that made me truly sick were the ones where Knox was also in the room. Balistar may have been ruthless and uncompromising, but he wasn't sadistic. Not like Knox.

Inside the docking bay, pilots and technicians prepare the ship. Some refuel it while others complete last-minute safety inspections. I walk slightly behind Knox, along with Crux and Onyx. They won't be accompanying us, but I wish one of them would take my place. Crux has no problem with Knox's . . . quirks.

Knox stands in front of the ramp of his ship and places his hands on his hips, taking in a deep breath. "She's a beauty, isn't she?"

Balistar's old ship adorns a fresh coat of bluish-silver paint. It's twice the size of Milo's and features all sorts of internal gimmicks, rumored or otherwise.

"You really cleaned her up," Crux says.

"It was a waste leaving her all locked up and collecting dust for the last ten years."

A pilot steps onto the top of the ramp and salutes, welcoming us aboard. It's a great honor to fly the Colum himself to Ashtanabo, but I can see the slight shake in the pilot's wrist as he lowers his arm.

Inside the ship, Knox goes toward the back, where a singular large seat sits in the middle of the cabin. Balistar vowed to never remarry, so he never fit it for two.

I sit down on one of the seats along the wall and rest my palms above my kneecaps. "Do we know who the detainee is?"

"A male. I know that much," Knox looks down at the tablet, propped up on his large armrest, at the report Commander Bellis prepared. "He's apparently incredibly stubborn too. Exactly my type."

Knox normally doesn't care much for tormenting men. He breaks them quickly, getting the information he needs and tossing them aside. But this time, there's an unsettling glimmer in his eye.

The journey goes quickly, and soon we pass through Ashtanabo's atmosphere into the western, unaffected portion of Ralia. One of the first things I see through the clouds is its functional temple point. It's only a matter of time until the west becomes just like the east if the rebels get to it.

It would be a shame for Ralia to turn to ruins. It's the kind of region that inspires paintings, books, and poems. As we fly lower to the water, I watch stray flowers float across it. If I ever got time off, this is where I'd spend it, in one of the villa-style homes along the endless rivers. But on the rare occasion I'm approved for leave, I spend it with my family.

In the center of it all is the chancellor's grand tower, made of stone and cerulean stained glass windows. The surrounding mountains and nature amplify its beauty.

Knox sighs from his seat. "I hate it."

"What?"

"Ralia. It's so . . . annoyingly colorful."

"Or maybe the Imnicus is just bland."

"Really? We're closer to the stars than anyone. Or do you not believe in the gods?"

"We worship different gods." Much to the dismay of the Vicars. It made growing up in the Mountains of Eskdale that much more difficult.

"Yet both sets of gods bestowed on us the same kind of powers."

I keep my mouth shut and continue looking out the window. There's no point in arguing with him. He knows damn well the only god he has is himself.

The ship touches down on the landing pad upon the lake, only a bridge connecting us and the tower. When we emerge from the ship, maids and soldiers stand in two lines facing each other and creating a wide walkway for us between them. Unlike the solemn awe I was used to when Milo arrived in different regions, the energy here is completely different. Everyone's shoulders are tense and their heads are down turned, not wanting to even risk meeting the eyeline of another full proditor-turned-Colum.

At the end of the line stands Chancellor Altus Ekon and the First Lady, Natacha Ekon.

Normally, the chancellor is pleased to see me arrive for my periodic check ins, and our time together is spent drinking, eating, and maintaining political relations. But this time, Ekon's eyebrows pull his ebony skin into annoyed creases. Natacha places her hand gently on his forearm, her colorful garments swaying with her movement. She's the glue that holds him together, and maybe one of the most beautiful women I've ever seen, if that's not too inappropriate to say about another man's wife. Golden strands weave through her dark braids, and sprinkles of silver have been smudged intentionally over the tops of her cheeks.

As we near, Chancellor Ekon buries his scorned emotions, helped only by his wife's touch.

"Proditor Knox, congratulations on the promotion," the chancellor says.

"You may call me Colum Arris now." Knox's eye twitches.

"How long have I known you and am only just now seeing your face? You resemble your uncle."

"My aunt used to say that I had his nose." *And his entitlement.*

"I speak for everyone when I say we're honored to host you. There have been so many casualties in the east, and nobody knows how to help the sheer amount of people displaced by the floods—"

"I'm not here for that," Knox says quickly. "I am here for the prisoner."

Chancellor Ekon's frown deepens and panic enters Natacha's eyes. Nobody knows how Knox will respond to defiance as Colum.

He used to have Milo to keep him on his leash, but now he's a ticking time bomb.

"Dear, how about we let our Colum do what he must," Natacha says. She has always been one to read people well. If she senses something off about Knox's current emotional state, we should all follow her lead.

Ekon's nostrils flare. "There are people dying."

"You already have access to the treasury, right?" Knox asks.

"Yes." Ekon stutters. "But it's more than that—"

"And you have a legion of planners, experts, and soldiers?"

"Colum, you don't understand—"

Knox raises his hand, and Natacha promptly squeezes the dear life out of Ekon's arm.

"There are rats within our walls, Chancellor. They scurry about, gnawing at the wires, unchecked and unpunished. Now, they've invaded my planet, destroyed one of your temple points, and plunged half of your region into chaos. I will focus all my efforts into this little roach you've flushed out, so I can prevent another catastrophe. So, please, tell me more about what *I don't understand*."

The tendons in Ekon's neck are showing, and if he says another word, I may personally seal his mouth shut. Knox could kill him in seconds. Natacha knows that. That's why her eyes keep dipping to the knives and firearms on Knox's belt, but it's his bare hands that are the true danger.

"Show our Colum to the prison, dearest," Natacha says. "We can manage in the meantime."

Ekon releases the visible tension in his body and turns toward the tower. Knox falls into a pace next to him as we're led toward the entrance.

Inside, there are fixtures made from brass antlers, indigo flora, and sunlight that reflects into moving beams. Guards are everywhere there's a doorway, and they guide us toward the underground stairwell.

"Per your orders, nobody has interrogated him. Yet," Ekon says. "I presume that's why you brought Proditor Dune? I hope you know that our Ralian proditors are more than capable."

"He may be the most important prisoner in all of Ashtanabo. The most dangerous one. I may be Colum now, but this is a job for an Imnicus proditor. Two, to be exact."

My muscles stiffen.

As a six-inch thick steel door opens to the prisons, things grow murky and musty. Water drips from the ceilings. As the prisoners see us, all of them stay silent, not a single curse or taunt. But it's not because we're proditors.

It's because they're nymbed or on track to be if they misbehave. Empty husks of humans that will never be the same.

We turn down the next hallway lined with interrogation rooms, then stop at the one at the end. A Ralian guard types in a code on the side of the door.

Guards follow Natacha and Ekon out of the interrogation wing, leaving me alone with Knox. This isn't something I can get out of no matter how much I deceive him. It will only make him ask questions.

The door slides open to an interrogation cell, a dark one lit only with two dusty bulbs.

"After you," Knox says.

I step inside.

A young man sits in the center with his wrists strapped to the metal armrests of the thick chair and his ankles cuffed to chains attached to the floor.

The rebel raises his head. Longish brunette hair slightly covers his eyes. Even if Ekon claims not to have tortured him, he must have been somewhat injured when captured. Knox won't like that.

His eyes rake over Knox's royal attire. "Who the hell are you?"

Knox chuckles as the door shuts behind us. "Is that how you greet visitors?"

The rebel's breaths grow shakier at the sight of me. But if I were him, I'd be focused on the one who's eyeing him up like his next bloodied meal.

"What's your name?" Knox asks.

"Dimitri."

"Last name?"

"Flynn."

"Interesting." Knox walks around Dimitri's chair, running his finger along his shoulders, studying every visible hair standing on edge. Every sweat gland. Every pain point. "You work for the rebellion?"

"What do you think?" Dimitri spits back.

Knox stops directly in front of him. He cups Dimitri's jaw, inspecting his face. Dimitri shrugs away roughly.

Knox grabs the back of Dimitri's brown locks and yanks his head back, exposing his entire neck. "I will forgive you for that infraction. Everyone in your situation has nerves. It's only natural to put on a show of strength."

Dimitri's teeth clench together. "I've already met Chancellor Ekon, so I can assume you're some kind of elite commander with that getup."

Knox inspects his own clothing. "My attire is a bit uniform, isn't it? Hmm, I was specifically trying to avoid that. I suppose the previous Colum impressed his sense of fashion on me."

I can't help but grieve for Dimitri. Whatever Knox already had planned for him is going to get so much worse. He needs to stop stoking the flame if he knows what's best for him.

"Knox Arris?" Dimitri asks.

Knox chuckles. "Seems my name is finally getting out there."

"You're a proditor then." What Dimitri says next means the rebellion must have given him some top-level torture simulations, because I can only deduce that he's fearless. "I've been waiting to get my hands on you for what you did to Margot, you sick fuck."

Knox's eyes light up and I wince, silently praying to the Nonakan gods. Whatever hope the prisoner had was sucked out of the airlock as soon as he mentioned *her*.

"What a small galaxy we live in. So, what is it? You're Margot's brother?" Knox runs his finger along the column of Dimitri's neck, like a butcher inspecting his next cut. "You know, I was wondering why you had such pretty eyes."

"Fuck off." Dimitri's teeth show as he thrashes to no avail. "I swear if you've hurt her again, you bastard—"

"No, your jaw is too dissimilar. Your nose too. Cousins, maybe?"

Dimitri closes his eyes and moves his lips inaudibly as if saying a desperate prayer. That fearlessness is starting to break. A proditor is bad enough, but Knox Arris is so much worse.

Dimitri speaks again, "She told me every gruesome detail. The scar on her back, the crows in her head . . . "

"How cute. So she does talk about me?"

"Only to tell me about the nightmares you've caused her."

Knox smiles, his face softening for a moment. "You have no idea how much that means to me."

He reaches out and grabs Dimitri's chin to study his eyes, searching for something. Then Knox frowns, letting Dimitri's head go and taking a step back. "I've delivered an ultimatum to your rebellion. Twenty Laven lives will be taken every day they don't turn themselves in. Though that number doesn't even come close to the lives affected by destroying the temple point. Your rebellion is quite bloodthirsty."

"We're nothing like you."

"That's what everyone thinks until the blade is placed against their neck. Or the last piece of bread has been devoured. We were starving, so we took what belonged to you. Now you do the same. It's an endless cycle, destined to play out for all of eternity. But me? I'm the only one outside the game. Where everyone fights for desperation, I ride the wave. The only way to escape the fight is to give in. To find enjoyment in the inevitable chaos."

The reality is, regardless of what he told Chancellor Ekon, both planets could burn and all he'd do is laugh.

"Now let's get down to it, shall we?" Knox folds his arms. "Are Anali Matsumoto and your rebel friend off to the second Ralian temple point?"

Of course now, of all times, Dimitri chooses to keep his lips shut tightly. But if he tells us the information quickly, he may be able to get out of this. I pull off my gloves and Dimitri watches me in his peripherals.

"Very well. We'll work our way up." Knox quickly steps forward, places one hand on Dimitri's forehead, then roughly plunges three fingers into the back of Dimitri's throat with the other.

Immediately Dimitri thrashes in his chair, gagging to the point of tears in his eyes.

Knox speaks lazily, "One of the specialties of skilled proditors like myself is the art of controlling bodily functions without invading the mind. It's why you're incapable of biting down on my fingers, even though I can feel you trying. It's why you can't breathe through your nose. And the reason you're unable to vomit."

Dimitri's legs shake, and his wrists desperately try to break free. The sound erupting from his mouth is difficult to listen to. The simultaneous desperation for both air and battling his useless gag reflex. It's enough to make anyone queasy.

"It's always an honor to be the first proditor to touch a mind. You know, yours feels so much like hers." Knox watches him like one would an opera. His lips part slightly.

My jaw ticks at the sight. It's a similar feeling to being forced to watch your closest friend bed a woman right in front of you, not caring that you're in the room.

Dimitri's lips turn purple, and Knox finally pulls his fingers out but keeps Dimitri partially entranced. He heaves for air, and his eyes roll into the back of his head, his hands trembling. And we've barely gotten started.

"I'll tell you the same thing I told your cousin." Knox leans to eye level with him. "I hope you don't give in. So why don't you put up a fight for me? Let me enjoy it."

Dimitri whimpers through the entrancement, spit dripping down his face and his blood-shot eyes watering. If he knew what was best for him, he would speak. This isn't a battle he can win.

"Let's try this again. Which temple point is your friends' next target?" Knox removes his fingertips from Dimitri's forehead.

There are tears of pain running down the side of Dimitri's face. He closes his eyes. All he does is shake his head. I've been witness to Knox's techniques before. Though I can't see inside Dimitri's head, I don't have to imagine much to know what the rebel is experiencing.

"Good boy." Knox cups Dimitri's face with one hand.

Dimitri's body goes catatonic and then seizes. This is the faction of proditor torture I'm more comfortable with—I prefer to break into someone's mind and get the information I need out of them quickly. Rarely do I ever need to resort to physical violence, and I certainly don't take pleasure in it.

Again, Knox releases him and steps back. "That was a phantom hallucination. It feels similar to the moment just before you wake from a nightmare, doesn't it? Except you can't wake up, not really. Some say it feels similar to dying and being pulled down into the planet's core."

Dimitri's head dips, sweat dripping from his face and hair. It almost looks like he has the flu. Knox is pulling out all the stops for this interrogation.

"You're up, Proditor," Knox says.

I shouldn't be shocked, but I hesitate. "If he's anything like Margot, he isn't going to talk no matter what we do to him."

"It wasn't a request."

Reluctantly, I step up to Dimitri. His exhales are so loud that, if it were a cold winter day, I'd be able to see his breaths.

"Mr. Flynn, it would be in your best interest to give us information to lead to the arrest of your friends. Or at the very least, the other rebel's name." I should be honest with him. It would put it into perspective that there's no point in letting Knox have his way with him even for the rebels' cause. "There are two temple points in Ralia, and we can only assume they'll attack the remaining one next, but we're not certain. Can you give us any information of what route they would have taken? Any plans they have up their sleeves?"

Dimitri stays silent. Damn him.

"How about a yes-or-no question? Is their next target the second Ralian temple point?"

Nothing.

"Have they left the continent?"

Still nothing.

It leaves me with no choice. I have to use force.

I place my thumbs on Dimitri's head. There's only one way to make this easy on him without Knox noticing, and that's giving it everything I've got. The only thing worse than my harshest entrancement is letting Knox have another go at Dimitri.

There was a moment during Margot's interrogation when she almost broke, and I was able to pull a fear from her psyche and display it into her mind as clear as day. When I was done, her mouth opened, as if she was finally going to tell me everything, but she gathered herself at the last second. I have to try it on Dimitri.

My crows enter Dimitri's head with a sharp force, and I focus intently on activating a similar trepidation I once did with Margot. I can see the surroundings, the lush fields and the clear sky, and I can hear the laughter of people. But my own powers block me from seeing things as vividly as Dimitri is.

The false memory is a happy one, one that takes place in a liberated Lavenai. The one Balistar took from him. I can hear Margot's voice, congratulating Dimitri on his nuptials to some dream woman. Wedding bells. The scent of cake and rose fields.

Until a dark cloud passes over. Iron mixed with sugar. Gunpowder with champagne. Screams entangled with a child's laughter.

Dimitri's body tenses, and he cries out as he becomes one with a memory he believes is real. He's losing everything. Everyone. Even those he's never met yet but one day dreams to. For one's dream isn't too far off from their worst fear.

But in the end, he still doesn't talk, much to Knox's pleasure.

Chapter 14

Margot

My dreams are unbearable and insatiable. I don't think I sleep for longer than thirty minutes at a time. When I am awake, it's easy to resist my crows' callings. I can meditate or do things to distract myself.

But resisting an addictive, horrifying thought is impossible when you're asleep. Sleeping means giving up control for a third of your life. It means trusting your subconscious not to betray you.

I am growing weary.

But my crows are sick.

So what can be done?

Alarik and I stand behind a rebel named Rian while he unlocks Lleu's room for us. She's probably completely out of sorts, stuck in this room with nobody to update her. For all she knew, the three of us were dead.

Meanwhile, Milo is currently in talks with Lucinda, willingly handing over information to help a team of rebels during the upcoming mission. Of course, the rational side of me says I need to stay cautious of Milo. Sleeping together and his desire to help the rebellion doesn't mean I've completely come around to his shift. But at the moment, we have no choice but to trust him.

Alarik will go on the mission at Lucinda's order, which sent some of the rebels into a frenzy. But when Imory explained the benefits of having a full-blooded proditor on their side, they reluctantly came around. With his powers and knowledge of Ashtanaban technology, he'll be able to get them out of any potential trouble that comes their way. Lives that would have been lost will be saved. Though that's not Lucinda's primary reason for sending him—she just wants to balance the scales.

The door opens, and Lleu is curled up on a twin bed inside of a small, dusty room. The second she sees us, she leaps out of bed and shrieks.

She tries to hug us at the same time, but instead gives me a tight squeeze and then practically leaps into Alarik's arms, kissing him and not caring about anyone else watching. She doesn't stop until Rian clears his throat.

"You guys made me worried sick!" Lleu narrows her eyes at me. "And you . . . I've been blaming myself since we got here. Just a little airsick, you said? Thank the gods you're okay."

"I promise I won't hide anything like that ever again." I smile.

"You better not." Lleu gently flicks my shoulder. "I don't think I can afford another sleepless night."

You don't deserve them, my crows remind me. *You've been enough trouble as it is. The longer you stick around, the likelihood of them dying increases. Don't believe us? Alarik might not even survive this mission.*

The pain of my crows' words zap through me. They show me memories of Lleu taking a bullet for me. Alarik locked in a rebellion cell. Even Milo being interrogated.

Your fault, your fault, they sing-song.

Alarik's words help me push them out of my mind. "They really haven't told you anything?"

"Nothing," Lleu admits. "No updates on either of you, and they left me with no more than a few games to play at my leisure."

He squeezes her hand. "Nothing about Knox?"

Lleu's face pales. "What of him?"

I sigh and tell her everything, from the temple point being destroyed to the broadcast.

She listens intently, her face falling. "Oh, Margot . . . "

"Milo has one idea," I tell her.

"An idea?"

Alarik starts, "I'm going to join the rebels on the mission to incite a planet-wide uprising. The Arris Reign can only exist as long as Lavens allow it, at least that's Milo's theory."

"You can't go." Lleu steps away from Alarik, her face dropping. "Listen, I support the rebellion and ending the Arris Reign, but I don't believe you should risk your own life for it, Alarik."

The logical part of me wants to tell her that Alarik technically doesn't have a choice. But the crows are so loud, blaming me for something that hasn't even happened. Forcing me to bear the weight of a false future. Their taunts make me want to pull Lucinda aside and get him removed from the mission too. What if he dies? Lleu would never forgive me.

"I love you," Alarik says. "But I want to go on the mission."

"I can't lose you—"

"For the first time, my powers will be used for good. It's what I've always wanted, to make a real change against the Arris Reign. I tried once, years ago, and it barely moved the needle. I want a second chance."

I study his face intently. What did he try? And why have I never heard this before?

Lleu sighs and places a fist against her forehead. "You're making it really hard to argue against you."

Alarik reaches out and takes her hands. "I will go on this mission tomorrow and be back in time for dinner, alive and well. Trust me."

Lleu looks at me. "Do you believe him?"

"The rebellion is happy to have him." I smile, masking my unease the best I can.

Lleu hugs Alarik and it's in that moment that something, or someone, catches the corner of my eye.

Lucinda stands nearby, watching the three of us. Her face is neutral, and I can't for the life of me decipher how her discussion with Milo went. My pulse leaps, and I excuse myself.

"Yes?" I ask as I approach her.

"We've been cross-checking every piece of intel out of Milo's mouth and running risk assessments on his mission plan. His idea is as solid as any," Lucinda says. "Not that I will ever trust him."

"Anyone he could possibly conspire with is already dead."

"Whatever Milo Arris is to you, he'll always be Balistar's son to me. A son who prolonged the Arris Reign for another decade. Thousands have needlessly died under his rule. Because of that, my plan is simple. We'll use him to stop Knox Arris, and then we'll ensure that the Arris Reign never continues."

I drop my hands by my sides. "Meaning?"

"No matter how helpful he ends up being, I will never let him see his throne again."

"Exile?"

"That will come down to him in the end. I've never known an Arris to lie down willingly."

A year ago, I would have been in the same camp as her—Milo Arris needs to die. But now, even exile is something I don't want for him. But I won't tell her that. The rebels are already cynical toward me. If I were in their position, I would also be wary.

"Is he back in his cell?" I ask.

"Imory said she wanted to speak to him alone."

Chapter 15

Milo

After another meeting with Lucinda, which felt more like a productive interrogation, rebel guards walk me back to my cell.

To my surprise, they take a left turn instead of a right, which has been my usual path during my imprisonment here.

"Aren't we going back to the cells?" I ask the guard holding my right bicep with a vice grip.

"Quiet," he bites back and doesn't offer an explanation.

If I hadn't just seen Lucinda, I would assume they're taking me to my execution. Or maybe the three of them want a moment alone with me to get out their rage.

If that's the case, I need to be ready for anything they try to throw at me. Already, I'm thinking of ways to take on three humans who have guns and tasers while I'm bound. It won't be easy.

We stop in front of a door within the residential wing, and I expect them to open it, throw me inside, and deliver me bloodied, or worse—dead—back to my cell. They haven't made a move of violence yet, so I won't either. If I'm wrong about this and become the aggressor, the entire rebellion will turn on me, and I'm already hanging onto my life by a thread.

Instead of opening the door, one of them knocks. My mouth is dry while the door beeps and slides open. I await the inevitable moment of them shoving me inside to where more rogue guards lie in wait.

But when I see who is inside, my heart stops.

My mother sits at a small table set with two cups of steaming hot tea. Her hair is braided over her shoulder, silver mixed with raven.

My jaw tightens as an unidentified but powerful emotion slices through me. She seems to tense at the sight of me too.

"We'll be back in an hour," one of the guards says. "If he acts up, hit the panic button."

"I'm sure that won't be necessary." My mother folds her hands over the lace napkin in her lap.

As the door shuts behind me, I stay frozen in place. My legs don't seem to work and my handcuffs feel too tight around my wrists.

"Take a seat, Milo."

My lips part slightly, no words leaving as I slowly walk toward the table, surprised by how natural it feels to obey her words. She eyes me carefully, maybe cautiously. Especially as I rest my cuffed forearms on the table.

"Sorry to do it this way," she says. "The rebellion has their protocols regarding detainees, and I must follow them too. You look well. Strong. You're twenty-eight now, right?"

"Yes."

"The same age I was when I had you. Where do all the years go?"

There's an ache in my jaw that brings attention to how hard I'm clenching it. My body can't seem to hold on to any one feeling. I want to leave just to escape the discomfort.

"If you'd like to drink, I can uncuff you," my mother says.

Something breaks in me. I let out a sarcastic laugh. "It's been twenty-four years, and you want to drink tea with you? Like we're extended family catching up after a long while?"

"Milo—"

"You left me behind."

"Milo!"

"Why did you leave me with him?"

"Is that what he said? That I *left* you?" She lowers her head. The whites of her eyes grow glassy with a hint of anger. "You were so young. I shouldn't expect you to remember the truth. Balistar was like that after his shift—manipulative. Nowhere near the man I married."

I say, "The truth? You were both fighting, and I don't think either of you remembered I was even there until Onyx's father dragged me into the hallway. But I could still hear your shouting through the walls, and by the time I broke free, Father was standing there alone, and you were gone. He told me you left on your own. He told me you were never coming back."

My mother's palm slaps the table, rattling the cups and splashing drops of tea across the tabletop like a blood splatter. "That's not what happened!" She inhales deeply, her fist clenching. Then more calmly, she says, "That's not . . . *entirely* what happened."

"But it *did* happen. And this is where you went? The rebellion?" I have the urge to throw my chair across the room, but I know that my fate lies in the balance of my controlled temper. "You didn't even say goodbye."

"Because he wouldn't let me." Her eyes burn red. "You remembered the argument, but what came before it? Don't you remember? We were in your bedroom, packing what we could in a small bag. Just enough food and clothing to get us to the next safe city. You kept asking me questions, and I told you we were playing a game to not alert the guards. You climbed onto my back, and we crept through the compound in the middle of the night while everyone was asleep. We were ten feet from the door when he caught us."

"What are you saying?" my voice shakes.

"Balistar ripped you from my back and almost killed me right in front of you. Instead, he gave me a choice. If I left quietly, he would spare my life, but I had to leave you behind. You have to understand, I would have ripped his eyes out to keep you! But I'm no proditor. I would've died, just like the others, and I would never have a chance to save you ever again."

"And that's all this is?" I gesture at the room, at the rebel base. "You allied with this rebellion to save me from my father?" My limbs go numb. Of course that's the case. Why wouldn't she? Even the few memories I have of her prove that she'd move mountains to get to me. What's another uprising for the sake of her son?

"*'My son is as wicked as you*,'" I whisper, barely audible. "That's what he told me you said on the day you left. That you couldn't bear the sight of me." But that was a lie. Of course it was. I remember now being carried through that compound late at night, holding back giggles at the game I thought we were playing.

"Milo, I wanted you more than anything. There isn't a day I fall asleep without grieving the son I lost. Years passed, and every day the doubt drew closer and closer to swallowing me whole, that I could ever have my son back. And for you to just show up here . . . ." She covers her mouth and closes her eyes tightly.

I watch her sob while my hands shake in the cuffs. She's telling the truth, and the worst part is, a part of me always knew it. I was so young, grieving the loss of my mother, that it was easier to believe my father's words. But now . . .

I reach past the tea set and hold on to her hands. I have no words to say, most of my thoughts dying upon entry as my memories scramble to right themselves.

She squeezes my hands back, finding her voice through the tears. "I remember the first time I saw you on television. It was shortly after your father passed. You grew as strong and handsome as any mother could hope for her son. Even knowing what he turned you into, I couldn't help but be proud, as convoluted as that sounds."

I breathe out, letting my shoulders fall. "That's why you wouldn't let Lucinda kill me."

"My goal was never to kill you. You're my only child, Milo. And what I told Lucinda wasn't a lie. I believe you can help end the Arris Reign once and for all. You can rectify your past wrongs.

I remember that Vicar boy who loved hugs and never stopped smiling. I had to believe he's still in there. But what about you, Milo? What made you willing to assist the rebellion?"

I almost answer by saying Margot's name, but I know she was only a catalyst. So I tell my mother the truth. "I realized that nothing I do in this lifetime will ever make a dead man love me."

She nods solemnly. "There was a time when he truly loved us both. It wasn't until he became interested in complementary magic that something broke within him. As a human, I didn't know the darkness it held. There was a war raging inside of him that I didn't see. Nor the degree his anger had built against the elder council. If I had noticed the subtle twitch in his eye, perhaps I could have stopped him from going into the Akumu forest. He was once a good man who adored both of us. The Vicars revered him, and when somebody needed help, he was the first to step up. That's why I fell in love with him."

I don't like to hear about how my father once was, before dark magic overtook him. It's why I can't stand being around the older proditors who have those memories. The man he could have been. How is it possible that there is a world in which he and I, along with my mother, were still living in Eskdale together? A world where he wasn't overcome with darkness and bitterness and simply let things be? Maybe, if he held onto his senses, he could have broken away from the Vicars and found an honorable way to help the previous Colum figure out why the planet was dying.

My mother continues, "The problem was he cared too much about helping others. Empathy broke him, and dark magic molded him into something I no longer recognized. It wasn't until the night he created an uprising within the Vicars that I realized the true extent of his shift. Once he started to kill, I could no longer look him in the eyes. When I heard he was assassinated, I did not grieve for him. My husband died long before that."

"Did his anger start because the council didn't want to help Knox?"

"Knox certainly needed help. I always told Zareena that she needed to find help outside the Vicar village, but she refused. Said it would go against Vicar protocol. In a way, I was thankful that your father was able to use the doves on him. But no, that's not what sparked it, and I'm not sure I'll ever truly know what did."

"His secrets died with the poison," I say.

"And you truly never found who did it?"

I shake my head. "Maybe it's good that I don't know. The planets are better off without him." I fold my hands together so tightly that my rings dig into my skin.

"With the way your father structured Arris law, you're the only one who can truly turn the solar system around, Milo. Lucinda knows it, even if she's not willing to admit it. And you *will* stop this mess. It takes an Arris to stop an Arris."

"Knox is not an easy enemy to have. He's more powerful than Father. His sick crows amplify his strength each time he hurts or kills." With a chill, I recall the way he hunted us down at the docking bay during our Imnicus escape. How he used the death of each soldier to take out even more of them like ants. "Sometimes I wonder what Father would think if he could see Knox now. If he'd regret it."

But I'm not so sure about that. With his death, he left Knox defenseless. A sick boy with no doves to keep him stable. He could have fixed Knox permanently but chose not to. It may be one of the cruelest things my father ever did. Maybe, in the end, he would have made Knox's doves permanent as he did the ravens and the other birds, but I don't think my father ever expected to die as prematurely as he did.

"I think he'd fear what he helped create," says my mother.

Chapter 16

Alarik

As a proditor stationed full-time aboard the Imnicus, I spent most of my days in relative comfort compared to those who work planetside. Dune had his own stock of personal missions, but Onyx, Crux, Knox and I were only ever sent when something needed a personal touch. Our missions were always the same—someone posed a threat to the Arris Reign, and they needed to be tracked down, found, and eliminated.

While Knox and Crux found pleasure in the hunt, I forced myself to become numb to the work. Every mission was just another notch upon the wall, a list of sins I would never rectify.

But now I stand in a rebellion warehouse, dressed in the garb of the very people I was once sent to neutralize. It's a strange feeling, one I struggle to pin down. My hand still flinches to adjust the mask that no longer sits upon my face.

Five rebels are gathered by the gray vehicle when I enter the enormous underground garage. Desmond, the mission leader, studies a map upon the hood. Nyra busies herself by cleaning a rifle with a thick rag. A crack shot, apparently. Rian and Brynn, the two tech specialists, tap away at tablets strapped around their forearms, readying for whatever contingencies they can prepare for. Connor, the muscle, pretends to inspect the vehicle, but I know I haven't left his gaze since I entered the garage.

Margot gave me some information about these comrades of hers. If I'm to build trust and survive, I have no choice but to do everything they say. They have instructions to put a bullet in my brain the moment Milo goes off script. I know they're less than thrilled at the prospect of working with me. If I were in their shoes, I wouldn't want to be within a hundred feet of my bare skin.

All of them spare me nervous, silent glances. Nyra starts her rifle inspection again, not wanting to be the first to speak. Desmond breaks first, locking eyes with me for a half step as he folds up the map.

"Alarik Walsh, is it?" he asks aloof, as if I were just another soldier, then he snatches one of the rifles at Nyra's feet and tosses it my way. I see what he's doing, and I respect him for it. Trust is a key part of succeeding in any mission, and as long as he acts like I'm no better than them, they won't have itchy fingers on their triggers. "You're in front with me. You've got damn long legs."

In truth, I know it's because none of them want to risk brushing against my skin, but I don't complain.

Within minutes, the whole team has piled into the vehicle and we've pulled away, out into the outer limits of Merth.

Desmond glances my way again, one hand relaxed on the steering wheel. "Have you ever been on a mission like this?"

"Plenty of times. Though, with a lot less firepower."

"His kind has no need," Rian grumbles from the back. His eyes haven't left the back of my head since we started driving.

Brynn punches his shoulder hard enough for him to curse. "I'm sorry about him. He's not used to being around . . . "

"Someone like me," I finish, and she nods. I don't take offense. It's a common enough reaction. "I'm usually called in when stealth is required. It's not easy for someone to sneak around corners with a gun a third of their size."

Connor leans forward on his elbows eagerly. "So what's it like to touch someone's brain?"

Brynn rolls her eyes but doesn't stop him.

My lips form into a straight line. That is a question I am less than keen on answering. "I don't take pleasure in it, if that's what you're asking."

"But you have to like it a little, right? I mean, if I could get anyone to do what I want with the threat of my skin, I'd be unstoppable," Connor adds. I better keep a close eye on him.

Desmond turns onto another road. "Save the questions for after the mission. We have to focus, so stop trying to step on Alarik's toes, Connor."

"Sorry," he mumbles back.

Alarik. Not Proditor Alarik, Proditor Walsh, or Sir. Just Alarik. Just . . . me.

We pull into a back alley near the heart of the city, then enter a small lot accessible only by a code that Milo gave us before we left. It's one of the reasons the rebellion has never even tried to infiltrate the broadcasting center before. Every approach would have to come from a wide, well-surveyed area. Except for one, entirely unbreachable until now.

Desmond parks in a remote corner, away from the other scattered vehicles. It's early in the night, but there will still be workers present. As well as a lion's share of security. Desmond lays out the map of the building on the center console, and we all crane to catch a good look.

"Okay, team, we're going to make this quick and simple. Minimal casualties, the fewer shots fired the better, but we have authority to go loud if we need to. Understood?"

We all nod. It's a job perfect for my crows, but for everyone's sake I will try not to use them. The team keeps glancing at my bare hands as Desmond talks us through the building route, but Nyra is especially jumpy. I'll have to keep that in mind.

As the clock hits the top of the hour, Desmond taps his earpiece. "We're in position, HQ."

A screech fires through our earpieces, causing us all to leap in our chairs, before coalescing into Lucinda's voice, scratchy from the transmission. "*The mission is a go, leader.*"

Desmond nods and the doors open at once. The six of us file out, staying low and quiet as we rush toward the back door. We slide up against the wall.

"Damn, could these old transmitters be any worse?" Connor asks, rubbing at his ear.

"We're lucky we have them at all," Nyra sneers.

Rian rushes to the front of the door, already tapping at his wrist-mounted tablet. "Time to pray to whatever gods are still up there for the Colum's code to work."

"We've resorted to prayer, have we?" Connor asks.

A dull thud resounds, and my eyes lock onto the little red light above the door. It would admittedly be a massive oversight for Knox to not change Milo's code, but that's the thing—Knox is naïve and has no idea what a Colum title really entails. The sleepless nights Milo endured. There are thousands of security protocols he'll have to sort through to really keep Milo out.

Rian manually types the last string of the code, and the light flicks green. With a flourish and a bow, he opens the door and beckons us inside. The whole team looks to me, as if they weren't expecting this plan to get further than the door.

Before Desmond even gives the order, I'm the first one through the door. If there are any doubts within their minds this might be a trap, I want them to know I'll be the first to trip it. I secure the first hallway, and Nyra and Desmond the next. Brynn follows close behind, using a small EMP gun to disable the cameras.

We follow Desmond's map to the first set of elevators. Our destination lies atop the fiftieth floor, but unfortunately for us, we can't risk using it traditionally. Desmond pushes in the ceiling door and starts climbing into the shaft. Brynn rips off the front cover of the button panel and hacks into the software controlling the whole elevator system. A simple line of code and the elevators will be locked to the bottom floor. They'll figure out the problem soon enough, but by the time they fix the glitch in their system, we'll be long gone.

I'm second to last up into the shaft, Nyra behind me. The others are busy securing themselves to the main cables, so I reach down to help her up. She flinches back at the sight of my bare hand, taking an unconscious step back. I wince at my own carelessness. Nyra hands over her rifle, and I give her space to leap up.

A faint whir sounds from above as Desmond starts his ascent, his motor belt carrying him up the thick central cable. One by one, Connor, Brynn, and Rian follow. I take the opportunity to hook myself up while Nyra closes the latch. She'd likely feel just as uncomfortable with me below her, out of sight, so I'll stay as ahead as I can.

I tighten the clip around the cable and start my own ascension. The whole contraption runs along the inside of our clothing, most of the weight held by one shoulder. It's a hell of a lot easier than climbing by hand, but it is still a challenge for such a height.

"Fuck, my arms are on fire," Rian complains. "How much further, Desmond? Your ass is in the way of my view."

"Just fifty more feet, you damn princess."

We slow at the final floor, and Desmond leans out to pry open the doors. He's first to unlatch from the cable and step through, shortly followed by Connor and Rian.

A gunshot cracks through the air, and a bullet ricochets off the far wall.

"They know we're here!" Rian yells.

"Go loud!" Desmond yells as more gunshots ring out. "Brynn, Alarik, Nyra, get up here, quickly!"

I curse, advancing on the elevator door as Brynn hauls herself through it. She rolls out of the way as another flurry of bullets spray through the door. I stop at eye level with the floor to use the bottom edge of the door frame as a brace for my rifle. I line up my shot. A single guard crouches along the far hallway, just around the corner. Desmond moves out of cover to advance on him, and the guard moves to take aim.

I take the shot, a single bullet ripping through the hallway and neutralizing the guard before he fully lifts his rifle.

Desmond doesn't break stride, but Brynn and Connor both shoot back surprised looks as I detach my arm from the elevator cable and leap onto the floor. I glance back only briefly, just long enough to see Nyra stumble as she dismounts from the cable, slipping backwards into the shaft with a yell.

I skid to a stop and dive back toward the elevator doors. Nyra hangs onto the cable with a white-knuckle grip. Her legs try to wrap around, to find some purchase, but our clothes are slick and she keeps slipping down.

Straining, I reach down for her. "Take my hand!" My foot hooks around the edge of the elevator door frame to keep myself from falling in after her.

Nyra's eyes go wide, and she shakes her head. Then her grip slips and she slides down another inch. Her palms are coated in sweat, and if her constant glances at the drop below is any indication, she's terribly afraid of heights.

Still, she doesn't even look at me. Is her fear of my crows really worse than falling to her death? Who am I kidding? Of course they are worse.

"I will not harm you," I shout. "I promise, I won't!"

Desmond appears beside me a moment later. I expect him to shout at her, to talk sense into her cowering form. Instead he seems almost indifferent. "Make your choice, Nyra. More are coming, and we need you."

There's hesitancy in her eyes. Enough that I almost expect her to simply let go and accept her fate. Yet somehow, that little speech must've carried the right words. I hardly even register her grip as her hand shoots up to take mine, but I do not waste a moment and haul myself backward. Desmond has a grip on my waist, pulling us both into the hallway.

Nyra pants heavily on the floor, barely able to catch her breath. Desmond lifts her to her feet and pats her firmly on the back. "Well done, soldier, I'm glad you made it."

Her resolve seems to strengthen at his words, and she nods sharply, retrieving her rifle with a final deep breath. Then she turns to me, giving me the slightest nod of acknowledgment before rushing to join the others down the hallway.

I chase after them, a certain adrenaline coursing through me that I'm not used to. Maybe it's the company. My missions are usually solo, and always one-dimensional. Extraction of somebody deemed guilty of crimes I had no way of knowing. But now I'm striving toward a goal I understand. For once, I feel like I'm doing the right thing.

Red lights shine and sirens begin to blare as we approach the main broadcast center doors. Rian is busy at the control panel, typing in Milo's code just as he did at the entrance. It's a long string to type by hand, and the rest of us post up around him, rifles trained on the twin hallways branching past us.

A long, tense minute passes, the blaring siren filling every inch of my senses, until the doors slide open behind us. Two thin men sit at the consoles in the center of the room, neither armed and both terrified.

Connor levels his rifle and yells at them to get on the floor. Thankfully, they comply, but Connor's anger still radiates as he searches their pockets. They're way too gaunt to be from Ashtanabo, but maybe that's what has him heated in the first place—Laven civilians manning the propaganda center.

Brynn moves to the consoles but freezes as she struggles to find her way around the command board. Considering how quickly she got us through the complex so far, this surprises me, until I realize this entire room is full of advanced Ashtanaban technology.

"It's over here," I shout to her, guiding her to the panel near me. "Everything will route through this console. Blue receives and red transmits."

"Figures you'd know that." She sits and gains her bearings. "Would you mind reading this out loud to me while I type?" She hands me the paper that Milo wrote the override instructions on. Then she plugs her wrist-mounted tablet into the panel.

"Of course." I look over my shoulder as Nyra, Connor, and Desmond secure the hallway outside of the command room.

As I read the instructions, I think of Milo and Margot, and of course, my sweet Lleu. All of them are likely with other rebels in a large room filled with computers and monitors, listening to our voices through our earpieces and watching our vitals. I imagine Lleu with her hands folded tightly, watching the smallest spikes in my heart rate with dread. Before I left, I told her to distract herself. But I know she won't do anything of the sort.

Brynn gets closer to the end of the instructions and then a red sign with the word "live" lights up over our heads.

Slowly, she reaches to her ear. "*Lucinda, he's on.*"

I freeze, waiting for Milo's voice to come over the intercom. And the second it does, Desmond yells for us to run.

We rush out of the transmission control room. This place will be swarmed within minutes.

"*Citizens of Lavenai.*"

Milo's modulated voice echoes through the speakers along the hallway. Of course, Lucinda wouldn't stop with transmitting this to just the live feeds. She'd want every speaker even remotely attached to the broadcast center to be connected. In city squares, subways, and public centers, Milo's voice will reach across all of Lavenai.

"*For too long we have suffered under the fist of the Arris Reign. One tyrant to rise, to oppress, to smother. Under threat of gun, gas and proditor torture, they breed a populace full of fear and hopelessness.*"

Milo's words don't belong to the Colum I once knew, but I know them to be his, nonetheless.

"Crushed under their heels, we are trapped within their cage, huddled around a kernel of hope. Hope that brighter days are yet to come if we just sit in silence and wait. But a tyrant came and tore us up from the roots, slaughtering our neighbors, our parents, our friends. Still, we waited, just for another to take his place. When one falls, another rises. An endless cycle."

A pair of guards leap in front of our path, but I'm faster. They're both unconscious before they have a chance to fire a shot. My mind is transfixed on Milo's speech.

"But no longer. Our cage is not made of steel and polished metal, but of brittle iron and rust. They keep us in the mud so we do not realize that we have the strength to rise. For every proditor, there are millions of us, ready to take back what is ours. For every gun, there are thousands of hands to rip it free."

Our descent through the elevator is swift. We flood out of the building and into the parking lot. The city is quiet, as if everything and everyone has stopped just to listen to the broadcasted message. The symbol of the rebellion shines on the jumbotrons as we pile inside the vehicle. Desmond turns the radio on.

"Knox Arris wants to round us up like cattle, to execute our friends and our neighbors. But we've learned our lesson. Let us rise and show him we will not be asleep anymore. The Arris Reign fears you. Fears the united force that Lavenai could become. My call to you is to answer the threat with one of our own. Rise up. Fight the Arris Reign!"

Milo's voice cuts out as we pull out of the lot and drive through the streets where citizens stand frozen, even with the transmission off. I can't read the expressions on their faces. All I know is there's a warmth of accomplishment welling up in me, and a foreign bond that I feel with these five rebels. I think they feel it too, even Nyra, who is arguably the most fearful of me.

All of us look out the one-way glass windows as Desmond parks on the side of the road. He lowers his window slightly. Our orders are to return to the base without stopping, but none of us can bear to wait.

We hold our breath, watching the crowd stare up at the rebellion symbol flickering on the displays. Displays that once belonged solely to the Arris Reign. Then, one by one, voices rise up.

"That's their plan? They expect us all to sacrifice our own lives?" one man shouts from the crowd, greeted by a flurry of hushed agreements from the rest. "They've done nothing but stir up Ashtanabo's anger for two decades, and now who is left to suffer?"

"We are!" The crowd answers.

"They should turn themselves in," a woman yells.

My heart drops while we all watch and listen.

The yelling rises, congealing its way into a single, resolute chant. *"End the rebellion! End the rebellion! End the rebellion!"*

For years, Milo and the arbitors feared that very message getting out to the Laven public. Milo just delivered the same speech that kept him up some nights, and it is being met with a response of complete rejection. Perhaps Knox is smarter than I've ever given him credit for, manipulating an entire populace against their own saviors.

The others have gone cold, watching the crowd with expressionless eyes.

"HQ are you getting this?" Desmond leans his transmitter closer to the open window.

"Copy, leader," Lucinda says in our ears. Her tone is simple, unreadable.

Imory answers back a moment later. *"It's the same across the globe. Every city, every town, every village, either ignoring our call or agreeing with Knox's order for us to turn ourselves in."*

"A message like that should have sent the planet into a riot," I say.

Imory takes a long moment to answer. *"Even a beaten dog grows comfortable in its cage. Once the door is opened, it may never choose to leave."*

Chapter 17

Margot

The rebellion was once a silent symbol of hope for the people. A hidden angel living right beneath their feet, reminding them that there were people still out there trying to free them, even as they grew to accept the polluted air and forced factory labor.

Now, we are the enemies. Tomorrow, people will be slaughtered in our place, and it won't be Knox they blame. It will be us.

The rebellion's command center is quiet as we process what just happened. How the reception of our organization has shifted and true feelings have emerged.

After the debriefing, and both Alarik and Milo's cooperation in the mission, Lucinda granted them limited freedom from their cells and gave them ankle monitors to prevent them from leaving the underground or going into unauthorized zones.

Milo and I are quiet as we walk through the halls, neither of us able to form a thought. I don't even pay attention to the occasional rebels who side-eye us while we pass. For Milo to deliver the speech himself was groundbreaking. It's something that should have won over the nations, and without his intel, none of it would have been possible.

But it feels like all of it was for nothing.

I bring Milo into the small suite I've been staying in. It's nothing special, no more than a bed and desk, and not even a dresser for my clothes so they're all stacked on the desk, but it beats rooming with girls who think I'm no better than a traitorous proditor.

Normally when Milo and I are alone together, the urge to rip each other's clothes off is overwhelming. But right now, all I feel is hopelessness. If not even the former Colum can help the rebellion, can Knox truly be stopped? Did Balistar really make his empire that unbreakable?

Milo takes a seat on the edge of my bed, still in a state of disbelief. "I just don't get it . . . I've had nightmares about speeches like that. A unified Lavenai gathered under a common cause was the one thing I thought could overturn my rule. Then Knox starts executing innocents, and this is how they respond?"

"Maybe it wasn't the message, but the timing. They're probably scared, but not desperate enough to do anything about it. Imory may be right—perhaps Lavens have grown too comfortable in captivity."

A vivid thought ignites of Lavenai burning with fire across every region. People screaming out as Ashtanaban soldiers raid their homes. Gallow machines wiping out the unfortunate ones who try to fight back.

And in all those thoughts, the people do nothing. They lie there and take it as they always have. Stuck in a pot of water as the temperature slowly rises.

It feels like Knox has played the perfect card. Whatever he has up his sleeve is beyond sick. He won't stop until he has our heads.

How he could throw Laven lives away with no more regard than tossing something into the trash. It's—it's—

I look at Milo and a faint whisper enters my head, the crows nuzzling against my neck. I feel a trembling under my skin. An ache I need to let out, but don't know how.

Strike him, says the crows.

A small, pained whimper escapes my throat. I stop in my tracks and press the heel of my palm against my forehead.

"Margot?" Milo stands and places a hand on my shoulder. "Have you taken your pain medicine recently?"

It's as if his hand is searing through my clothing and if he doesn't stop—"Please, don't touch me." I whip back, my body colliding into the wall.

I shrink to my knees, then curl in on myself. Even righteous anger for the well-being of others is triggering the crows now. *"Margot?"* Milo's voice sounds like it's underwater.

My vision turns to static, and then to nothing, but I don't care. How can I ever control them if they can warp goodness itself? My heart pounds, the sensations from the crows overwhelming and unrelenting.

A black cavern surrounds me, flickering with wing-like movements. I don't know where I am within the confines of my own mind. I normally try to claw my way out of hallucinations, but I'm growing weaker to them each time they happen.

I stand, blind to my surroundings, hoping I'll walk off a mental cliff and back into the real world just so I don't have to fight.

I swipe out my hand to feel around in the dark. The air is cold and prickly. It's unlike other hallucinations I've been in. The more time that goes on, the more I can sense.

I feel everything that surrounds me, and I know I'm not alone. *He's* here.

It's as if he's right behind me, wearing his crown and capelet. If I squint, the gold in his hair shimmers. Any time the crows place him in my hallucinations, I know they're being particularly sick.

Knox's boots ripple in the pitch black, like a stone hitting water. A finger points at me like static, and I slide back as it nears my face.

"This is strange, isn't it? Meeting like this."

I turn my back to him, hoping that the crows' sick joke will be over any second now. *"Go away. You're not real."*

"Really? Sure about that?" He's in front of me again, his face just on the cusp of being seen behind the darkness. *"Tell me, where are you right now?"*

"Go to hell."

"Trust me, I will. Both *of us will."*

"Margot!" Milo screams from somewhere outside the void. His voice briefly frees me as my consciousness tries to return to my room.

A hand roughly grabs my face, pulling me back in. I dig my heels into the ground, trying to free myself. Crows swoop down and peck at my forearms, but I don't give up.

"We'll be together soon enough, Little Fennec," Knox says. I feel him everywhere yet nowhere. His breath on my skin and his nails clawing down the scar on my back, yet it's like he's light-years away.

"Margot!"

I snap out of the dark trance. Milo is holding my face, panic in his eyes.

I try to speak but my mouth stutters wordlessly.

"Where on earth did you just go? Your eyes turned black!"

"I . . . I don't know." There's a lump in my throat. "The crows were taunting me." I leave out the part about Knox. It felt so real, but there's no way it could have been him. Not for real. Telling Milo would only make him panic.

Milo backs up to give me space. "They talk to you?"

I nod.

"How often?"

"Too often."

"What did they tell you?"

I swallow. "Please don't make me say that."

"Margot—"

"They wanted me to hurt you." I don't know that I've admitted that to anyone, and it's like a weight lifts off my chest and then is thrown back upon it. How sick is it to want something like that? To hurt someone for the sake of pleasure? "Whenever they speak, I feel a genuine—temptation."

Milo's frown deepens. "Tell me everything."

And I do. Everything. It's physically painful when the words leave my mouth. Milo stays silent the entire time, listening to how I felt when I battled Crux and Proditor Tatuc. Even when I made my first kill.

Once I'm finished, Milo stays quiet for a minute before speaking. "And you still feel this way?"

"Yes."

He extends his hand, and I take it, letting him pull me to my feet.

His half-proditor crows skim over my skin. But it's unlike when a full-proditor does it, where even the most innocent of mind invasions leaves a mark. When Knox showed me a projection of a beach, I couldn't stop dreaming and thinking about beaches for a week, like a terrible song stuck in my head. Milo's crows aren't mind-bending at all. In fact, I don't see anything. I only feel.

They nullify my power. Knox's crows fall asleep, just like they did when I battled Milo at the Susukan temple point. Or any time another proditor has temporarily disabled my powers. And just like that, the sadistic thoughts are gone as if they were never in my mind in the first place.

Milo keeps my hands in his. "When I nullify the crows within you, you can't enhance your fighting or strength with them. But now his crows cannot torment you. Temporarily, anyway."

I look up at him, heat spreading across my chest from his soft eyes on mine. My heart skips a beat. But that thought is quickly replaced by the reminder that all proditors can disable my powers whenever they want because of my human blood. Torture me whenever they please.

I quickly pull my hands away. "It never lasts long."

"As long as I'm around, I can keep them contained. Promise me you'll tell me if they're bothering you? If we're in public, just tap me twice. I'll know what you mean."

With a clear head, I wrap my arms around him. "Thank you."

When I go to pull away, he stares down at me, studying my face. That craving for him returns, and as much as I try to talk myself out of it, I don't put up any kind of resistance when he holds the back of my neck and brings my mouth to his.

I hold on to the collar of his shirt, yearning for his touch. Pleasured shivers shoot down my spine all the way to my toes. It's one of those kisses where we can't get enough of each other, no matter where our hands travel or how deep we let ourselves go.

I break away from the kiss breathlessly. "Should we be doing this?"

He dips his hand down the front of my pants. "I've been trapped in a cell for days. If you think I'm not going to take advantage of every rare second I have alone with you . . . "

My neck arches as he finds that perfect spot. But I grab his wrist and pull it away. "Then let me."

Milo seems frozen as I take the lead and push him back into a chair. He visibly shudders in pleasure as I sit between his legs and undo his belt.

When I free him from his pants, I can't help but watch his reactions as I take him into my hands. His head falls back and his breaths grow deeper, lips parting as I work faster. And when I replace my hands with my mouth, his hands grip the armrests. He covers his mouth to stop his groans from leaking out into the hallway.

With the way he's twitching, I can tell he's close. And just before I'm sure he's going to spill out, he quickly pulls himself out and hauls me to my feet.

"Take off your clothes . . . please," he says with the cadence of a beg.

I waste no time undressing completely. He's not even undressed when I straddle him, because I don't think either of us can wait a second longer.

As I lower myself onto him, and we both grow sweatier and louder, I think back to the time I first saw him after my memories were erased. How much I despised his rough demeanor. How I wished to throw my fork across the table, hoping it would land straight in his eye.

But it's that same roughness I crave now, gripping my hair, rocking his hips rhythmically with mine. He picks me up and moves us to the bed, finally discarding his clothes in the process.

Before he enters me again, I say, "I love you." Then I close my eyes. "But . . . " I take a deep breath. "You hurt me, Milo. Had me tortured. Then kidnapped me *again* and treated me like some prisoner. Threatened Lleu . . . "

"I know." He slowly joins with my body again, and I can't contain the noises that leave my throat as he sets the pace.

"That doesn't just go away."

"Would you like me to stop?"

"No!" I say quickly as he thrusts harder.

"Well, if it's worth anything, I love you too. But you already knew that."

My nails leave marks on his back as we rock together, sweat beading on our skin. His lips skim against mine as he chases his release.

Pleasure seizes my body, heat exploding across my body with a vengeance. I don't always understand how we got here, and how against all odds, I fell for the one man in the galaxy I was destined to hate. And if I had to guess, he feels the same way.

Milo follows shortly behind, gripping the sheets and my leg as he groans into my neck.

His body weight falls on top of mine as we both come down. His thumb strokes my waist. Eventually he moves off, pulling me into his chest and rubbing my arm like in the early days when I thought I was his wife.

Even with the veil lifted, and all our truths revealed, I still want him as much as I did when my memories were erased.

Chapter 18

Margot

Late in the night, Milo is fast asleep next to me, his arm resting over my stomach. I, on the other hand, lay wide awake, feeling every minute more heavily than the last.

I don't know what to call Milo—my lover? My partner? Not my husband, like I once did.

I turn my head, watching him sleep. To be honest, I think he gets better rest here than he ever did on the Imnicus. He was always a light sleeper during our brief faux marriage. At any moment during the night, he could be called on and often was. But right now, I could dump a bucket of water on him and I don't think he'd wake up.

It pains me that I can't stay in this moment where my biggest conflict is my relationship status with the former Colum. Tomorrow, lives will be lost unless we find out where Knox is holding the executions. That thought alone brings a terrible ache to my chest.

I give up on sleeping and slip out of bed without waking Milo, then I head into the bathroom.

My reflection looks beyond tired. Exhausted from fighting an unending war that seems to be growing more and more complicated by the day.

I turn on the sink, running my hands under the water, and splashing my neck. The underground subway rumbles in the distance as it passes near the rebellion, the lights in the bathroom flickering. I was once used to it. Sometimes, I even enjoyed the white noise of it in the dead of night. But now my fingers tremble, and with each flash of the bulb, I feel heat against my neck, like the sensation of fingers pressing into it.

The rumbling stops and I wait for an eternity for the lights to stop flickering.

But they don't.

Don't panic, I tell myself, but it doesn't do much to help. The rebellion hasn't had an outage in five years.

The bulbs grow brighter and brighter, buzzing like they are screaming. I shriek as one pops, then another, glass hitting the mirror and the floor.

I fumble around, trying to find the door in the pitch darkness, but am met with nothingness where it once was. This bathroom is tiny, so I should at least be feeling a wall. But when I feel around for the sink, nothing catches on my desperate fingertips.

A splitting headache zaps through my skull, a high-pitched ringing shattering my eardrums.

Oh gods.

I fall to my knees, clutching my head. Am I bleeding internally again? Are my crows playing tricks on me?

Water drips from the ceiling. Or rather, rain, pouring down with the intensity of a thunderstorm.

I try to yell for Milo, forcing out the smallest sound. But no words come out.

A soft chuckle echoes around me.

No. No. No.

My body trembles while water drips down my face and hair. My surroundings brighten just a twinge. Enough for me to see a thick, dark fog around me.

Movement ripples in the fog. A human form, though I can't see his features. And I don't need to. I know exactly who it is. I think I'm going to be sick.

"Margot, Margot, Margot. What a strange place for us to meet." I can feel him standing a few feet in front of me, smirking down at my fearful state. *He can't be here.*

I quickly crawl away as fast as I can. There's something about the smoke I taste on my tongue and the dark chills running along my spine. This isn't like anything I've experienced before with the crows. It doesn't feel like an entrancement or hallucination, nor reality.

"How adorable. But this is my world, Little Fennec."

His form moves quickly, stopping in front of me just as I make it to my feet. A phantom hand grasps my chin and I gasp, grabbing his wrist.

How . . . how am I awake? How is he in my head?

This is real. He's really here.

"Let go of me," I bite. "Or I'll kill you."

"What if I like to touch you, Little Fennec?" Knox's thumb runs across my jaw then over my lower lip, pulling it down. A crow caws in the distance.

"No, you like to hurt me." I try to back away, but my legs are heavy like lead. "Are you really here? Or have you meddled with more dark magic to do this from Imnicus?"

"Interesting. I was just about to ask you the same thing."

"I don't understand . . ."

"It seems my crows have found the ones I lost in you. I'm not here of my own will."

Surely that can't be true. Crows communicating across a solar system? "That's not possible."

"Well, I would have agreed with you, if we weren't in this current predicament. I suppose it might be my own fault. You see, I had an interrogation with a prisoner recently, and let's just say that it brought me quite a bit of *energy*."

"You're disgusting."

He's done terrible, horrible things to me in the past. Yet whatever he did to some fool was enough to transport his crows all the way here?

I try to push him away, but every time I go to make contact with his chest, my hands are back at my side. I have no control here. Hell, I can't even see him.

Knox hums disapprovingly. "Is Milo nearby?"

"That's none of your business."

"Oh, and you've been *together* recently too. What a disappoint-ment."

"What I do with him is none of your concern."

"Tell me, does he know you? The *real* you? The one who craves? Who wishes nothing more than to be exactly like me?"

"I'm nothing like you!"

"You'd tamper with dark magic if it meant your mental freedom from me, wouldn't you? If you knew you could save your planet with the help of it, I'm sure you'd do anything. It's why nobody is truly different from Balistar."

"At this rate, I won't need any dark magic. Staeziemie is thriving once again, no thanks to you. And though the Laven people aren't ready to stand up yet, it's only a matter of time before they grow restless and rise up after you go through with your murderous ultimatum."

"Ah, so you are on Lavenai." His tone is more than self-satisfied. "I had a feeling you were involved in that jumbotron stunt."

Shit.

Shit. Shit. Shit.

I grit my teeth together, furious at him for getting that informa-tion out of me. Furious for damning myself. If I had any control, I'd pull Knox apart, limb by limb. And since this is the dream world, I'd do it over and over again until I'm satisfied.

"Now, now, what's that I sense?" Knox pushes strands of hair out of my face. "Beautifully vile thoughts? You know, you could indulge them here. With me. I wouldn't tell anyone."

"Never."

"How much longer will you deny the crows? Margot, give in. Let them overtake you. It's a feeling like no other."

I try to hold back the tears that form, but they fall down my face one after the other. An ache like no other builds in my stomach at his offer. I've pushed those dark, sadistic feelings away, day after day. Night after night. It's been hell. But now he's here, amplifying them to such a degree that the horrid temptation enters my mind.

"Tomorrow, you're going to kill people who don't deserve it," I say bitterly.

"Give in, Little Fennec. When they die, I will feel as you do now. Power will radiate through me just from the sight. Or do you not remember the way you felt when you watched the prelude live on television? Did you hear the way they screamed?"

"I don't want to be anything like you."

I sense his lips resting centimeters from mine, and I want to scream.

"Do you think you have a choice when I'm in control?" Knox whispers.

Crows fill the fog surrounding us, cawing as if they're laughing. Taunting.

All they've done is control me. Ruin me because of my human blood.

I'm sick of it.

"Knox, get them the hell away from me."

Knox ignores me. Instead, I sense him kneeling in front of me.

Then he yanks me down with him.

He moves me to straddle him and grips the back of my hair. His arm laces behind the small of my back, holding me close.

"Memories of the pain of others aren't enough to satisfy the crows, though the remembrance is enough to make you go mad with desire." He leans his mouth close to my ear. "Remember when Crux's face turned blue as you cut off his airflow? More importantly, the way your body *responded* to it?"

Gods, no. My stomach tightens, but the memory grips onto me, as if it's happening once again—those chains tightening into Crux's neck. The ecstasy it brought. I had never felt anything like it. A dark insatiable energy that only the gods can experience.

Now it all makes sense. When Knox tortures, it amplifies his magic, enough for him to transport his crows all the way to Lavenai, even unintentionally. It's how he amplifies crows and ravens to control armies. What would it be like to have that kind of power?

No, stop it, Margot. You're not like him.

I push against him, but he holds me tightly. I whimper, tears falling from my eyes.

"That's more like it." His hand tightens into my curls. He moves his mouth to my other ear. "Do you have any idea what it does to me when I see you cry?" His exhale is filled with pleasure.

The more I give in to this twisted vision, the more powerful he will become in it. I have to get away from him. Away from these thoughts. If I don't get out of here now, I will succumb.

I mentally resist the temptation, steering my mind in the direction my crows abhor. I've done it repeatedly, every hour I'm awake, even when it's difficult, which means crows aren't always in control. They can be contained.

I think of anything that brings me happiness. My friendship with Lleu and Alarik. My love for Milo. And even the mother-daughter bond I have with Lucinda. Dimitri and his contagious laughter.

The thoughts steer me into a new direction. A confidence to imagine Knox's crows are my own. *Truly* my own.

"Think of it, Little Fennec. With my crows and more training, you'd be one of the strongest humans in the galaxy. Wouldn't you want that? To prove your strength to everyone? To me?"

"What are you asking?" I keep my thoughts focused on the crows as I indulge his terrible fantasy.

What would it be like to control the crows for myself? For them to do my bidding instead of his or even their own? To hold the reins on their uncontainable power?

The thought is strong. Tangible. But it's hard to hold on to. Enough that I let out a pained gasped, which Knox probably assumes is from his tight hold.

"For you to stand by my side." He smooths his hand along the back of my skull. "As my Columess."

My lips part and my eyes widen.

I'd rather die than ever be joined to him.

It's enough for me to find a single crow out in the distance and mentally grab on to it. I bring it face to face with me, tearing it through the fog, staring deep into its eyes.

You obey me now, I tell it.

It cocks its head, and I free it. At first it flies away, joining its friends.

Turn on them, I command.

It doesn't obey me at first, and a pit forms in my chest. I almost accept defeat. To succumb into this eternal darkness.

Then the crow lunges forward. Its beak flies into another crow's eye.

Knox's breath hitches and he shoves me off his lap. "What . . . what did you just do?"

I place my hands flat on the ground to steady myself. Keeping this control over them sends a searing pain through my skull. It's something I won't be able to hold on to much longer.

I find the crows weaker than the rest of their flock. It takes all my concentration, but I do it again, gaining control of one after the other. As for the ones who resist me, I knock eggs out of nests. Start fires in their trees.

"No . . . no!" Knox yells. The sound of his back hitting the ground resounds through the Nexus. "You . . . you shouldn't be able to do this!"

Knox screams in pain at my feet. It feels so good for him to finally be the one hurting. For me to be the one in control.

Not only that, but it's amplifying the crows that now belong to me.

I bend over, searching for his invisible form until my hands find his warm torso.

With all my might, I grip his neck while he pants out of control. Using all my mental energy, I pull his head from the fog.

For once in this horrible simulation, his face is visible. Rainwater drips down his features, his pupils dilated.

"The next time we duel, proditor"—I bring his face close to mine—"only one of us is walking away alive."

With that, I release *my* crows on him.

When I let go of him, his torso hits the ground hard. Crows launch at him and he screams. They peck at his skin. He covers his eyes and kicks, but their beaks do everything to pierce between his fingers.

While they pick him apart, I stand there. Watching carefully. Taking in the beautiful sight that I know I shouldn't enjoy. Yet I savor every second of it.

The world cracks around me. Through the fog, I swear I can hear Dune's voice somewhere in the distance.

A vision of Merth's town square surrounds me. The place where my parents were executed. I hear the future screams, the smell of blood that hasn't been spilled yet. The feeling of morning dew on my skin.

Everything goes still.

I jolt, the bathroom reappearing around me. The sink and door back in their places.

And if I didn't believe it was real before, my hair and clothes are sopping wet, a puddle around my feet, as proof.

Things are changing. If there is a reality in which I control the crows, I can defeat Knox. I can save everyone tomorrow.

But since it was real, he knows Milo and I are in Merth.

Chapter 19

Dune

The Imnicus is quiet as I patrol the halls deep within the north wing. It's peaceful this time of night, and with Knox's new orders for me to stay tied to the Imnicus, there's no chance of me being pulled planet-side unexpectedly. Even though I would escape this palace if given the chance, I have to admit there's a certain tranquility to finishing up my shift in peace.

That is, until a chilling scream pierces through the Imnicus.

I freeze in place, trying to track down where it's coming from through the shock of it all. The scream is male and it's coming from the north wing. The royal quarters.

I sprint through the hallways, past fear-stricken night shift servants and A.S.O.P. units hiding in corners. As I near, a slew of guards who also heard the scream rush behind me to find the source.

The scream hits us again, bordering on a pained yelp.

It's coming from Knox's new room.

I quickly run to his door with guards flanking me and use my security clearance to barrel my way inside. He didn't want to use Milo's old room. A surprise, considering it also once belonged to Balistar.

Water is strewn across the tiled floor in the middle of the bedroom, Knox thrashing in a claw-foot bathtub, pulling at his hair. The pain he's in looks excruciating, as if he's being stabbed in the chest or burnt alive. Yet he's here. Alone. No blood. Untouched.

And though Knox has always been crazy, he's not hallucination-type crazy.

The guards gather around him, uncertain and nervous. The certainty of danger had passed, but no one approaches. Ironic, really. He leads with such an aura of fear, no one dares even help him.

They glance at each other, then at Knox's flailing form. Then to me.

"Proditor Dune? What's happening to him?" one asks.

Knox screams, seemingly unaware of our presence in the room. Even when his eyes are visible, they're somewhere else. He's more helpless than he's ever been in his life.

"I'm not sure," I say, wondering if I should call for a medic.

Knox doesn't let his guard down, ever, and has always been the strongest of us.

My crows flicker against my mind, warning me about something, but it doesn't seem to be Knox's crows for once. Whatever is happening is new to them.

"Leave." I tell the guards who entered with me. "This is a matter between proditors."

The guards nod and quickly shuffle out. By the looks of it, they're more than relieved to be dismissed.

When the door shuts, I kneel down next to the tub with my hand hesitating just above Knox's forehead. His screaming has begun to die out, his eyes staring wide at the ceiling above, his breathing fast. I take a breath and touch his skin, bracing myself for an attack that doesn't come. His skin is clammy, but I sense nothing.

What am I doing? I'm not like Milo. I can't diagnose the true state of crows. When my hand retreats, the veins on his forehead and arms bulge out, blood vessels breaking under his eyes. He still doesn't know I'm here.

A terrible thought crosses my mind.

I could slit his throat.

End his life. End this idiotic reign of his. Within my hand lies the power to change worlds. The daggers hidden beneath the folds of my uniform grow heavy, like lead. An opportunity like this may never present itself again. A simple flick of the wrist. A tiny nick of his artery, and this would all be over.

Memories flash of our days as boys in the Vicar village. There was once a time where Knox fended off bullies for me. The ones who cursed me because of my gods and my tribe. Their rejection often hurt worse than their beatings. But when Knox ever caught them hurting me, he gave them hell, even at such a young age.

But a few good acts don't excuse what he has done. What he will continue to do.

He has no allies. No true friends to seek vengeance. It would be a crime with no victims, no grieving parties.

I reach for the hilt of my dagger.

Knox's eyes open fully and he takes a sharp, gasping inhale. Whatever trance he was in vanishes.

My own breath catches instead, my trembling hand releasing its grip. *Never hesitate, Dune, even for a second. The smallest delay may lead to detrimental consequences.* Those were Balistar's own words. Words he instilled repeatedly when he'd occasionally oversee proditor training.

My hand moves to the water flask on my belt, and I offer it to him as his eyes frantically search the surrounding room. "Are you all right? What just happened?"

Knox flinches back when he notices me, then he relaxes. He swipes the flask from my hand, gulping it down before resting back. His muscles are still tense, his breathing labored. "That vixen . . . She's on Lavenai."

I stand and cock an eyebrow, but inside I'm panicking. "What are you talking about?" Maybe I was wrong. Maybe he has gone hallucination-level bad.

"Margot . . . I found her through our crows. No." His grip tightens on the flask, denting the metal. "My crows. They'll do good to remember who their master is." He takes another swig.

"You mean . . . you saw her with your own eyes? From within your mind?"

Knox sets the flask down and rests his arms on the edge of the tub. He dips his head back against the rim. "I was thinking about her while I bathed and then . . . she was there. In front of me in the flesh."

"Our crows can't do that. It had to have been a dream."

Knox scoffs. "Are you hearing yourself? Your crows are bonded with Milo."

"Yes, but I can't communicate with him." Or so I thought until Knox almost ended his life, but I won't tell him that. There was once a time I thought my bond with Milo would fade after Balistar's death, but it's grown stronger by the day. Still, it's not like I've ever seen him in the flesh from within my mind.

Water sloshes out of the tub, joining the rest of the growing puddles as Knox stands and reaches for a towel, not caring in the slightest about hiding himself. "Plans must be changed, but we cannot let the rebels know. They already got into Lavenai's ear once, and it can't happen again. Thankfully for us, Lavens are fickle people."

"Plans? You mean the execution?"

Knox nods. "There's no doubt Margot's joined back up with the rebellion, which means she's in Merth." He pauses, his frown deepening as if recalling a distant memory. "I think she knows where the execution will take place."

"Should we cancel? Or move it to a different location?"

"Of course not! Quite the opposite. We have a pawn of our own in case they decide to attack, which is almost a guarantee at this point. They won't give themselves up and they also won't let those people die. It's what I was counting on."

"But—"

"That will be all, Proditor." Knox waves his hand dismissively, disappearing into the walk-in closet.

I remain at the edge of the tub, staring into the pools gathered on cold tile. My kaleidoscope mask warps within the water's reflection.

If Margot is with the rebellion, Milo won't be too far behind either. He'd never leave her side, which only means he got himself captured or did something stupid, like join their cause. Knox wouldn't be too far away from that conclusion himself, which can only mean he has a plan to draw Milo from the shadows.

My throat goes dry. Milo has nothing left to be baited with, no family, no cause that would cause a misstep. But Margot certainly does. With Dimitri as bait, Margot will run straight into the lion's den.

Where Margot goes, Milo will have no choice but to follow.

That leaves me only one choice.

I breathe in deep and make for the door. My oaths are to the empire. To the Arris Reign. To the betterment of our people. To Knox. But when my oaths conflict, I take the one of greatest importance. Before them all, I gave a vow to Milo Arris, to protect him with my life, and I cannot sit idly by and watch his destruction. If that means keeping him safe by damning my own life, then so be it.

The guards at the prison doors don't pay me any mind. Thankfully, my proditor status still means something, and they allow me into the ward without a second thought.

After I get past the next security check, I enter Dimitri's cell. The boy lies on the ground, his body covered in bruises and cuts. The ones on his chest are the worst of them all. Based on the sweating, I presume he has a fever. Probably an infected wound or two.

I've been torturing people for as long as I can remember, but I've never witnessed anything like . . . like that. It was like—now that Knox is Colum—he no longer cares about keeping the other proditors' respect. And he was already bad before.

Dimitri's eyes are open, unfocused but present. He's been watching me since I entered, but he hasn't said anything. He's barely stirred. Knox did a number on him during their last session.

"We're going to Lavenai in a few hours," I say.

He mutters a pained prayer. He knows as well as I do how Knox will use him there.

He'll be too good of leverage against the rebellion if Knox uses him to lure out Margot. I need to get him as far away as possible from Knox the second we land on Lavenai. I can imagine it already—Dimitri mysteriously regaining his strength, him slipping out the emergency hatch of the ship shortly after landing, a guard being blamed. But to do that, I'll need to actually restore his strength.

I kneel down next to him and he winces, and I'm pretty sure he's trying to cry. Proditor magic is funny like that. When I first met him back in Ralia, he was the kind of guy that would have given his life before conceding. But that's the terror of crows. Death is a mercy.

"Don't—please," he begs.

I remove my gloves and he's already scooting away. As if that would help in a locked room with a proditor.

"Relax. I'm not going to hurt you," I say with an air of annoyance. I place my bare hands on his exposed shoulder and close my eyes. There isn't much I can do for his injuries, but I know most of his current immobilization is caused by Knox's crows. I must reverse them.

"W-what are you doing?" He weakly grabs the back of my hand, but his own quickly falls back by his side.

"You're going to need your strength."

"What?"

I sigh and look over my shoulder. Thankfully, if a guard enters, they'll likely think I'm just finishing up another round of torture and promptly get the hell out as quickly as they can. "Once we land on Lavenai, you're going to escape out the back. To do that, you need to be able to use your legs."

"They're paralyzed. I don't even know why. He didn't touch my legs." By his voice alone, his strength is already returning.

"Proditor entrancements often cause catatonia."

"So you guys *are* civilized enough to be all technical about it?"

Yes, he's coming back to his senses. I can feel Knox's crows wearing off quickly, but only because they've turned their attention on me. They don't want to stop, so they're trying to peck at me, unsuccessfully I'll add. Wicked little things.

Though Knox never told me why he was screaming in pain. Is communicating with someone through crows that painful? What isn't Knox telling me?

It doesn't matter. I need to focus on protecting Milo.

Dimitri finally softens his muscles as he lets me work. "I don't see why you'd want to help me."

"Margot is a friend," I lie. Well, maybe we're friends. Or rather scorned acquaintances. He seems protective. I probably shouldn't mention that I kissed her once.

Dimitri laughs. "She really did leave her mark up here, didn't she? She's good at that, you know? Getting people to like her."

He's not wrong. Even if not evident from her words, there's something I've always liked about her. She's balanced in a way that not many people are. It's hard to describe.

He continues, "Not like me. I have a habit of pissing people off, which she likes to remind me of."

I smile under my mask. It's good if he keeps talking. It distracts me from these horrible crows trying to peck through my proditor blood. Fortunately, they have little power over me, but they're annoying enough.

Dimitri sighs. "So, she escaped with the Colum? The old Colum, I mean."

I want to tell him that I know she's on Lavenai, but I'm already risking my neck as it is healing him. "For the record, you need to pretend to be out of it or they'll realize someone has healed you. Then we'll both have hell to pay."

He tries to sit up, but he winces at the bruises on his side and drops back. "Pretend? Yeah, I can do that."

I hope he's right, because once he escapes, he'll have a good minute before proditors and soldiers alike are after him.

As do I, because once we're there, I'm running with him.

Chapter 20

Dune

The Imnicus docking bay is as busy as I've ever seen it as the staff prepares for Knox's journey to Lavenai. Commander Aisil shouts orders at employees. Onyx and Crux keep a close eye on the mechanics servicing Knox's ship, and I escort Dimitri up the ramp. His eyes are vacant, jaw slack. To my relief, he's doing well at playing the part of someone who can barely walk. Maybe too well—I'm practically dragging him.

When I volunteered to collect him from his cell, Knox wasn't remotely suspicious. It will work to my advantage once we land. I'll lock Dimitri in the back, as is standard with prisoners, and then sit near Knox to keep his mind occupied with other affairs until we touchdown.

Nobody is inside the ship yet, besides a lone pilot who doesn't even process my presence as he intently finishes his final inspection.

"You can cut it out for a second," I tell Dimitri after we disappear into the back of the ship, out of the pilot's hearing range.

He looks around and straightens his spine slightly. "Am I convincing?"

"It's making me wonder if I even healed you."

"I'll take that as a yes."

I shake my head and guide him to a small room, directing him inside. I clamp one of his cuffs to the magnetic lock upon the wall, then pull out the small magnetic key from my pocket. "Use this to unshackle yourself when the ship touches down." I pull out a longer key used by the maintenance staff in power emergencies. "This will override the door. After you get out, there will be a hatch farther back where you can climb out to the tarmac."

Dimitri gathers them both in his bound fist. "Do you think it will work?"

"It's your only shot at getting out of this alive. It has to."

"And you're really doing all this because of Margot?"

"I have my reasons, and it's best you don't know them."

In the distance, I can hear Commander Aisil shouting something and more feet scrambling. I can only assume that Knox is about to board.

"Sit tight," I say as I step out of the room. "And remember, pretend to sleep for most of the journey. We don't want to give off any indication that you've been healed."

"Act half dead. Got it." Even through his jokes, his gray-tinged skin and dark circles are telling enough of his internal state. It's the dark reality of proditor magic—how permanent it is.

I shut the door and make it back to the main deck just as Onyx ascends the ramp with Crux in tow.

"How is our prisoner, Dune?" Onyx asks, taking his time to get comfortable in his seat.

"Stuck," I answer as I buckle up. It's an old phrase we use to refer to someone whose sympathetic nervous system hasn't processed that they are no longer in a trance. It results in a numbing effect in the brain that leaves someone without an ability to speak, and their movements are limited or paralytic.

"You both really were hard on him, then?" Crux asks, impressed, as he takes a seat next to Onyx.

"He is a danger to the crown," I reply, hoping to steer away any suspicion.

"*Those who follow the heart, follow their own doom,*" Onyx recalls a Vicar proverb.

"Perfectly said," Knox remarks, standing in the entrance way. His eyes meet mine, an unreadable smile spread across his lips. He takes his seat in the large chair in the middle of the deck.

I inhale deeply, allowing my nerves to dissipate through my tense muscles. I must not let them show. One wrong move, and Dimitri will lose his chance to escape. If that happens, his life will be used as a pawn, which will only further endanger Milo's life.

Soon enough, the ship takes off and everyone gets comfortable in casual conversation. It is difficult for me to join in, knowing that, as we speak, unfortunate souls are being kidnapped from the streets of Merth and dragged to the town square as rebellion bait. It's another added weight to my shoulders. Even if I don't personally agree with the rebellion's methods, this path to their destruction does not sit easy.

Freeing Dimitri could potentially delay the event another day, as Knox will be too preoccupied trying to get his prized toy back. By the time they discover Dimitri is gone, I will have slipped out the back and joined up with him.

There's a lull in the talk. It's the sort of quiet that brings about a discomfort, making me overly aware of every microexpression on Knox's face.

He fiddles with an empty glass of champagne. "This is rather boring."

"That's because you're the one normally piloting the ship," Crux counters. "Maybe you should hop up there and show that pilot how it's done."

"Hmm. You know what could be fun?" Knox rests his fingertips on his jaw. I can't decipher the intention behind his eyes. My breath heats up under my mask.

Knox looks at me and smiles. "Fetch him."

"What?" I ask.

"The boy. Grab him and bring him here."

I freeze. He wants to use Dimitri as entertainment? *Now?* That sick bastard.

Even if I let it happen and bring him to Knox before landing, there won't be nearly enough time for me to heal him. "He's completely out of it. It wouldn't be worth it."

Knox doesn't so much as inhale, only his lips move. "Go get Dimitri, Dune."

Three pairs of proditor eyes follow me as I stand and head into the back of the ship. Not all hope is lost. If Dimitri puts on a good front and acts overly paralyzed, Knox may not want to do anything to him. I hope.

I punch in the code to the door, running a thousand scenarios through my head. I'm successful in barely any of them.

As the door opens, I put my finger over my mask where my lips are.

Dimitri is slumped, doing his best to pretend his mind is still stuck. But once he sees it's me, he lifts his head with confusion in his eyes.

"The Colum wants to see you," I say as monotone as possible.

Dimitri stays quiet, his jaw twitching. There's a terror that builds in his face that I don't think I'll ever wipe from my memory. The kind of terror that only Knox can bestow and still sleep at night.

He slowly nods. I can't explain anything to him nor communicate any last-minute plans. Knox might overhear from this vicinity.

I adjust the cuffs behind Dimitri's back, grabbing the two keys from his hands and securing both his wrists before dragging him toward the main area of the ship.

As we emerge and Knox lays eyes on him, the corners of his lips curl. He moves his legs apart. "Sit him here."

I do as he says and place Dimitri on the floor facing the rest of the room. Knox's legs are positioned on either side of him, as if he's some kind of pet.

Dimitri lets his head droop and fall onto Knox's thigh. If he puts an ounce of tone into his muscles, I can't protect him anymore.

When I go to sit back down, Knox snaps his fingers. "Stay."

My jaw tightens and my heart begins to race. But I do as he says and stay standing.

"You know . . . " Knox rakes his fingers through Dimitri's brunette hair, delicately as if playing a harp. "Sitting on a throne is incredibly taxing. A crown weighs heavy upon the brow, it seems. When I ousted Milo, I really thought that this elevation of power wouldn't come between us proditors. I thought we could all remain friends. I woke up this morning thinking we were."

Onyx and Crux exchange confused looks, but my gaze is locked upon Knox.

His hands still rake through Dimitri's hair, and his words have but one direction. "Did you know that real crows are quite unique in their intelligence? They can solve simple puzzles, follow basic instructions, and can even warn their flock of impending dangers. And they don't forget the faces of those who seek to harm them. All traits we utilize as proditors.

"My crows have minds of their own. They speak to me. Call to me. Each. And every. One." His hand tightens painfully on Dimitri's scalp and the rebel cries out, thrashing upon the floor.

"I was wondering when you'd come out to play." Knox laughs at Dimitri, then slowly lifts his head. His eyes narrow at me, that implacable smile unwavering. "And my crows tell me that you've been altering them."

My breath halts. Dimitri's hands are clutching at Knox's grip, shaking uncontrollably.

"Oh?" Knox chuckles. "You thought I'd never find out?"

I barely have the strength to speak. "I don't know what you're implying."

Knox turns his attention to Crux and Onyx, who both seem confused. "Who upon the Imnicus has authorization to access the hyssopite bombs from the weapon's cellar?"

Neither of them respond at first, glancing at each other. "Commander Aisil, the two heads of security, the Colum, and . . ." Onyx pauses, his eyes flicking to mine. "And the proditors."

"And did you know that all security clearance logs can be wiped by that same level of access? Of course, we all know that my uncle was a paranoid, *paranoid* man in his final years. He gave power to the people he trusted, but he never *truly* trusted them. When he constructed the Imnicus, he made an override that only he could access, to monitor all the little machinations happening beneath his floorboards." His eyes meet mine again. "Including the logs for the weapon cellar."

"Dune . . . no." Onyx's head dips in disappointment.

Crux narrows his eyes. "I told you I was right, Knox."

I go numb. This entire time, he knew Alarik and I betrayed him to save Milo from following the same fate as the arbitors. But he kept the information to himself, waiting for the right time to use it against me. A time when I'd be stuck in a small ship with three men of equal strength.

I have no defense but the truth. "My oath to the Arris—"

"No, *no*, don't you say another word," Knox yells, his face flooding a shade of crimson. "Your oath is not to the Arris Reign, it's to *Balistar's direct line.* And with that little bond of yours, I'm sure you felt like you had no choice but to save him. You stood and spoke allegiance in my name, all the while conspiring against your new Colum. All in the name of *honor*." He spits the last words, but his temper simmers. His grip on Dimitri returns to his sadistic combing. "It's why you healed my toy. Why you were planning his escape. Perhaps even your own."

If that's how he's going to be, then I have no reason to appease him. "I'll say what nobody else dares to tell you: Your entitlement to the throne is nothing more than an illusion of grandeur."

I place my hand on the hilt of my gun. Crux follows suit and draws his knife out too. Onyx stays seated, as if paralyzed, his eyes blankly staring at the floor.

"We grew up together, Knox," I say.

"Yet you betrayed me." Knox sighs. "How's that for old friends?"

Knox catches Dimitri's neck and begins to squeeze. Dimitri claws at Knox's fingers and kicks his legs while he tries to breathe. There's a flutter in the air and a glaze in Dimitri's eyes that I can only assume Knox is using crows to amplify the pain.

"Knox, stop it," I seethe. "You've proven your point."

"I don't think I have." Knox lets Dimitri take in a single heaving breath of air before he throws him on his side and lands a kick in his stomach, knocking the wind out of him.

I want to tell Knox to stop again, but I know as well as Onyx and Crux do that, once Knox sets his mind to something, stopping him is almost impossible.

So I watch. Watch as Knox kicks Dimitri repeatedly without reprieve. As he kneels over him and places his fingers on his forehead, injecting his sick crows. And I watch as Dimitri grows paler by the second, blood flow slowing.

When I look at Onyx, he averts his gaze, but his reservations couldn't be more obvious. If he wanted, he and I could team up together and stop this. Sure, I may die in the process, but it will have been worth the sacrifice to get Knox off his throne. But without Onyx, it's hopeless.

Finally, Knox releases Dimitri from the trance and he's as paralyzed as he was in his cell yesterday. Everything I had planned was for nothing. The worst part is, both of us will pay for it, and he'll pay even more for me getting him involved. Dammit.

Everything is quiet as Knox paces around me, but I don't dare say the first word.

"Take off your mask," Knox says.

Bitterness runs through me at his words. "I earned my proditor status as much as you did."

"Take it off or I will make you."

I don't have a choice. Hesitantly, I lower my hood then work at unfastening my mask before handing it over. Knox rubs his fingers over the smooth engraved material, a kaleidoscope design. "I've always liked your mask. It fits you, somehow. Unreadable and ever shifting. The closer you look, the more you realize you never knew the man underneath." With a crack, the mask shatters in his grip, and he lets the remains fall from his fingertips to the floor. I stare down at it, blood running cold.

For a proditor, our identity is everything. We hide our faces from the world, like an executioner does from his victim, too ashamed to be seen. We carve patterns upon the surface, searching for identity among a sea of anonymity. Now I'm forced to watch the artificial light bounce off the shattered kaleidoscopes.

I devoted my lifetime to the Arris Reign. Enduring years of training, of beatings, of ridicule, to build myself toward a title I did not deserve. Now, in the snap of a moment, it's all gone.

The moment the ship lands and the hatch opens, my identity will be revealed and my creed broken. All in a single act by my Colum.

My mind empties, all reservations leaving with it. Power floods into my limbs, compelling me forward. My eyes snap up and my fist follows, arcing toward Knox's steady, sadistic smile. If I'm to abandon my creed, I'll abandon all that goes with it. If Onyx doesn't join me, so be it. I'll at least have fought for something.

Before I even have a second to process his movement, Knox bats my hand away. His other hand darts beneath his capelet, and then a small bitter object is shoved into my mouth. I step back, pivoting for another hook, but a weakness descends over my arms. My legs give out and my crows go with them.

He's so fast, fueled by a dark magic I can never truly understand.

Knox is upon me with his hand clasped over my nose and mouth. "Swallow it."

My body doesn't give me a choice. I do as he commands, floral notes flooding down the back of my throat.

Hyssopite.

My body slumps.

Knox steps back as I fall onto my side and the world around me becomes blurry. "You know, when I had the Imnicus's lab make this for me, I knew I needed more than just hyssopite to keep you down. After all, you're strong beyond the crows. So I had them add a little something . . . extra."

Whatever it is, it takes me deeper and deeper. My mind is drowning, and no matter how much I resist, I can't outswim its consuming waters.

"Your pending death will not be in vain. I have a use for you." Knox says. "Goodnight, Dune."

I'm dragged into the depths. The last thing I see is Knox's cruel, constant smile.

Chapter 21

Oliver

The wind is picking up, slicing against my face as I run among a sea of Ashtanaban guards. I swear a bug or two splatters against my skin from the sprint. Right now, dead bugs are the least of my worries.

"It's destabilizing!" an officer shouts somewhere behind me. "Get to safety!"

Anali runs next to me, also disguised in an Ashtanaban uniform. They were her idea. *"We'll walk right up to it, no problem,"* she had said. I didn't expect her plan to actually work. Just an hour ago, this place was being patrolled by unprepared guards who had been sent here after our near-destruction in Susuku.

I look over my shoulder at the temple point and the way it shudders like a house made of toothpicks. Okay, maybe her plan worked too well. We're going to be crushed if we don't drive out of here as soon as possible.

"Keep up, Parrow!" Anali shouts, now a few feet in front of me.

I huff, somewhat annoyed by how much quicker of a runner she is. Fighter too. If I was bred to stop a war, maybe I could match her. But no, I'm just a rich boy turned rebel. Some of my friends call me crazy for leaving that life behind in favor of this one. But what can I say? I've always hated caviar.

Dimitri clouds my mind as we near our stolen vehicle. He used to call me things like 'count' or 'lord,' never letting me forget my roots. *Dimitri, you damn bastard. Why did you have to get yourself caught?*

After his capture, Anali and I decided the western Ralian temple point was too risky. Too predictable. Instead, we made the journey to Iverat, rationing out geeds and food the best we could.

Once we get to our vehicle, both of us leap inside. I quickly turn on the ignition. Only minutes remain before the land will collapse like dominoes, just like it did in Ralia.

A smaller group of guards rushes toward our car, desperate and out of breath.

"Wait for us!" one shouts.

But I'm already putting the car in drive and slamming onto the accelerator. Now isn't the time to grow a heart. Besides, if they knew I was Laven, they would have done the same to me.

I pay as much attention to the road as I do the rearview mirrors, waiting for the ground beneath us to split open or an earthquake to fling us off the side of a cliff. Other vehicles are driving just as erratically.

"Oliver!" Anali shrieks.

I quickly turn the wheel to narrowly avoid the edge of a fence. "Sorry."

"Pay attention! You're going to get us killed."

I do my best to keep my eyes ahead of me as we peel onto the main road, but any moment, a mountain could have a landslide. Or the weather could change and lightning could strike our vehicle. We need to be prepared.

"Take a right here," Anali says. She's breathing harder than she normally does, even with the sprinting. I can't confirm, but it seems the extra power it takes to deactivate points has built up a toll against her. We need a longer break before we take out the next one. That is, if we can get to it before starving to death first.

"Has it happened yet?" I ask.

Anali turns in the passenger seat and narrows her eyes. "No. Just vehicles scrambling."

"That's strange, isn't it? In Ralia, the flooding started within thirty seconds."

"Perhaps the damage is building below ground. Volcanic or something, I don't know."

My own mention of Ralia brings back the familiar jolt of pain that has been seizing me by the day. None of us anticipated how hard it would be to leave the region in the days that followed. It was only a matter of time before we were recognized. And being chased down on foot while the enemy had boats? When land broke, Dimitri was separated from Anali and me. The current was too strong for him to risk jumping and swimming to us. He said he'd take the long way and meet us back at our campsite, but within minutes guards were on him. Anali and I were helpless to stop it. Dimitri screamed for us to go. To leave him behind.

The mission doesn't stop. It didn't when Margot went missing. It couldn't with Dimitri either.

My grip tightens on the steering wheel.

We drive for gods know how long, but with the adrenaline coursing through my veins, it feels like minutes. Nothing has happened. Absolutely nothing. I don't know what Ivaret was like before the Arris reign, but the mountains still stand, the trees still blow in the breeze, and the weather remains unchanged.

Once out of the range of the temple point, we pull into our pre-planned stop behind an abandoned farmhouse, perched on the edge of a rocky outcropping, overlooking the valley. It's as good of a hotel as we're going to get ever since we ran out of geeds. We're lucky we have enough food to last us until the morning. But after that . . .

I open the sunroof and stand up, using a pair of high-tech binoculars to see the other half of Iverat.

"Anything? Anali asks. I feel her stand next to me.

"Something isn't right." I hand her the binoculars.

She sighs and takes them, inspecting the land. "I don't see anything."

"Exactly. The temple point was destroyed, but Iverat hasn't been affected." I pull out the stolen communicator with a still-perfect signal, then I open a live local Ashtanaban newscast, the banner reading, *Iverat temple point destroyed, leading to questions about Ashtanabo's health.*

"Look at this," I tell Anali.

She rolls her eyes and leans over to watch the stream with me.

The newswoman speaks, "Reports say that Iverat's temple point was unexpectedly destroyed, leaving top scientists with numerous questions. Ralia's eastern temple point destruction left half the region in ruins, but Iverat remains untouched. It begs the question, 'Is Ashtanabo healing itself?'"

"Holy shit," Anali whispers.

I sit back down, toss the communicator into the cup holder, and rub my temples. The lack of destruction has been weighing hard in its own way, but maybe this alternative is the better outcome after all. If Ashtanabo is slowly healing, it could change everything. Ashtanabo never learned what caused the planet to fail, but if Iverat really has been repairing itself on its own, it opens up the possibility for the planet's independent health without stealing Lavenai's.

"That's good, right?" Anali says, following the same line of reasoning I did. "We can just keep taking out temple points and freeing up the energy that's being used for nothing. And there won't be ceaseless destruction in our wake."

I sigh, fingering the antenna of the communicator. "Very true. But that means our work is a lot less effective as a message. Not to mention we're at a crossroads regardless of the success of this temple point. We're only days away from starving to death, we've lost half our team already, and every time we go to a temple point, we risk losing you and your powers."

"What you're saying is, you *do* think I'm one of a kind?" Anali winks.

I narrow my eyes. "What I'm saying is, if it's true Ashtanabo is healing, it's something that should be investigated from another angle. Perhaps there's another way to go about this that doesn't risk devastating entire regions back to their former form."

"Negotiation doesn't sound like it's going to go over well with the new Colum, if he's as horrible as Margot described him."

"Forget about him. Our mission parameters have changed. The best thing for us right now is to get in contact with the rebellion, but I don't know how in the world we'll do that."

I pick up the communicator again, as well as the geed device. Maybe I can't get into contact with Lucinda or Imory, but I know one person who may be able to help.

It takes me hours to find a way to establish a connection, calling contact after contact to link us to a Laven line.

Meanwhile, Anali snores in the back seat, out cold. She might be cute if she didn't sleep with her mouth open. Or find every way imaginable to push my buttons. Though I can't deny she has been invaluable, even if she is a bit of a nuisance.

I place the communicator against my ear, waiting with bated breaths until I finally hear a buzz on the other line.

"To whom do I have the pleasure?"

"It's Oliver," I say. "We need an extraction."

Chapter 22

Margot

Everything in the Nexus felt so real. I could feel Knox's touch, his breath on my skin, and hear his screams as I overtook him with the very crows he cursed me with. But I'm human. Controlling crows is supposed to be impossible, right?

Regardless, I know where the executions will take place. Knox lost control of his thoughts, handing over information to me against his own will. Mind reading isn't supposed to be possible with crows—then again neither is a human controlling them and attacking their original master. I can only assume it's a result of our warped crows. Even if by some chance one of my relatives had Vicar blood, it still wouldn't explain it, considering that Milo is half-blooded and he cannot use them for more than detective purposes, among a few other things.

Milo was still asleep when I clawed my way out of the bathroom, my energy drained. I abruptly woke him and told him everything. Well, almost everything.

"Stand by my side, as my Columess," Knox had said.

Now, I sit next to Alarik and a group of rebels in the pre-briefing room, all of us dressed and ready to save the hostages. If my vision was correct, everything will happen at sunrise, which didn't give much time between me pounding down Lucinda's door to deliver the news and rallying a last-minute team together.

Though Milo won't admit it, he is beyond nervous for me to go. Both he and Lleu will be subject to watching us through the live broadcast, helpless to do anything if something happens to Alarik or me. But we both need to do this. I know Imory will try her best to ease their minds while we're away.

Our team heads to the supply room to gear up before we leave. Alarik stands next to me, hiding weapons under his clothes and securing his utility belt. I chose a handgun whereas others chose larger semi-automatic rifles.

I volunteered for the role of getting citizens to safety. And yes, given my fighting abilities from the crows, it left the other rebels with raised eyebrows. I accepted the scrutiny, letting them assume I didn't want to risk my life.

But the real truth? My crows are out of control, to the point that my mind isn't thinking rationally. At any second, they could snap and cloud my judgment. If I kill guards, hell, even if I simply injure them, it could be enough to set the crows off.

Alarik taps his heel rhythmically beside me, and I glance at him. It's still unusual seeing him without his mask, at least not in private. It suits him, somehow, now that I've seen him so much without it. As if the mask itself never quite fit him.

"Nervous?" I ask him. He glances over, embarrassed, and forces his foot to still.

"It's the first time one of my missions will be televised. I'm not like Lleu. I guess you can say I have a bit of stage fright." He pauses for a prolonged moment. "It's a strange feeling. I've never really struggled with nerves on missions before."

I laugh, but I quickly realize he isn't joking. "Not even during your last mission with the rebellion?"

He just shrugs. "For the first time in my life, I returned from a mission without being haunted by ghosts."

"I'm not sure I realized how often you were sent out on missions."

"Not nearly as much as Dune, but often enough. Mostly to Ashtanabo. The majority of them ended in bloodshed. Never in Eskdale, though. Balistar would never let me within five hundred miles of my former home."

"Do you remember any of it?"

"Distant memories. They seem to fade every year. Replaced by . . . " He grows still, his eyes fading to stare at nothing for a brief moment before he shakes his head.

"Maybe the Vicars will remove their shields once the world is back in order," I say. "You could see the mountains again. Your family." Lleu told me all about Alarik's past. The way Balistar kidnapped him and molded him into a proditor just to spite the Vicars.

"I'm not convinced they'd want to see me. Their isolation was their own doing, and that barrier won't come down easily. Not even for me."

"Sometimes I'm surprised you weren't born Laven," I joke. "You have far too soft a heart for your line of work."

Alarik turns to me, his jaw stiff. "All of us have secrets. There are things I'd never admit to Milo."

I laugh. "What, have you been Laven this whole time or something?"

"No, he wouldn't care about that. He's half Laven himself. No, mine is far worse. I doubt he'd ever forgive me if he ever found out."

I frown, trying to search his face, but I find nothing readable. "What did you do?"

He considers for a moment, as if standing at the cusp of a precipice he'd never been down before. "You have to understand, those first years were hell. I'm not even sure how I survived them. It wasn't without consequences, though. Day by day, bitterness and rage grew within me. Every mission, every trance, every beating and berating, and all the blood upon my hands . . . it built up. I grew to hate my captor and hate my very existence. I missed my parents terribly and mourned what I had lost. Death was my only way out, but I never took that route. One day, I realized I was far too valuable to waste my life like that. I was in far too unique a position to throw it away."

I furrow my brows. "I'm not following."

"Margot—" Alarik's breath catches for a second. "I've been breaking apart the Arris Reign from the inside for years. Undermining the smallest of orders, sabotaging lines of communications. Things that would easily go unnoticed. It's why I helped you escape. It's why . . ."

Alarik's eyes widen as his confession pours forth like a valve opening a dam. "It's why when the opportunity presented itself to do something more, I took it. I barely even had time to think, barely had time to consider the consequences. He left himself open and vulnerable for the first time in decades. A man so paranoid, he didn't even trust his own son, but he turned his back to *me*? The child he ripped from his own parents?"

"Alarik, I don't understand."

His eyes darken. "Perhaps my heart is not as soft as you think, Margot. Because I'm the one who poisoned Balistar Arris."

Sunrise nears as we approach the town square in a packed, windowless van. Alarik sits to my left in silence, holding his long weapon diagonal against his chest.

Balistar's death was always a mystery. Though there was a manhunt to find Balistar's assassin, they never found the person who did it. Some Lavens even said it was an angel of death sent down by the gods to collect his soul for judgement.

All this time . . . it was Alarik.

It makes sense. How else could somebody kill a Colum and get away with it? It was a crime only another proditor was capable of committing.

I wanted to ask him how he pulled it off. How premeditated the plan was. But before I could find words, Desmond began shouting orders for everyone to get moving.

All I could say before we left was, *"I promise, I will never tell anybody. Not even Milo."*

To my surprise, Merth's roads are quiet. It's only after a few more turns that we realize how many roads are blocked off.

"It's a ghost town," Desmond comments. "Any heat signatures?"

Brynn sits in the passenger seat, typing away on her laptop. "Further up north near the jumbotrons."

"Makes sense," Alarik says. "He said it would be televised."

Which makes me all the more relieved that our respirators will cover our face. But it will be no secret that we're part of the rebellion.

"Wait, wait. Slow down." Brynn points outside. "What is that?"

Desmond brings the speed down to a mere coast. I can see him squinting through the rearview mirror. "It's . . . Is that them?"

I don't wait for him to explain and push past the other rebels to the front of the vehicle, crouching between Brynn and Desmond.

Covered by the morning fog, figures kneel on the ground with their hands tied behind their backs. Other figures pace around them, which I can only assume are armed guards.

"Have they started the broadcast yet?" I ask Brynn.

"Not yet," she answers.

From the looks of it, security isn't as heavy as I thought. None of the Ashtanabans look like proditors. Do they really think blocking off all the streets will be enough to shield them from an attack? So far, our vehicle has snuck past the barriers without any issue. Hell, there aren't even checkpoints the way there usually is when politicians from Ashtanabo arrive.

Desmond parks the car on the side of the road. From this position, it's easier to see amid the fog. Some hostages are crying. One looks like he's begging a pacing guard, only to be ignored completely. Others whisper to themselves in prayer.

"There isn't any indication of hidden traps or heat signatures beyond what's normal for this area of town, so there are no hidden army of proditors waiting to ambush us," Brynn says. "No snipers either."

"I say we should go for it," Connor says from the back. "We can use the fog to our advantage."

All of us look between each other in agreement. Now is as good a time as any. We know what we signed up for with this mission.

One by one, we exit the vehicle crouched. Brynn stays behind to monitor the mission and instruct us through our earpieces.

We use the other cars parked on the street to our advantage, hiding our approach. The better view I get of the town square, the more shocked I am by the set up. Yes, there are cameras, and yes, there are armed guards ready to execute the hostages. With the skills of our team and the amount of Ashtanaban guards, the success rate of this mission is climbing dramatically, confirming my theory that Knox has no idea I saw into his mind.

Desmond throws a hand up for us to stop while he looks over the hood of a car. He then uses his pointer finger to assign each assassin a guard to eliminate. While they do so, I'll be ready to free each hostage. My handgun is heavy on my hip, and I pray to the gods I don't have to use it. My crows are already whispering sweet nothings into my ears, begging me to pull the trigger anyway.

After our teammates spread out along the row of guards and aim their guns, Desmond swings down his hand.

Shots fire out. Then screams.

The hostages cover their heads while our team takes out the surrounding guards. They must be horrified and think the execution has started early. I need to be quick.

A few other rebels and I stay low while we rush into the square, putting full trust in the others to cover us from any stray guards.

The purple sunrise peeks out from the horizon as I rush into the sea of hostages. A guard aims his gun at me, but I quickly duck before he can shoot, then I slide on my side to trip him before knocking him out with the butt of his own gun. The crows reward me with a rush of euphoria, and I bite the inside of my cheek to suppress the accompanying thoughts.

A girl around my age is sobbing, and I briskly kneel in front of her. "You're going to be okay. We're here to rescue you." I keep low as the battle around me roars on, bullets firing and men grunting. Desmond, Alarik, and the others have advanced now, brawling with guards in close range.

I use my dagger to saw off the girl's cloth binds and then hand her a dagger of her own. "Help me free the others. Then run south."

She nods and turns to an older man on her right, continuing the chain. It's one of the few ways to make this go as swiftly as possible.

Everything smells of gunpowder and smoke as I continue to free people. One woman is passed out from the sheer terror of it all and I use smelling salts to revive her.

I scan the area, sighing in relief when I see Alarik alive and well, skillfully knocking out two guards. We've already lost a few of our members, but Ashtanabo has lost even more. They weren't prepared for an ambush. But why? They know the rebellion resides in Merth.

Lavenai is a large planet. Why have it here in the first place?

It's at that moment that I see the red light of the cameras turn on.

By now, nearly all the hostages are freed. They know the rebellion has won. There's nothing to ambush us with either.

Why televise it now? Were the cameras automatically set to go live and showing our victory is just a catastrophic mistake on Ashtanabo's end?

The jumbotron turns on. I straighten up as the last few hostages run to safety and the final Ashtanaban guard is neutralized.

No. It can't be . . .

Upon the screen are around twenty people bound and gagged in some kind of warehouse, surrounded by proditors and guards.

I shoot a look at Alarik across the square, who is just as pale and shocked as I am.

A mic'd up voice reverberates over the town square, sending a chill up my spine. "Where the rebellion goes, death follows. And yet, it's not the rebellion that is punished for their own disobedience, but all of you, the citizens of Lavenai."

I didn't see him at first, standing on a nearby building balcony stories above. Knox Arris stares straight at me. An overwhelming nausea overtakes my entire body. And he's not alone. Onyx and Crux are with him and—

Dimitri.

Oh gods, Dimitri.

My knees go weak and I catch my body on a nearby light post to steady myself. The details on the jumbotron amplify his state. He's barely able to stand. Knox's hand grips the back of his neck to keep him upright. His body is bruised, bloody, and battered, and he has that look in his eyes. The one he could never understand when I returned to the rebellion with it myself. There's a shudder beneath his skin, a quiver to his breath, and a begging in his eyes.

Knox's lips curl. "The rebellion ignored my threats at the risk of all of you. I'm not naïve, dear Lavens. I will never be taken for a fool or a bluffer. We all know what happens when a child tries to dodge the whip of their father—things only get worse."

Crows chuckle in the back of my head, and I can't stop the shake of fear and fury that overtakes my fingertips.

I flinch when the echoes of bullets ring out through the jumbotron, people shrieking and blood spraying. I'm completely numb while I watch, and I'm not sure why I can't look away. Their blood is on my hands. I should have known this was too easy.

Tricked you, tricked you, his crows taunt inside my head.

I didn't extract a thought from Knox's mind. He implanted lies into my own.

Knox tilts his head and looks down at Dimitri, pleased with himself.

No, not him too. Please don't, I beg internally, knowing that, even if I shouted, Knox wouldn't be able to hear me from here. Not without a microphone.

I have to save him. I don't know if it means scaling a building or trying to shoot Knox from here, but I can't let him have Dimitri.

Knox continues his speech. "Shame to have lost so many good people, but let this be a lesson to you all. Though I have a different ultimatum for tomorrow's festivities. Instead of my previous demands, there's only one person from the rebellion who must themselves in—Margot Tavish. If she does not, twenty more people will die." He looks down at Dimitri. "Forgive me, twenty-one."

Nausea fills my stomach. No, I can't let that happen. I can't lose him. I'd risk a thousand bullets to save him.

My crows peck at my mind, begging me to step forward so they can be reunited with their true master upon the balcony. They promise me life—Dimitri's life.

You're lying, I tell them. But I don't believe myself.

Do it, and we promise you'll win in the end, they say.

I consider their words. No one knows where the crows' true allegiances lie. No Vicar or proditor does. Could they be telling the truth?

I find one foot moving in front of the other, seemingly without my control. I've grown weary, failure after failure. I can't let any more innocents die on my behalf. And Dimitri isn't allowed to leave me alone on this planet . . .

"That's it . . . " Knox coos.

A body quickly steps in front of mine, completely covering my view of Knox and Dimitri.

"Margot. The hostages are all freed. Get inside the vehicle," Alarik says.

My bottom lip shakes as I stare up at Alarik's blood-speckled face. "But—"

"You have to leave him. Don't you see? It was never about the hostages. This entire time, he only wanted *you*."

Knox's voice rings out again. "I'm a merciful Colum. Margot Tavish has until midnight to turn herself into the Cymru Hotel, and all detainees will be released in her place. But after that . . . "

Dimitri's mouth moves as if screaming. He thrashes painfully and I'm completely incapable of stopping it. It's as if I can feel the edges of the entrancement by my own memories alone. The emptiness, the physical torment, the lost dreams. It's like standing near a fire and holding your hand close enough to barely tolerate the heat, but it opens a world of possibilities of what sticking your hand inside may actually feel like.

An overwhelming numbness takes over as the vehicle speeds up next to us. And before I can consider dropping to my knees and surrendering myself, Alarik wraps his arm around my torso, dragging me against my will to the vehicle filled with rebels screaming for us to get in.

Alarik practically throws me inside and slams the door shut behind us. The vehicle takes off and I'm forced to watch as Knox unhands Dimitri and lets his unconscious body and broken mind crumble to the ground.

Chapter 23

Milo

When I see my cousin on the screen from the rebellion's control center, restraining none other than Margot's cousin, I can't stay seated a second longer. As if it wasn't bad enough that Knox had secretly kidnapped twice the amount of people he said he would, now I have to watch Margot make a decision in front of the rest of the world.

"Dimitri . . ." Lucinda says to herself, watching him carefully. She tries to hide her shaking hands as she zooms in on his face on the screen.

Of course, most people watching don't realize that the Margot Tavish he speaks of is already on their screens, but I do. I see the hopelessness and defeat in her eyes. Her raging crows. Once I see her take a step forward, I curl my fists.

My mother is also in the room and steps close to me, placing a hand on my arm to try to calm me down. But I barely register it.

Don't do it, I whisper to Margot, as if she can hear me. *This is exactly what he wants from you. He planned all of this.*

When Alarik stands in front of Margot, preventing her from going any further, I wipe the sweat from my brow and decide against shattering a nearby glass screen.

But what else would I expect from my cousin? Of course he would blackmail her. She's his lethal pawn. I want to kill him. Choke the life out of him.

After Margot and Alarik's team successfully escapes the city, I follow Lucinda into a debriefing room to await their arrival.

Lucinda sits across from me, things painfully quiet. She taps her foot. Checks her watch.

"She almost did it . . . " I say. "She would have given herself up to him."

Lucinda pretends to sort through papers in front of her instead of meeting my gaze. "I'm well aware."

"She can't go on any more missions. Not with Dimitri involved. It's too risky. Her crows are too sick. She won't be able to trust herself any longer."

"You don't have the authority to make such calls." But I can tell by the look on her face that she agrees with me.

"Knox planned all of this from the beginning. A decoy execution? I shouldn't have underestimated him."

"And he will continue to have the upper hand if we let our emotions control us. He does have a rebel hostage, after all."

"And what about you? If Margot is like your daughter, isn't Dimitri like your son?"

The papers crinkle slightly under her touch. "I train spies. Soldiers. I would never do myself the disservice of letting you learn a single one of my weaknesses."

She could have just said yes.

The doors slide open, and I can smell the metallic stench of blood even before I crane my head around to see the group. One by one, rebels find their seats.

A gray cloud fills the room and the pain is contagious. Something tells me Margot wasn't the only one who was shaken up about leaving Dimitri behind.

Alarik files in, then lastly behind him, Margot.

Her skin is sheet white, her lips pressed tightly together as if she might lose her breakfast. I remember having a similar feeling too when I saw my father's cold corpse lying stiff upon his hard bedroom floor.

Knowing your family member is in the custody of one of the most sadistic men in the solar system is enough to play with anyone's head.

Margot sits diagonally across the oval table from me, but I wish she would've taken the empty seat to my left, which Alarik is now getting comfortable in.

"Lives were lost today, even rebellion ones." Lucinda straightens her posture. "But I don't want any one of you to see this as a loss. Though we couldn't have accounted for the second group of hostages, the core of our mission was a success. You saved every life you set out to rescue."

She rattles on about some other elements of the mission, but I watch Margot the entire time. She doesn't even seem here right now while she chews her bottom lip bloody.

Finally, one word pulls her back into the room.

"Dimitri," Lucinda starts, "is in custody of the Arris Reign, and from the looks of it, they've been torturing him for a while."

"And what do you suppose we do about it?" Margot interjects. Everyone looks at her and her fist clenched upon the table.

Lucinda frowns. "For one, we are not going to give in to the demands of Knox Arris."

"But we could use it to our advantage. I could trade places with Dimitri, and if you equip me with tracking and mic equipment, as well as something to assassinate him . . . "

"Absolutely not," I interrupt.

"This doesn't concern you, Milo," Margot shoots back.

"You really think you'll be able to overtake him? He might be reckless, but he's also intelligent and is a masterful manipulator. Don't you see this is all a big trick? Considering the state Dimitri is in, he's probably already going to—"

Margot furrows her brows and stands, slapping her palms on the table. "Are you saying I just go about the rest of the plan and let my cousin die?"

"Yes."

Pain flashes across her face. "It's easy for you to say. You almost killed him twice yourself."

My lungs constrict at her words, enough for Alarik to notice. She might be right that Dimitri has been in his fair share of near-death scenarios because of me, but it's not the same. She knows it isn't. Hell, I've almost ended her life even more than his. But I can't stand the weight on my chest that I could have been the one to take away what little happiness she has.

"Margot, that's enough," Lucinda snaps. "Though I don't disagree with your analysis, you're losing control of your emotions. Milo is right that you cannot give yourself over. You know I won't stop trying to find an alternative way to free Dimitri. But you are absolutely not allowed to turn yourself in. Do you understand?"

Margot turns her head, refusing to look at Lucinda or me. "I understand."

Lucinda eases back into the meeting and goes over combat scenarios, and what rebels could do better in the future to avoid death and injuries.

I've seen a lot of emotions from Margot over the last year, but I've never seen her like this. It's like she's a different person, and the next time I'm able to touch her, I'll give her a break from her crows. Grief is bad enough without Knox's crows amplifying every feeling.

After the meeting concludes, the rebels pour out. Alarik goes to stay with Lleu, a privilege now awarded to him for gaining Lucinda's trust.

Margot looks like she wants to strangle me or whatever imaginary projection of Knox is floating around in her head. I can feel their inaudible whispers to herself through the air. My own crows try to hide from her crows' mere presence.

I follow Margot back to her room, even though she's clearly trying to outpace me.

Once she gets there, she tries to shut the door before I can get inside, but I place my hand on the sliding door and shove it back open, almost breaking the internal mechanisms. "Margot."

She ignores me and sits on the bed, removing her boots.

I sigh and pull out the desk chair, spinning it to face her before sitting. "You know I wasn't trying to hurt you. I just want you to be safe and think logically about this."

"Logically?" Margot scoffs while she tosses her shoes across the room. "The second I saw Knox on that balcony, I knew that logic no longer existed, only the will of the crows." Margot closes her eyes and pinches her nose.

"You blame yourself. Nothing of this is your fault. You have to know that."

"But—"

"Do you think Dimitri was captured after your dream? No, he was clearly already in Knox's care for much longer than that. Lucinda said as much. Your presence only sped up the inevitable."

"If I lose him, I don't know what will become of the crows. I spend half my energy every day pushing them down. But if he dies, the final thread may break."

"Come here."

To my surprise, Margot slowly pushes out of her bed and comes toward me. She wraps her arms around me and straddles me in the seat.

I hug her back tightly and bring my hand to the back of her neck, nullifying Knox's crows. It's getting harder each time to do so. They are incessant, fighting back against my own flock. All I know is that Margot isn't well. In fact, I'm not going to let her out of my sight for the foreseeable future. The crows will do everything they can to tempt her into saving Dimitri. I won't let that happen.

Once Knox's crows are finally asleep, she breaks down into a sob. I say nothing while her cries soak my neck. Nothing while her body shakes in my arms. Sometimes the forewarning of grief is worse than mourning itself.

I am taken by surprise when her lips find mine. I kiss her back and shudder with pleasure when she sighs and melts into me.

To her dismay, I break the kiss. "Margot, you're not well. This isn't the time . . . "

"Please, Milo. Distract me." Margot's lips find my neck and her hands snake up my shirt.

Pleasuring her doesn't seem like what she needs right now. She needs to rest.

My thoughts are sharply interrupted as she cups and strokes me through my pants. I groan, blood rushing to one place.

I don't fight her when she kisses me again, nor when she finds her way under my beltline, stroking me bare. All rationality goes out the window whenever she touches me like this. Like she's solely in control of my every instinct and desire. And I wouldn't have it any other way.

Margot pulls me to the floor and gets on top of me, but I take the lead by rolling on top of her, pecking her jaw. Sucking her neck.

I get both of us undressed, positioning her on her stomach and licking up her back. She trembles once I reach the back of her neck.

"You scared the shit out of me today. If I lost you—" Some of my senses come back, even as I hook a hand under her leg and adjust it for better access.

"I know . . . I was reckless." Margot whimpers, turning slightly so I can see her face. She's so beautiful like this. With her swollen lips and flushed cheeks.

"I'll never let him have you, Margot. You hear me? You're mine. Not his. *Mine.*"

"I don't want to talk about him. Please, just take me."

I enter her with a seethe, and a moan consumes her. Gods, she feels so good.

I rest my forehead against the back of her head, taking her in like she's the only thing that exists in this universe filled with pain and horrors. For a second, I forget all about pleasure itself, even while she trembles beneath me with her own.

Instead, I think about how I want nothing more than to see her happy. Safe. How I wish we could leave both planets behind and live out our days in peace. How, if I were ever Colum again, I could give her both worlds and more. I would give her the universe and the stars if I could. I would wear her pain as my own.

As Margot climaxes, it stirs my own along and I angle her head to kiss her as I spill out. Whatever we were before doesn't matter. It's who we are now that does. And somehow she still loves me, despite everything.

She sits up, and I hug her tightly. I never want to let her go. I'd trade my soul if it meant never letting this moment end.

"You're everything to me, Margot Tavish." I kiss the side of her scalp and rub her back. I extend my crows' healing touch, no matter the toll it takes on me. Even the small number of Knox's crows that have reawakened brings an unsettling chill down my spine. They are furious with me.

I stay with her all day, reading a book while she showers and then forcing her to take a nap while I run my fingers through her hair. Knox's crows are fast, and I swear they are getting stronger every hour. Even after removing my hand from her head for mere seconds to turn the page of my book, they've already started to nip at her again by the time my touch returns.

That night, I try to stay awake as long as I can before I drift off into sleep, holding her tight against my chest. As I do, I dream of sweetness and bitterness and everything in between. Mostly, I dream of Margot. I dream of her as the wife I wish she knew she already was.

I'm awakened by a frantic voice knocking at the door.

I shoot up and immediately soak in the coldness of the mattress. The empty divet in Margot's pillow.

I rush to the door and have a near heart attack at seeing Lucinda standing on the other side. I awkwardly scratch the back of my neck, knowing there's no excuse she'll accept for me being in Margot's room so late at night.

But she doesn't seem to care about that in the slightest. She barrels past me. "Margot!"

Lucinda sticks her head into the bathroom and then slowly backs out, her eyes widened in panic.

"What's wrong?"

Lucinda faces me, clutching her chest. "There is poison missing from the stock. It disappeared an hour ago without prior authorization. I think Margot is turning herself in to Knox."

Chapter 24

Dune

I sit in an old-fashioned cell with walls of steel bars in the basement of the Cymru hotel. My arm rests on my propped-up knee. The odors from previous prisoners bring a scrunch to my nostrils. This cell doesn't even have the decency of a cot.

In the cell next to mine, Dimitri lies on his side, scars and bruises along his chest, his breaths irregular. As the hours have passed, I'm never sure when he is in or out of consciousness. Sometimes, I think his soul has finally given in, but he always heaves in a single large breath a moment later.

Seeing him reminds me of all the ways I've failed. Not just him, but my oath. I should have known Knox would stumble upon my true ideals in time. My face is bare, and my soul is naked. I've been stripped of my identity and left to rot.

I've thought of a million and one ways to get out of here, but none of them will work. The hyssopite hanging from the high ceiling makes sure of that. I can feel its floral scent tickling my nostrils, weakening my muscles. It takes a proditor to think like one.

At one point, a guard enters the prison to deliver our dinner. He slides mine through the slot under the barred door and does the same for Dimitri. Then they leave, not even giving Dimitri a second glance. He hasn't had the strength to even stir, let alone to eat. At the very least, he needs the water.

"Dimitri?" I scoot to the bars that separate us and reach for him through the bars, shaking him. My bicep almost gets stuck. "Wake up."

Dimitri adjusts his head, his lips trembling. He can hear me, thankfully. But he doesn't move an inch. His mind is still stuck, one foot inside the world of the crows and the other in reality. I look up at the hyssopite. Its presence is overwhelming. If only I had even a fraction of my crows, then I could at least wake him. Allow him to regain his own strength.

Suddenly, I feel the flutter of feathers upon the back of my mind. I look closer inside, but my crows are asleep—dulled by the hyssopite, as expected. Then I spot it, hidden among the deep recesses of my mind. Two crows, heads cocked and standing together, unaffected.

Milo's crows.

When I draw near, they coo at me. At that moment, I know they're willing to save me the way I once saved them. Balistar always said oaths could do strange things to crows, that they could morph into something unlike their kin.

It certainly won't be enough to overpower any guards, but I can at least slowly untie Dimitri's mental binds.

I don't hesitate, touching the bare skin of his arm. With none of my own crows able to bear the burden, I take Knox's dark residue upon myself, letting the two crows fly toward Dimitri's mind. A dark shiver runs down my spine, and then I'm inside.

I stand upon a plush red rug inside a pristine venue decorated for a party. The tables are set, the floors are clean, and the windows are scrubbed.

Shadows play at the edges of my vision, but I ignore them, walking among faceless party guests, noteless music, and flameless candle light.

My vision glitches twice, and within seconds, the party becomes a place of horrors.

The string quartet plays off-tune, screeching notes. Many of the lights flicker out. There's so much discarded food and ripped-up decor that I cannot even see the floor. Chairs have been thrown through windows, glass in piles.

It's all familiar, though—it's the mind of someone tormented by a proditor.

It's only when I see the chandelier hanging by a thread from the split-open ceiling and the bloody handprints streaked along the walls and floor that I sense the ill crows and pervasive ravens.

The party guests are ghostly now, floating around the room with stale faces, mouths stuck open in frozen screams.

I try my best to find Dimitri, dismantling the perversions one by one as I go. I shout his name. I don't have much energy, and with only two of Milo's crows, I won't have long before I'll be kicked out of his mind entirely.

Then I hear a small cry under a table.

I bend down and lift the tablecloth to discover a small child hiding underneath, covering his ears. He is shaking and crying.

"Quickly." I extend my hand to him. "We don't have much time to get you out of here."

Young Dimitri squints one of his eyes open briefly and then shuts it tightly again. He can't speak, and I can hear the new monsters that now roam around the tablecloth, the steps of their large feet vibrating the fabric around us.

He's petrified, unable to move even with the threat of new monsters closing in around him.

I have no choice. I must pull him out by force. It won't be as effective as if he left his fear willingly, but I don't know how much longer either of us have.

I grab Dimitri's arm and pull.

"No! They'll find me!" Dimitri thrashes. His form in this section of his mind may only be a young boy, but he fights me like a full-grown man. "Let go!"

I pull him out from under the tablecloth, and as he screams, the prison comes back into view.

As I suck in a breath, Dimitri's eyes open. *Thank the gods.*

He groans as I pull him across the ground toward me until he rests against the bars between us.

"What on earth did he do to you?" I say mostly to myself. Dimitri's even worse off than he was before Knox knocked me out. I can only imagine Knox had a last hurrah with him, putting him through the wringer in a way he doesn't even do to women, his preferred targets. There are bruises along Dimitri's wrists and ankles and across his neck.

Dimitri scans his battered body and the surrounding room, as if searching for the monsters. When he sees me, he breathes in relief.

"Here, you need to drink." I reach through the bars and place his water cup in his hand, making sure he has a good grip on it before I let go.

"Margot . . . She's not here, right?" Dimitri asks.

I shake my head. My gaze dips to where his other hand rests protectively against his side. He needs a doctor.

"I need to send a message to her," he says. "She can't come for me. I know she will."

"Milo will not let her."

"Yeah? If you think that, then you don't know my cousin."

In this case, I believe him.

With a sigh, Dimitri says, "I suppose that's the thing about family, though. When there's no one left, there's nothing left to lose." He takes a few gulps of his drink then grimaces. Still, he's improving drastically. Well, his mind is, anyway. "What about you, proditor? Do you have any family?"

"My mother, father, and sister." I pause. "All alive, back on Ashtanabo."

"An intact family of four? Luck is on your side."

"I guess I never thought of it that way. I've been busy. It's been awhile since I've checked in."

"No girl?" Dimitri asks.

I stiffen. "The responsibility of an Imnicus proditor is extremely time-consuming."

"Ah, so there *was* a girl." Dimitri smiles wide, but then winces at a flare of pain. He takes another drink, shaking off the aftereffects. "What's her name?"

I shake my head. "It doesn't matter. She's been claimed for years now."

Dimitri frowns. "So? Get her back."

"I don't approve of breaking up marriages."

"I see." Dimitri nods, conceding his point. He swirls the small remaining bit of water left in his cup. "This must be from Ashtanabo's tap. I wonder what kind of ship liner they use to carry water through space."

"What?"

"You know, how different regions have different tasting water? This one has an over-purified taste." Dimitri takes another sip with his eyes scrunched, as if downing terrible medicine.

The prison doors open and two guards enter. I narrow my eyes at them. Even without the strength of the crows, I won't make it easy if they try to round me up. Then again, if Knox wanted to see me, he would have sent at least one proditor.

But the guards don't pay me any mind, and all of them funnel into Dimitri's cell. They grab him, and he drops the cup on its side. He's barely able to walk as it is, but the movement seems to be hurting him as they haul him to his feet.

"What's going on? Where are you taking him?" I stand, gripping the bars.

"I don't have to answer to you anymore," one spits.

"Tell Knox I demand to speak to him."

He ignores me, and I can't help but study Dimitri once again. Yes, he's been through the wringer with Knox, but he's declining again. Rapidly.

They drag him out of the cell, then the door to the prison closes behind him. I'm left in silence, my circling thoughts as my only company. The timing of their return was certainly erratic. Something must have happened, and if they took Dimitri, this can't be good.

Still, with only two guards, it was quite a gamble that he'd be conscious enough to cooperate. Unless, of course, they were watching us through the cameras. If that's the case, it's strange they'd allow me to free Dimitri from his trance, but if Knox was that worried about it, he wouldn't have placed us in these primitive cells where we could reach through the bars to each other.

All blood floods from my chest. Knox is not a man of convenience. Every act, every detail, he does with intention. He's a trickster, playing the fool when it best suited him. What good does it do to place us here, free to conspire through the bars?

And Dimitri's comment about the water—we do not ship water from Ashtanabo. Everyone on this planet uses the same water. Noble, citizen, proditor, and Colum all drink from the same purification centers.

I scramble forward, dipping my finger in the tiny puddle left from Dimitri's overturned cup. The water is bitter upon my tongue, and my heart skips a beat.

Knox knew I would free Dimitri. He wanted me to.

He knew I'd be the reason Dimitri could drink that whole cup, knowing that whatever happens next will be on my hands.

I slump back on my knees. My hands fall limp by my side. Knox had won again, and he didn't even have to step foot in the room.

Chapter 25

Margot

The chilly night nips at me. A poison pen hidden under my bra presses against my skin. Most streets are empty besides a scant vehicle or two that passes on occasion, paying me no mind. Often, when things were still somewhat safe for rebellion members, I would throw on a respirator and take midnight walks. Sometimes, I'd take Dimitri along with me. Other times, I could convince Oliver to join while Dimitri was dead asleep.

I imagine Milo chasing after me. His voice pleading, *"Please. Turn back."*

But the crows swallow up his words, ripping the picture of his face from my head. *We're with you, Margot. This is the choice you were meant to make. Without you, Dimitri will die.*

Yes. If I don't do this, I will lose him forever. Whatever Knox did to my cousin . . . I know it was despicable. Life was drained from Dimitri's eyes. He looked like he'd been through hell and back. But saving him isn't my only goal.

I'm going to kill Knox. Poison him when he least expects it. And if I fail? Well, I'll have no choice except to use the poison on myself. When it comes to Knox, death is a better fate than staying alive.

As I approach the Cymru hotel, fifteen minutes before the deadline, I take in the guards patrolling the courtyard in a staggered fashion, all of them armed. It doesn't take long before one stares at me through his helmet's visor. He presses a finger to the left of his helmet as more start to take notice.

I won't give them the benefit of seeing me cower, so instead I focus on the statue of Balistar Arris, who looks rather pleased with himself even in stone form.

When I enter the lobby, a gust of herbal-scented air whooshes at me from the airlock, rustling my curls. I remove my respirator as I walk and discard it on the floor without stopping. The lobby is definitely Ashtanaban-owned with its boxy cathedral ceiling and pillars of black marble. Artisan paintings hang in gilded frames. Crystal-clear water flows in a fountain in the center.

"Something told me you'd come."

My stomach tightens. On the other side of the lobby, past the fountain, stands two familiar proditors.

And, of course, Knox Arris, with his eyes lost on my form.

He sits on a pillowed chair, exactly how I'd expect Balistar's protégé to—arrogantly, yet like he was meant for power. His smile is small and satisfied. I shiver as his bottom lip moves slightly as he drags his tongue along the inside, hungry for this newly trapped prey.

Crux's lethal gaze hits mine and I evade it by looking at Onyx, who immediately breaks the contact. I grimace.

I stop walking once I'm around twenty feet away. "We have business to attend to."

"Come closer," Knox says.

My brows furrow. "No."

Knox laughs and crosses his legs. "Smart girl. Though, I'm the one with the bullets, or should I remind you?"

"If you wanted me dead, I would be bleeding out in the courtyard."

"Yes, and you haven't even thanked me for not doing so." Knox taps the armrests with his fingertips. "How rude."

Blood churns through my pounding heart. It's too late to go back. What's done is done, even if I'm on the brink of pissing myself. This is the path I've chosen, so I intend to follow through. But my mind and my crows remind me of each time Knox has gotten ahold of me. The invasions. The scars.

"Release Dimitri," I demand.

"Oh, come on, we'll get to that. First, we have a lot to catch up on, don't we? Linked crows, broken temple points, traitorous proditors."

"Are you referring to yourself?"

Knox narrows his eyes. "I did what I had to do to protect my uncle's wishes. After all, treason is only defined by its relation to the Arris Reign."

"Yet you don't truly care for Balistar's ideals, do you? Only the violence it takes to accomplish them."

Knox straightens his back but says nothing.

"Let Dimitri go," I say firmly.

"Your cousin is safe and sound."

"Define safe."

"Fine. Sound then." Knox pushes up from his chair and saunters over to me, studying every inch of my rebellion attire. "You came alone, I hope?"

"I am here by my own volition, against the rebellion's orders." *And Milo's.*

Knox stops behind me. There's a beat of silence before I can feel his chest lightly against my back. "Good."

A tremble forms within my chest, and I constrict my limbs to stop it. Controlling the shake in my voice is almost impossible. "I won't ask again, Knox."

"Hmm." Knox places his hands on my shoulders.

My entire body is stiff. His warm hands sear through the fabric. At any second, he could lift his thumb and stroke the side of my neck, temporarily stealing his crows back and my strength along with them. Leaving me defenseless.

"There he is, the man of the hour."

I turn my head as pained gasps echo through the lobby.

Two guards roughly drag Dimitri across the smooth floor.

Dimitri . . . what in the gods' names . . .

If he looked bad earlier, he looks awful now. His face is whiter than paper, striped with swollen gray-green veins.

"Dimitri!" I yell and try to rush forward, but Knox holds me back. His fingers tighten around my shoulders. "Knox, what did you do to him?"

"Nothing I wouldn't do to you."

"Let me go to him," I demand.

The guards unhand Dimitri, and he folds onto the floor. He lies there for a second and then groans as he pushes himself up to look at me. "Margot . . . You shouldn't have come here."

"And leave you to die?" My voice cracks.

"He's a liar and you know it. Go while you still can."

I can't tell him that saving him isn't the only reason I'm here. Even if it was, I could never leave him to die.

Knox unhands me and takes a step back. "I will keep my word." He motions to the exit. "One of you stays and one of you leaves, as promised."

Dimitri shakes slightly while he forces himself to his feet. Have they been feeding him? His face is so gaunt. There are bruises along his jaw and neck that disappear down his shirt's collar. He just looks at me, heartbroken.

"I know you're worried about me," I tell him. "Just . . . go, please. You know you have to."

"You don't understand . . . " He places a hand on his abdomen as he grabs back the words.

Knox clears his throat. "Be on your way, before I change my mind."

"Please go, Dimitri," I beg.

He looks between Knox and me and shakes his head, a small tear running down his face. I know he's scared for me. I'm scared for me too. He needs to trust me.

Dimitri's feet drag toward the exit, and I pray that rebels have already noticed I'm gone and are scanning the area. The only way he'll get back in his condition is with their help.

I watch as he passes under the threshold and walks down the path of the courtyard. His legs wobble slightly, and then he almost loses his balance, catching himself on the tall base of Balistar's statue. He pushes away from it and freezes.

To my horror, he collapses on his side.

"Dimitri!" I scream.

Knox doesn't stop me as I run out of the lobby and into the courtyard.

My cousin shivers as I approach. Whatever is happening has nothing to do with crows.

I roll him onto his back. "Are you okay? Say something!" I feel his pulse. It's too slow.

He tries to reach for me, as if he's trying to hug me, but his hand falls limp against the ground. "I'm so sorry."

"What are you sorry for?" Seeing him like this is unbearable.

Dimitri coughs, and it sounds like his lungs are full. "Please run while you still can."

Yes, I know that Knox tortured him. Yes, I know his body is weak from it. But he should be strong enough to walk. Something else is happening here.

"Margot," his voice cracks slightly. "You can't save me from this. Before, I didn't understand why you changed so much after you escaped the Imnicus." He forces a laugh that turns into a cough. "Life has a funny way of humbling you."

Dimitri looks up at the night sky. A tear falls down his cheek. I only notice it now, the clamminess taking over his face. "Do you know what my most fond memory is? It wasn't when we'd make pillow forts or steal extra snacks in the middle of the night. It was when we would make up stories about our valiant parents, and how in the afterlife, they went on adventures together, all four of them."

He's growing colder by the second and I don't understand what's happening. He's not . . . he couldn't be . . .

Knox now stands a few feet behind me. I sharply scream at him, "Tell me what you did!"

Dimitri grabs my arm. "Please, Margot. Give me this."

"You're . . . dying. Why are you dying?" I hold him close to my chest as if it will stop what is about to happen.

Dimitri ignores my question. "Be the victor that our parents wanted to be." His eyes are barely open, and his lips are turning purple.

"Stay with me, Dimitri." I tap the side of his face. "You still have so much to do. Remember? The wife and the cabin in the mountains? The children? Aren't I supposed to be an aunt?"

"The gods will give me everything I've ever wanted," Dimitri's neck loses tone as his head tips back. "Now, fight back."

As Dimitri's body goes limp, my ears ring so loudly that it drowns out all other sounds. Everything becomes a void so loud and quiet at the same time. I don't notice Knox anymore. Nor Crux or Onyx.

I'm out of my body. If it weren't for the crows trying to numb me, I'd be sobbing on a lifeless chest then screaming up at the gods.

The ringing deafens for a second as I sit back on my knees. I can see Dimitri, far across the courtyard, standing in the shadows and smiling the happiest I've ever seen him.

"Please," I whisper. "Don't go."

He takes a few steps back into the darkness as I reach for him to stay.

The world speeds up again and I don't recognize it . . . this world that now exists without his lifeline in it. Somehow I feel as though it's all my fault. The crows withdraw the blind confidence they gave me, forcing me to feel the weight and stupidity of my actions.

What they don't withdraw is my anger, and I look at the proditors around me. The final straw in me breaks.

I'll kill them all.

I grab a dagger off my belt and charge at the closest proditor to me—Crux. He takes a step back, but my fury hastens my pace. Before he can grab me, I slide on the ground, ramming a dagger into his thigh.

Crux curses and yells, holding on to his leg. "Shit!"

"Restrain her," Knox commands, and I hate the laziness in his tone. The lack of urgency. As if he knows he's still going to win.

Onyx runs at me next, and everything becomes a mess of strikes, dodges, and blocks between us. He's fast, but I don't let up. My crows drive me. For a second, there's a glimmer of fear in Onyx's own eyes, like he might not be able to block my blows any longer.

Until he rips the tip of his glove off with his teeth and catches my hand in his. The second I feel that bare sliver of skin, my strength drains out of me. *No.*

I'm grabbed by Onyx first and then Crux limps over to take hold of my other arm, as if I stabbed him with a mere toothpick.

Two of the nearby guards throw a sheet over Dimitri, as if this has been planned from the beginning.

"Don't touch him!" I scream. "I said don't fucking touch him!"

Knox steps in front of me, and for once he doesn't have a smile to wipe off. It might be the most serious I've ever seen him. He looks down at me while the guards drag my cousin's dead body away.

"You said you'd let him go!" I yell and thrash.

"And I did. He is now free."

"I'll fucking kill you!"

"I look forward to it." He motions to Onyx and Crux. "Take her to my room."

"No!" But I'm cuffed now, and it takes no effort for both proditors to take hold of my arms and drag me back into the hotel.

I give them hell the entire way. Even as they haul me into the elevator. As the doors close, I try to elbow Crux, but he evades it. Barely.

"Do you want to die?" Crux seethes and clenches his fist, ready to knock the wind out of me.

Onyx quickly puts his hand up. "Stop."

"Do you have a better idea?"

Onyx removes his glove and touches my neck. It's a lighter proditor trance, not one to torture, but one to subdue me. I'm on the edge of dreams, my legs weakening until I can't use them anymore.

Onyx picks me up bridal style, and Crux mutters something under his breath.

My vision is blurry, the side of my face resting against his proditor armor. The elevator doors open on the highest floor, and they take me down a hall and into a room.

I can't see anything anymore as Onyx lies me down on a mattress and the world shuts down.

Chapter 26

Milo

Chaos has fallen over the rebellion. Rebels scramble, pulling up camera feeds all over the city from here to the Cymru. Lucinda barks orders to the deployed search teams.

Margot, where are you?

I shouldn't have allowed myself to sleep. I knew the ways Knox's crows were affecting her judgment. They're exploiting her emotions, pulling on her bloodlust.

My mother uses a communicator to speak with someone across the city, but by the look on her face, I don't think she's any closer to finding Margot.

Lleu enters the large surveillance area and locks eyes with me, heading in my direction. She sighs as she spares a glance to the monitors with absolutely no sign of Margot.

She takes a seat next to me, and her eyes dip to the now-bulging veins of my forearms. "Alarik told me she was distraught. But I didn't think she'd really give in."

"Knox is messing with her head. He's good at that. Growing up, he'd play tricks on all of us to convince us to do his bidding. At the time, it was giving him the last cookie . . . "

"And now it's the balance between life and death." Lleu folds her arms. "Still, you need to mind your expressions. Your body language." She signals to a male rebel across the room eyeing me with unease.

I grit my teeth and release as much tension as my body allows. "Knox won't play fair with her."

"She's smart. And when survival is involved, she always manages to keep herself alive. I mean, she escaped you, didn't she?"

"Don't remind me." My jaw ticks. "Though you and Alarik were instrumental in that. At the Cymru, she has no one."

"And that's why we'll do everything to help her again."

Across the room, Alarik signals to Lucinda and points to his computer station. She rushes over to him.

Is Margot all right? Did Lucinda's spies stop her in time?

My heart stops as Lucinda's head drops and she releases a long exhale. "Call off the search."

Typing comes to a halt and chairs spin to face her. Lucinda folds her arms, her face an indecipherable mask of rage and sorrow. The very same emotions storming within me.

"She is in custody."

Nobody says a word. Lleu places a hand on my shoulder, a preemptive gesture to prepare for an outburst that does not come. I don't know what to say or do. How to feel.

But I'm not given a chance as my mother stands.

"Another update just came in." My mother looks nervously at Lucinda. "It's about Dimitri."

"Are the spies bringing him back here?"

My mother stays still for a second and slowly shakes her head. "He was released from the Cymru . . . His body was placed in front of one of our compromised entrances . . . "

His body . . .

My mother doesn't even have to say the word "dead" to get her message across. Her eyes are already watering. Everyone gives Dimitri a moment of silence, though sporadic cries break through. Some people even excuse themselves, unable to handle the news.

Lucinda is pale, refusing to cry. But even she can't hide the pure devastation.

In true Knox fashion, he kept his word while remaining the trickster he is. He's sharp and cunning. Deception won't be enough to stop him—he's already two steps ahead. He does not think like we do, not bound by even a sliver of morality.

My mother takes another call from her communicator. She lowers it after a minute of listening. "Lucinda, Joriel Sinclair is requesting to speak with you."

She pinches the bridge of her nose. "Now is not the time. I don't care what it's about. Send him away."

"Oliver made contact with him. He has news about Ashtanabo."

Lucinda looks as though her head is about to explode. She looks to my mother, who nods solemnly. This information is too important to pass up.

"Tell him we'll meet him at his club," Lucinda says.

"He is insistent that he will only deliver the news if he can meet you inside our walls," says my mother.

Alarik and I exchange glances. There's no way in hell she'll let him in here. Honestly, I don't blame her. My interactions with him have been few, but he knows how to create enemies out of people quickly.

"Send him in," Lucinda says.

There's a collective gasp and murmurs that ring throughout the rebellion. Seems Alarik and I weren't the only ones with the same thought.

"If he's so set on seeing inside the rebellion, then let's humor him. Is he available now?"

"Yes," my mother answers.

"Bring him to my office immediately. None of his bodyguards are allowed in. Only him. That's my compromise."

I don't know what Joriel's plan is, or if he has any ill intent at all. Perhaps he's like a toddler who can't bear not knowing what's on the other side of the door.

Lucinda motions to me. "Milo Arris, you'll come with me. Imory, you too."

I straighten my back and nod firmly once. Perhaps she'll use me as a human shield.

Joriel Sinclair enters Lucinda's office with a self-satisfied smirk, his cane twisting with a certain panache that raises even my blood pressure. Lucinda can barely keep her impatience under control.

He studies the walls and taps his cane against the ground. "My, my, Lucinda. You really have been hiding a city. I see why you've kept it to yourself."

"Sit," she says firmly.

"I'll have black tea, no sugar," he says to the rebel guard who's positioning to leave.

"Uh . . ." The girl looks at Lucinda.

Lucinda rubs her temple. "Indulge him."

The girl nods and leaves Lucinda, my mother, Joriel, and me alone for the time being.

Truth be told, I can only assume Lucinda wants me in this meeting to confirm the validity of Joriel's words. But what news is Ashtanabo hiding that hasn't made its way to Lavenai yet?

Joriel begins, "My father and your old superior, Donovan Mac-Manus, got along nicely enough. They often had tea down here, you know? Perhaps we should make it a habit. Keep old traditions."

"That's when this place was a drug haven and Laven tea was made from real plants," Lucinda says. "I don't keep the same habits as Bastien Sinclair."

Joriel frowns and places a hand on his chest, as if hurt. "Aren't we old friends?"

"I babysat you twice, and you're as spoiled now as you were then."

Joriel laughs as the rebel girl returns and sets down his tea. "Your memory is better than mine, Lucinda. Even if you're a bit . . . older."

Lucinda furrows her brows at the jab. Truth be told, she looks good for her age. "I hope you've brought truthful information. If you lied just to gain access, know you've made a dangerous mistake by coming here today."

He runs his fingers over the edge of his saucer. "I don't have a death wish. But I'm not the rebellion's errand boy either, am I? Running around carrying messages, smuggling your members between planets. It's humiliating. I had to get something out of it to balance the scales."

My mother interjects. "How is Oliver?"

Oliver, as I recently learned, was the other boy who tried to destroy the Susukan temple point with Margot, Anali, and Dimitri. I barely remember him. I was too busy fending off Margot and nearly shooting her cousin.

Joriel sighs. "Alive and well thanks to me. He mentioned that he recently took down a temple point in Iverat."

I breathe in sharply. That news hasn't reached our ears. Lavenai is isolated, fed only the information the Colum permits. However, it surprises me that Knox wouldn't use that fact to accelerate his executions. But why would this Oliver risk making contact?

"Iverat?" I ask. "That point is heavily guarded as of recently."

"It didn't seem to matter. You see, nothing happened. The temple point went down, and nothing changed. The land is healing or something. You know, while we're on the topic, Lucinda, you should warn me before you go about such things. I have investments on Ashtanabo, and these attacks have been—"

"What do you mean the land is healing?" I ask firmly.

Joriel shrugs. "The region is still intact, according to your little strike team. Oliver did no more than rustle a few trees."

This is impossible. Susuku and Ralia are evidence enough that Ashtanabo is nothing without its Laven life support. Without it, Susuku's flora shriveled and its water sources dried up. Ralia became so flooded that there's practically no land left. So, for Iverat to have restored itself . . . Well, they're lucky volcanoes didn't erupt when Oliver pulled that stunt.

Lucinda turns to me. "Milo? Did you know about this?"

"Of course not. If I had, there would have been no purpose for the temple points. There's a whole division of climatologists monitoring the land. What Joriel says should be impossible."

Joriel clears his throat. "Don't believe me? Phone in one of Miss Nolan's connections."

My mother chimes in, pulling out her communicator. "Already on it."

Lucinda ignores his challenge. "What is Oliver doing now?"

"Traveling back to Lavenai, with my help, I might add. Don't worry, he's paying his own debt this time."

Ashtanabo has been sick for as long as anyone can remember. What is happening now for my planet to heal itself as if it had no more than a scraped knee? Has Ashtanabo's poor health been a lie? Another convenient explanation weaved by my father? No, I've seen footage of the changes. Seen how Ashtanabo once was for myself. I maintained my justification of the temple points out of those facts, believing that the horrors we doled out to Lavenai were worth the benefit for my home. If even a shred of those facts are not true, if these temple points are not as necessary as I was led to believe, what grounds have I ever had to stand upon?

I swallow bile and move forward. It does not matter. Because right now, I am not the Colum. And with Knox on the throne, this new knowledge won't change anything in the slightest.

He'd enslave Lavenai even if both planets were perfectly healthy, just for the thrill of it.

Chapter 27

Margot

I thought what I felt for my parents all these years was grief. That the gods had created a space in my heart that only a mother and father could fill. Both that I would forever be without. My entire life I have felt their absence, missed them even without ever truly knowing them.

But true grief? No, I had never felt it fully until now. It's like a foe trying to mask itself as a healing friend. It's relentless, like nails scraping down the walls of your chest. A hand squeezing and contracting your heart. It's a pain you can't escape from. Even when your dreams are sweet, it's always there, watching and waiting. Yet I don't want it to leave.

More memories flood in—trying flavored ice chips for the first time as a child, and Dimitri crying when the cold froze his tongue.

His pale eyes staring lifelessly from where he lies on the dark, stone ground.

Chasing each other through the rebellion hallways, too young to know where we truly were but old enough to avoid restricted areas. Places we hid in anyway.

Blood pooling in his throat, bubbles of air struggling to escape.

It's relentless. A hand vise-gripped upon my heart. The joy of every friendly memory ripped away by the ceaseless battering upon my soul. Inescapable, even in my dreams.

As I claw through sleep, I push past the dreams, searching for him.

And when I find him, he's within a crowd of people, his back turned.

"Dimitri!" I rush toward him.

But he walks deeper into the crowd as if my voice was nothing more than a wisp.

A crow lands on my shoulder, its head nuzzling mine, trying to comfort me. I keep chasing my cousin, pushing past faceless people and shouting his name.

As I emerge from the crowd with labored breaths, I find him standing by a fountain with his back still turned to me.

Just let me see your face again. One last time.

"Dimitri?" I slowly step forward. The crow makes a small noise as I do.

I stop behind him and extend my hand, reaching for his shoulder.

When I touch his sleeve, his skin rustles like dead leaves.

"No!" I quickly spring forward, wrapping my arms around him from behind to try to keep him here. "Please!"

He says nothing as his body turns to crow feathers in my embrace. They fall slowly into an obsidian pile at my feet.

I fall to my knees. The crow on my shoulder caws as the feathers get caught up in the wind.

Come back. I'll do anything.

Even as the dream collapses and I open my eyes, no tears come.

I stare up at the high ceiling, lying in the bed. A formless pain runs through my body, pumping through my veins like blood. I can't seem to move, grief paralyzing me.

That is, until the sound of trickling water brings my thoughts to a halt.

It turns grief to fear, allowing me enough energy to turn onto my side.

The lavish bedroom comes into view. It's so large and well-furnished that it may as well be an apartment. The floor-to-ceiling windows overlook purple clouds and tips of skyscrapers.

Steam leaks out from under the bathroom door.

My knee-jerk response is to hide or escape. Knox is here. Showering.

But I didn't come here for that, otherwise, I would reach for the poison and free myself from Knox's imprisonment in my own way. Knox Arris needs to die when he least expects it.

Get up right now, I tell myself, allowing myself to replace all other feelings with anger. The crows are going to make an assassination attempt difficult. They have been lying to me, and I've been unable to convince myself of the real truth. Even now, I can't tell if I'm acting on logic or idiocy.

As I stand, the sound of the water stopping brings my thoughts to a halt.

Crows are already swarming my head with the anticipation of seeing Knox again, enough that a shake moves through my arms. The thoughts are the hardest they've ever been to control. The fantasies of how I want Knox to suffer are overwhelming. Because of them, I know this isn't the time to kill him. If I do, it will be sloppy. I think? Or is the energy they bring me exactly what I need to follow through with it?

A few moments later, the bathroom door opens, and I go still.

Knox steps out from the bathroom. My jaw ticks with blood lust just at the sight of him. He stands there, studying me, with nothing but a towel low around his hips. I quickly avert my eyes.

"Enjoying the accommodations?" Knox asks. It's laughable of me that there was ever a time I thought of him as a friend. A confidant. The person who was nothing but easygoing while Milo was insufferable. What a fool I was.

I take my time answering. "You think you can just flash a smile, and I'll forget all about what you've done?"

Knox takes a few steps down the tiered room onto my level. "Aren't you the hero you wanted to be? Laven lives have been spared because of you. Today's execution has been cancelled and people were freed. Or was there only one life you were truly concerned about?"

"Killing him was senseless!"

"But I got what I wanted, didn't I? Look at you, Little Fennec. You cannot contain my crows any longer. Any rational person would have known he'd still end up dead, yet you turned yourself in regardless. You need a teacher to control and appease them."

"I need you dead."

Knox doesn't stop walking until he's only a few feet from me, and I instinctively take a step back. With his chiseled body on display and his golden hair soaked from the shower, I can only imagine how many girls have fallen victim to his charm when he was off-duty.

How many of them he carved marks into.

A tremble of anger courses through me. Before I can throw a punch, he grabs my forearm and pins it above my head against the wall behind me. I try to slap him with the other, but he subdues that one too, as if reading my mind.

"Our bond is growing stronger by the minute." He stares deeper into my eyes. "It's like looking into a mirror. Have you had time to consider it?"

"Consider what?" I narrow my eyes.

He releases one of my arms and traces my collarbone. I turn my head slightly, a strange weight filling the room. What does he think he's doing?

"Becoming my Columess," he says.

Time stands still, and I don't know how to process what he's asking me. I had barely processed the words when he had said them before. He can't mean it, can he?

To stand by my side, he had said, *as my Columess.*

I shoot my gaze back to his dark and sultry eyes. I wait for a break in his expression. For him to crack a smile or start laughing, as if it's the most insane request he could ask me.

But it never comes.

Risking his wrath, I slap his hand off my collarbone. "I'd rather die."

Knox tucks a strand of my hair behind my ear, then he gently cups my face. It takes everything in me to resist kicking him between the legs. Instead, I grasp one of his wrists, ready to tear him off me at any second.

"Let go," I demand, becoming overly aware of how little he's wearing. His face is so close that I notice a small scar where his jaw meets his neck. It's as small as a nick.

Knox's thumb moves along my cheekbones, wiping away tears that aren't there. "Love and pain aren't that dissimilar of emotions, you know? I find that combining the two erases all complexity." He moves one of his hands to the front of my neck and grips just hard enough for me to whimper. "See?"

"Knox—" I grimace and squeeze my eyes shut as his chest presses against mine. My pulse races out of control. At any second, he could deactivate my crows and spend the rest of the night trapping me inside my own mind.

He lowers his head to my ear, speaking softly. "Just say the word, and I will give you everything. Money. Power. *Pleasure*." Knox grazes his nose across my jaw and down my neck. "Though I never take a woman without her permission. I've never needed to."

"But the same doesn't apply to pain, does it?" I need to unlatch myself from him, but I'm scared he'll do something even worse if I do. I'm locked in a room with him, completely at his mercy. I'm surprised he hasn't tortured me already. "Release me."

He sighs against my neck and takes a step back. "How boring."

My skin crawls as I cover my chest, wishing I could sink deeper into the wall away from him. "I'd never accept any of that from a senseless killer."

"A killer?" Knox scoffs. "Should I tell you about all the lives Milo has taken? Prisoners who vanished without a trace by his bidding? Bodies floating in space at his mere command? And if we're talking about Lavens, well, his death tolls vastly outnumbers mine. Am I really so much worse?"

Even though I know he's trying to get under my skin, a pull in my stomach reminds me that he's right. But the way Knox has gone about it is what makes it truly sick. *Right?*

Knox smirks. "You know everything I'm saying is true."

I become hyperaware of the poison hidden under my bra. All I'll need to do is uncap it and slide the sharp, poisonous edge at least an inch along his skin, and he'll be dead within minutes. But figuring out how to get close enough to him without garnering suspicion will be its own battle. Which is why I need to wait until the perfect time. I can't rush this.

Kill him, the crows say anyway. *Now.*

No, I tell them. *Not yet.*

"Our crows are loud, aren't they?" Knox studies the back of his nails.

Panic floods me. Did he just hear my thoughts? When our crows linked in our sleep, he was able to place thoughts into my head under the guise that I was reading his mind. Who knows what other hidden powers he holds under his sleeves. "You heard them?"

"They're mine. Remember?"

"They betrayed you."

Knox frowns. "It was a fluke. They're not used to dreams."

"Yet they healed my body from the injuries you created. Or is that just an anomaly too?

He doesn't look happy at all, and it brings me great satisfaction to see him so peeved. "My uncle once told me that there are no bounds to what forbidden magic can do. But my crows are loyal. Anything they're doing for you is nothing more than to benefit me in the long run. They only want to give you the illusion that you have any control here."

What if Knox is wrong? I was there. I told them to attack him and they obeyed me. Could I do the same thing next time I'm stuck in a proditor entrancement, or was it truly a stroke of luck?

Knox steps away from me and moves toward a wardrobe. He throws open the doors and sorts through the fitted coats. "If you'll excuse me, I have an appointment with Dune."

My ears perk up. "Dune?"

Knox chuckles. "You think I don't know he helped you and Milo escape? He even tried to give your poor cousin a second chance at life. It's annoying, really. Now I have to spend the day deciding how to punish him."

My stomach drops. Dune tried to save Dimitri? And now he's suffering for it? "He's imprisoned here?"

"Of course. Even proditors are not immune to punishment."

"And how does anyone punish a proditor?" It's not like Knox can use the crows against him. And Dune will heal fast with his Vicar blood.

Knox pulls a dark garment off a hanger. "I'm not that boring, Little Fennec. Hyssopite does exist."

A knot forms in my stomach. They'll weaken him? Drain him of his healing abilities and physically torture him like they would to an ordinary human?

Knox spares me the sight of his body and changes in the bathroom, emerging soon after in ivory attire fit with gold buttons and chains. His crown fits snug around his forehead. "Don't do anything too rash while I'm gone."

Chapter 28

Milo

After Joriel leaves, my mind is swarming with thoughts. From the devastation of Margot's capture, to Iverat staying healthy despite the destruction of a temple point. Everything in me wants to hack into the jumbotrons again and spread the news all throughout Lavenai. But right now, the reality is that Knox has my wife in his grasp, under his control. He's able to do anything he wants to her. My tense muscles shake at the thought.

Lucinda pushes up from her desk, and my mother follows, both of them leaving the office to head back to the rest of the rebels.

Something has to be done. I'll be damned if I'm stuck underground, sitting on my hands, while my cousin has his way with Margot.

I rush out of the office to find Lleu and Alarik waiting for me. Before either of them can ask me how the discussion with Joriel went, I push past them.

"Lucinda," I call down the hall.

She and my mother stop. Lucinda's shoulders rise and fall with a sigh before she turns around. "What is it now? We have Oliver and Matsumoto's arrival to prepare for."

I tighten my fists. "We have to go after Margot."

Lucinda gives me an exhausted look, like she's regretting letting me off house arrest and wishes to throw me right back into a cell. "Absolutely not."

"I'll give you more information: locations of additional weapons bases, experimental labs, underground caves with secrets. Everything and anything you want. I'll spend hours locked away, drawing out the inner workings of Ashtanaban technology. I'll even teach you how to create your own humanoids."

"Margot left of her own free will. I will not risk more rebel lives to save her."

My blood boils. "So you're just going to leave her there? Stuck with powers she clearly can no longer control? Powers that enticed her to go in the first place? You think she had free will, but that couldn't be further than the truth. You've never met Knox's crows. I have."

"She broke protocol. There are consequences for that. I won't risk this entire operation for one soldier. We don't have the manpower."

"Then let me go."

Lucinda glares. "That's completely out of the question. Besides, you don't think he's expecting you to go after her? You don't even know where she's being held, or if she's even still *at* the hotel. For all I know, Margot has been taken to the Imnicus."

"Your cameras would have caught that if she had."

"The most I can do is send an undercover spy, but only if they volunteer willingly."

"I can spot a Laven gait a mile away," I reply. "As can most other Ashtanabans."

I feel someone step next to me from behind. "I'll go in."

My gaze shoots over to where Lleu stands to my right. I look at her with parted lips then to Alarik. He has gone completely pale at her offer.

"No," Alarik says firmly. "You're not trained for it, Lleu."

Lucinda chuckles to herself and folds her arms, seemingly not opposed to Lleu's idea. "What more is a spy than an actress? She already played the part as lady's maid once, and Margot never suspected a thing."

"And it would solve the issue of blending in naturally," I add. "Lleu is Ashtanaban, after all."

Alarik moves toward us and pulls Lleu into his side. "It doesn't matter because she's not going."

Lleu pulls away from him and takes both his hands in hers. "What did you tell me when I didn't want you to go on a Laven mission? I'm warming up to what you taught me. I want to be useful and help bring both planets back to their former unity too. And, most importantly, I want to save Margot."

"But Lleu, after what Knox did to you . . . " Alarik shakes his head. "What if he does it again? You don't sleep well anymore. You rarely finish your meals . . . "

"All the more reason to stop him from doing it again to anyone else."

"The only people who would recognize her are Crux, Onyx, Knox, and Commander Aisil," I argue. "As long as she avoids those four, nobody would be the wiser. She'd be in and out. Once we know where Margot's being kept, a team can more easily get her out."

Alarik closes his eyes, and I know with every fiber in his being that he doesn't want Lleu to go. It's the way I felt when Margot went on her last mission with him, but I kept it inside because I knew she wouldn't let me talk her out of it. And what right did I have to try?

Alarik places a hand on the side of her face. "Lleu, if you're caught, you'll be right there suffering with Margot, if not worse."

She places a hand over his. "Knox has already taken so much from me. Let me take one thing from him."

I look between them, praying to the gods that Alarik will let her go, because if he doesn't, my only choice will be to escape the rebellion and likely fail at finding Margot.

Alarik looks at Lucinda. "She'll be given a bug to wear."

"Okay," Lucinda agrees.

"And tools for self defense."

"Everything you want will be provided."

"And if she goes dark for even one second, I'm infiltrating the Cymru, my life be damned."

Chapter 29

Margot

Knox has been gone all day. I don't know what he has planned for me. Whatever happens, I need to kill him before he gets any ideas, like taking me to Ashtanabo or the Imnicus.

I slip the poison pen out of my bra and take the cap off. The pointed tip glimmers. All it will take is a single scrape. Then all of this will be over.

Carefully, I put it back together and slip it back under my clothes. Knox is too strong to drown in the bathtub or shove out the window to his death. Poison is my only option.

I approach the floor-to-ceiling window and place my hand on the glass, watching the cloudy purple pollution blow past sky-scrapers.

Still, the hardest part of killing him will be keeping control over my anger and fear. My need for revenge. My desire to see him suffer. Truth be told, poisoning him is a mercy. He'll die never truly paying for the things he's done. Even if the stories of the gods are true, and he will be punished in the afterlife, I won't get to see him suffer. That thought itself grieves me.

I want to see him tormented in the same way he tormented Lleu and me. He killed my cousin without so much as breaking a sweat, and now I wish I chose a poison that could kill Knox slowly and painfully over the course of days, just so I could pay him back tenfold for what he did to Dimitri.

I hear the bedroom door slide open and I stiffen, but I don't turn my head. No matter what happens next, if I do not succeed, I need to do everything in my power to poison myself.

Knox's shoes tap against the hard floor behind me. "Enjoying the view?"

"No." I rest my hands at my sides and keep my eyes focused on the clouds. "How can I when I know you've just returned from torturing someone you used to call a friend?"

Knox stands next to me, admiring the eagle-eye view of Merth. "He'll recover in time."

My stomach ties into knots. I don't want to ask what Knox did to him, but at least Dune is still alive. "So it's true then. The crows make it impossible for you to feel any kind of mercy?"

"I consider myself very merciful . . . when I believe the perpetrator deserves it. That he or she is truly sorry for what they have done."

"And how often does that happen?"

"People only beg for mercy because they fear the pain. But if they weren't being punished, they wouldn't care at all for committing treason," Knox explains. "Dune didn't beg, though. He knew what he had done. I think he is proud of it even as we speak."

Knox furrows his brows at a building in the distance. Proditors don't break easily like humans do. Hyssopite or not, Dune was probably the least satisfying torture he's ever performed.

"Why do you want me to marry you, Knox?"

Knox's lips fall into a straight line. "Politics. Why else does a Colum marry?"

"A Colum marries the daughter of a wealthy arbitor for *politics*. Not only that, but you've already broadcast both my last names as traitors. The planets will have questions."

He still doesn't answer, and I take the opportunity to sidestep closer to him. "All this time, I thought you wanted to skin me alive and deliver me to an early grave. Now you've had a change of heart."

"Fine. It's because I want to piss off my cousin."

I frown. "I don't believe you. All you've wanted since our first meeting was my blood."

He whips his head in my direction. A darkness overtakes his eyes as he stares me down. "You have no idea what I want."

All at once, realizations and ideas hit me. I don't know how I didn't see it before. Or rather, I saw it but chose to ignore it. It was too complex. Too fucked up. But now it's the only pawn I have. The poison pen burns under my bra.

Love and pain aren't that dissimilar of emotions, he had said.

"Kill me, Knox. I won't resist. I'll even scream for you."

"Crux and I didn't kill you. What makes you think I'll do it now?"

"What changed, Knox?"

Knox looks away. "Stop talking."

"You've tormented me and targeted me even though there are millions of other girls out there. Why don't you want to take my life anymore?"

Anger burns in his eyes, and he stays silent. But he doesn't have to answer. We both know what has changed on his end.

I know what's going to happen next. That I'll let it happen as guilt eats me away. It will feel like light-years, but I will do what I have to do.

I hold his gaze, softening my face and forcing my breaths to grow heavy. *Forgive me, Milo.*

Knox gently grabs my neck, swiftly backing me against the window. His lips capture mine ravenously, his breaths filled with craving. He's wanted this longer than I've ever known or realized. Yet I can taste the venom on his tongue. The loathing on his teeth.

My body tries to reject him without my mind telling it to. My hands go to his shoulders to instinctively push him away, and I quickly redirect it by digging my nails through his clothes and into his skin.

He groans in approval then moves his hands to my thighs. His touch is rough, almost branding me. I ache to reach for the poison, but he'll notice if I do in this position.

The crows caw in my head as he kisses my neck, dragging my carotid artery through his teeth.

Good. His eyes are further away now. I try to ignore my body's physiological reactions as he picks me up to straddle his waist, but an unintentional gasp escapes me as he drags his tongue across my throat and kisses my other artery.

I find the hem of my own shirt and slowly reach beneath. Even if he looks, he'll hopefully think I'm stirring myself on more. But I don't want him to realize my attention has shifted, so I arch against him like I'm overwhelmed.

It's the wrong move. He pulls me away from the wall and lays me on a nearby marble table. I'll be damned if I actually sleep with Knox Arris. Repulsed with myself. But I can't let him think that.

He peels off his upper garments, putting his well-worked chest on display. When he leans over me to kiss me again with his warm mouth, his kisses are desperate, his tongue soft yet slicing. I let one of my hands thread through his golden curls. But the other goes beneath the hem of my shirt again toward my breast. Toward the poison. I can't let this go much further. I'll never forgive myself. I already don't.

I just have to grab the pen then flick the cap off to expose the sharp tip. After that, Knox Arris will lie dead at my feet in a matter of seconds. Dimitri and Lavenai will be avenged. I'm almost there . . .

I gasp as Knox's hand grabs my wrist. My hand freezes mere centimeters from the poison.

He releases the kiss, mostly. When he speaks, I can still feel his lips' slight graze. "Let me."

"I—"

"Don't you want to go higher?"

Not with you. "Yes—but . . ."

Knox's eyes darken. He looks incredibly turned on but also . . . something else. I'm not sure what that look is. I don't like it.

He smirks, staring into my eyes deeply while he moves my hand up more toward my breast. Even with this hiccup, I could still grab hold of the poison. But my wrist isn't nearly mobile enough to scratch him without risking my own life.

I don't realize my bottom lip is trembling until he drags it once through his teeth. "Why the nerves, Little Fennec?"

With my free hand, I reach for his belt, trying to distract him. He takes that arm and pins it above my head on the table.

"I don't have to do this . . . " I start.

"Are we still talking about sex?" Knox leans down to whisper in my ear. "Or do you think I'm a fool?"

His grip tightens to the point of pain and I yelp. Oh gods, he knows. He knows.

I grab the poison anyway and flick off the lid with my thumb. Even if I accidentally scratch myself, I'll take him with me.

But Knox is faster, yanking my hand out from under my shirt and laughing when he sees the pen. "I'll give it to you, you almost got me. But a girl like you who hates a guy like me, well, I know that's a malice that doesn't leave. Forgive me for being naïve. It was a moment of weakness."

I use the strength of the crows to push against his thumb with my wrist, freeing my hand with the poison briefly. I throw my arm forward, aiming for his neck.

"Oh no you don't." Knox catches my forearm a mere inch from his skin. He carefully pries the poison from my hand, then he places his shin on my torso to keep me contained. The sunset reflects the poison tip as he inspects it. "Brilliant. Is this a nerve agent?"

I cower as he disables my crows and points the sharp point at my neck.

"Stop," I grit.

"Don't tell me you're tapping out of the fun now?"

"Screw you, Knox."

"You could have," Knox jests. "You know, being seduced into my own assassination is a first for me. I liked it. We should try it again sometime."

Even though I'm ready to die, my body shakes in pure fear while I wait for him to scratch me with the poison. The way he's compressing my chest prevents me from taking a full breath, making me overly aware of how each breath could be my last.

Knox watches me carefully, studying my fear. His tongue passes once over his bottom lip. "Let's try something else." He tosses the poison behind him and grabs my neck, raising my upper body slightly and slamming me back on the table.

I cry out, pain seizing my body. I barely have time to catch my breath before he grips my hair and brings my lips mere centimeters from his. If he tries to kiss me, I'll bite off his tongue.

"You were wrong about one thing, Little Fennec. I do want to kill you, but not within seconds or hours. I want you to suffer for years, begging for each day to be your last." He buries a fist into my abdomen.

The wind is knocked out of me and I gasp at nothingness, my lungs burning in desperation. It's like choking on your own body. It doesn't feel like I'll ever be capable of breathing again.

"I understand myself better now. My true desires. Maybe a part of me thought that even a kiss from you would shake the world as I knew it. But it wasn't your obedience and submission I wanted. It was your resistance. And for you to just walk into my grasp willingly? Well, that's not thrilling in the slightest." He breathes in deep, and I feel my crows respond to his ecstasy. "You still have some fight. I'll make sure that's never beaten entirely out of you.

"I'll worship you as much as I'll torment you. You'll feel as much pleasure as you do pain. You have my word." Knox blows air behind my ear, sending nauseating shivers up my spine while I struggle to breathe. "I don't even care if you love me back, or if you enjoy even one minute of my attention, as long as you, and your power, belong to me, and *only* me."

Just as I regain my first full breath, Knox throws me off the table. I roll across the floor until my back slams into the side of the bed.

When he held the poison to my neck, I should have lifted my skin to it and ended my own life. I shouldn't have let myself be afraid. How foolish of me to want to stay alive when living with him will be so much worse.

Knox approaches and grabs the collar of my shirt, yanking me off the floor and throwing me onto his bed.

I try to crawl off of it but he quickly pins me beneath himself. I kick and scream, but the crows are nowhere to be found. I still haven't caught my breath fully.

"Just kill me. Please, kill me." I thrash around, trying to land any kind of kick or punch.

"Patience. It's the key to all good art." Knox grabs a pillow and presses it onto my face.

With my hands free, I scratch at his forearms, but he doesn't care. He steals my oxygen, laughing while I am left with burning lungs.

As unconsciousness starts to take over, I think of Milo. Of what it would be like for him to storm into the room, see what Knox is doing, and slit his neck. For him to hold me and tell me everything's going to be all right. Through all my pain, and all my risks, I regret letting Knox be my last kiss.

Before I pass out completely, Knox releases the pillow and I heave in as much air as I can. My vision is half-covered with static, and I can barely move from the deprivation.

Knox cups the side of my face. "Do one thing for me, then all of this will be over."

"What?" I force out.

"Cry for me."

Aren't I already crying? But I realize that even though my body is trying to, not a single tear leaves my eyes. I'm dehydrated, and the only saliva in my mouth is Knox's. He knows I'm not capable, so that's why he's asking.

"I can't."

"Cry." Knox's hands wrap around my throat.

My body moves like it wants to weep, but it won't.

Knox continues for an hour, cutting off my air and telling me to cry, but no matter what I do, no tears fall. All I can do is beg. And that's what I do until I'm so air deprived that I cannot stay conscious.

Then he and his crows continue his sadistic torment into the dreamworld.

Chapter 30

Lleu

The Cymru sticks out like a sore thumb in the heart of Lave-nai. It must have been one of the few buildings built during the Arris Reign, considering its Ashtanaban architecture. Crystal clear windows cover its domed cream exterior. Pristine in a city of smog and mud. If it had a little greenery, it would fit perfectly in Ashtanabo's capital, though it's several hundred feet too tall for our standards.

My heart trots while I approach the back entrance, armed with nothing more than a small dagger and a miniature emergency transmitter in my ear. A transmitter that I'm only to turn on and use if things go array. After I enter that door, I'll be completely on my own.

The old me would have been horrified to accept any kind of mission. I wasn't trained to spy or to fight. But within the last year, I've been shot and tortured. The fibers of my mind have been split in two. The girl I was and the girl I am now are only remnants of each other.

Lucinda was right—an actress isn't that much different from a spy. As much as Alarik begged me not to go, even after we finally were alone together, I knew this was something I had to do.

Once upon a time, I took everything in my life for granted. Food, wealth, clothes, and even air. If Milo had never kidnapped me for his plan, I probably would still be the same girl I was—happy, yet ignorant of the needs of another planet.

And right now, the best way to save both planets is to save my best friend from a psychopath. If it came down to it, she would do the same for me. I don't care what the rebels or Lucinda say about the gravity of the mistake she made in turning herself in. None of them have been stuck in proditor hallucinations before. They have no idea how mad they make you. Not even Alarik or Milo understand, and they never will.

But I do, and it's why I'd still save Margot even if it didn't move the needle to stopping Knox at all.

As I reach the large employee entrance, I do my best to blend in with the small group of people entering at the same time as me. They're also dressed in cream garments. I even ask a girl how her night was. Through her respirator, she says that it was as dull as every night is.

My stomach is a ball of nerves as I enter the Cymru with the group, a single guard nodding to us on our way in. I sigh in relief once we're past him, and a ball of excitement swells in my chest from the victory. I can see why Margot chose spying over other roles in the rebellion. It's terrifying, but it's a rush like no other.

I mentally recall Milo's directions. *Go left, then right, then take the glass elevator.*

While the others are distracted, I slow my steps until I'm out of the small crowd.

As I turn a corner, I nearly crash into a humanoid.

It furrows its metallic-blue brows and glares at me, rebalancing the tray of carefully folded crane napkins. "Watch it, human."

"Sorry," I mutter back.

It stares at my respirator. "Are you going to wear that thing all day or are you going to get some work done?"

I quickly snap the respirator off my face. "Force of habit."

"I don't want excuses. Just get to your posting." Its metal feet stomp against the ceramic tile as it pushes past me. I can't blame robots for being on the more aggressive side. Their programming often dictates their life's purpose, and sometimes that means de-livering drinks to politicians.

As I follow Milo's instructions, I grab an apron and a cloth bandana off an unattended cart. After stepping into the elevator, I press the button for one of the higher floors and the elevator ascends. First, I put on the apron. Then I start tying the bandana around my head, pulling my braids back. Before I left this morn-ing, Lucinda gave me a few pointers, one of them being to use additional accessories to blend in. I think these will do nicely.

The Cymru may be a hotel at its heart, but over half the building is used for military operations and housing high-ranking commanders. Which means I need to watch my back. Soldiers and proditors could be lurking anywhere.

The elevator slows ten levels from my desired floor.

Don't panic, I tell myself and take a slow inhale and even slower exhale.

I nearly collapse as the doors open. A proditor stands on the other side, his mask embossed with diamond and square patterns. Msannian patterns. He's not a proditor I recognize but a proditor nonetheless.

Imnicus protocol takes over, and I bow my head slightly. "Good morning."

He steps inside, presses his floor number, and stands beside me. "A bit too gloomy to be a good morning."

I was hoping he wouldn't respond. My throat dries and my palms sweat. Fear is overwhelming me now. Almost like stage fright.

But I know better than anyone that stage fright is curable.

I force a smile until it feels real. "Isn't everyday on Lavenai gloomy?"

The proditor laughs. "The day I'm finally reassigned back to Ashtanabo will be the best day of my life."

"What got you posted in this cesspool?" I feel somewhat guilty of my choice of words, but it seems to be keeping any of his suspicions at bay. Plus the small talk is easing my nerves.

"Behavioral, unfortunately. I was once stationed in Diyu Prison. A prisoner escaped on my watch, and Milo Arris himself found out."

I pinch my lips together. "Hopefully with a new Colum comes a new assignment."

He shrugs. "Maybe if he'll ever review my appeal. But from what I've heard, he's barely speaking with Ashtanabo's leaders, let alone pardoning proditors. So as far as I'm concerned, both Arris' can burn."

The elevator dings, and I tighten my bandana. "This is my stop."

Before I can make it a few steps, his arm reaches out to stop the elevator from closing.

The blood drains from my face as I barely bring myself to look back at him.

But instead of suspicion, I find only kind eyes. "You know, ever since I arrived, most servants won't even look at me."

Thank goodness. "Is that so?"

"Not that I can blame them. They run this place like a prison camp. Even Diyu Prison was a tropical paradise in comparison. Anyway, for what it's worth, thank you. For being decent."

I smile back. "Glad I could oblige. Have a nice day."

The doors close, leaving me alone in the hallway once more. I've only met a handful of proditors, but none were that pleasant during a first interaction. It's a strangeness my own mind struggles to wrap around. In a just world, he'd love being stationed on the Imnicus. It might have been the only place in the galaxy where servants and proditors get along. As long as everyone stays in line, that is.

This floor is filled with maids busy in the heart of cleaning hour. A time where all the commanders are off at meetings, and there's a moment of peace for everyone to get their work done.

In the corner, there's a stack of baskets filled with dirty laundry. I pick up one full of pillowcases, holding the metallic basket handles to blend in. Another thing Lucinda mentioned was to keep my hands busy, so I'll do just that.

I walk down two halls. Milo gave me a list of floors she may possibly be on. Still, this place is huge. Finding her may take all day.

Apparently there are prisons in the basement, but I was told to check there last. Milo has a feeling she's not being kept there and I'd be more likely to get caught there due to all the guards.

I find a tired maid and ask if I can borrow her keycard to clean, claiming that I misplaced my own. She rolls her eyes but lends me hers without a fuss.

For hours, I override empty rooms, searching the grander ones first before going through the smaller ones. No luck.

As I loop around the corner, I barrel into someone and fall back, the basket in my hands escaping my grasp. Pillowcases and dirty sheets tumble across the floor. Dammit.

Assuming it's a humanoid by how hard I hit them, I immediately start apologizing. "I'm so sorry, the basket was so full and—"

My stomach dips as a familiar set of eyes stare back at me, as well a mask embossed with circular Susukan designs.

"I was hoping I was wrong when I saw you back there." Onyx smirks. "But it is you, Lleu."

I try to rush past him, but his leather-clad palm slams into the wall, blocking my path with his armored arm. He steps closer, boxing me in completely with his other arm.

I stuff my hand into my pocket, ready to transmit my status to Alarik, who will likely come barreling in the Cymru like it's war. Which is the only reason I don't press it immediately—Alarik will get himself killed.

"You shouldn't be here." Onyx leans down to face level with me.

"Neither should you," I bite, ready to snap. Onyx and I have always had a comfortable dynamic whether we were drinking together or arguing. "Joining up with Knox? You know you're better than that."

His eyes flinch. "Don't act like I had a choice."

"Poor little daddy's boy unable to say no, hmm?"

"I told you that in confidence," he growls. It wasn't an easy feat, but after a particularly rowdy evening, he spilled the depths of his complicated relationship with his father. He was at my door the next morning, equally hung over yet demanding my secrecy. Onyx is glancing around now, as servants continue to filter through. "We shouldn't talk here. Come on."

Onyx drops his hands from the wall and opens the nearest bedroom. I sigh and follow him inside, letting him secure the door behind us.

I near the window, fully knowing it would be impossible to escape from this high up. The neon city has a warm glow to it this early in the morning. I remember photographs of Lavenai in its prime. It had destinations worthy of emptying your entire account of geeds to travel to. There was nothing equivalent anywhere in the solar system, even on Ashtanabo. Before Balistar was in the picture, Lavenai's technology was decades ahead of Ashtanabo's.

"Did Milo send you?" Onyx takes a seat on a chair in the corner. In the privacy of the hotel room, he removes his mask.

"What do you think?"

"It's a lost cause, Lleu. Knox will hardly let Margot out of his sight. Or his room."

"Has he hurt her?"

He doesn't answer at first, and when I turn to face him fully, he quickly looks away. "Last night I heard screaming."

My fingers curl into claws. When Milo finds out, he'll absolutely lose it. I already am. "And you didn't try to save her?"

"What do you want me to do, Lleu? Barge in there and throw the Colum across the room? Not to mention he's stronger than I am. Stronger than . . . well, probably any proditor to ever live. Even *if* Crux ever took my side, I doubt the scales would tip even an inch."

"At least you could say you died honorably." I rest my back against the window, facing him. "Tell me what his plans are."

"I shouldn't—"

"Onyx, please tell me. Despite all of this, I would hope we're still friends."

His eyes grow distant for a second, then his shoulders slump. "He's going to marry her at Dune's execution."

My lips part, my mind barely catching either of those bombs he just dropped on me. Holy shit.

Onyx continues, "He's using Margot's grief against her. Right now she's resistant, but he's slowly cultivating her anger into something more. He wants to make her his pawn. She's powerful for a human, and his crows have taken a liking to her. It should be an impossibility, but Knox has secretly hired researchers to investigate further. Already they have found that crows truly do have minds of their own. They can willingly choose someone with human blood, but it's dangerous. Proditor blood keeps us in check. Binds our powers to a specific vessel. As a human, she'll operate exclusively outside of those boundaries. A crow's power without limits could be unstoppable. It's unheard of. If the Vicars didn't curse proditors before, they will now."

"She'll be able to break into minds?"

"Human minds, no. But proditor minds, yes. Not even Knox can do that."

That could change everything. Only proditors are capable of stopping Knox. But if he had someone like Margot on his side that could break into their minds too . . . "When and where will it take place?"

"Haven't I given you enough?"

"You betrayed Milo and Margot. Even me . . . What is wrong with you, Onyx? Why can't you say no to Crux?"

"I'm a lost soul, Lleu. He's my best friend."

"So is Dune."

He flinches back.

"Knox has killed hundreds already, and that count won't slow as time goes on. You know this better than anyone."

Onyx tightens his fist.

"You can still rectify this," I say. "The fact that you're speaking with me in private at all means you know this is wrong."

"Do I? I've been dragged around my entire life being told what's right and wrong. What to say. What to do. First, it was the Vicars, who were easy enough to follow. Next, Balistar rises and the code changes. Now this?"

"Then help me. Earn your freedom, Onyx, just as the rest of us are. The planets don't have to be like this anymore. Haven't you sensed the shift? Things are changing, and not even Milo could hold on to his father's wishes anymore."

Onyx rubs the back of his neck. "Later today at the old arena. Knox is inviting the wealthiest from Ashtanabo to fly in and view the start of his new empire. He'll use Dune as an example and have Margot torture him. Their marriage union will show everyone that he's not to be messed with." Onyx replaces his mask. "Now let's get you out of here."

Chapter 31

Margot

I fear opening my eyes like one might fear jumping off a cliff, unsure if they'll land safely in the ocean or splatter upon concrete.

But I know I'm on no cliff with the sharp metal cutting into my wrists and dried sweat coating my body. My lips are chapped, and I desperately need water. Still, everything I feel, and even everything I think, could all be a hallucination. One used to trick me into thinking I'm once again safe, only for me to open my eyes and find myself in another timeless trance.

When my crows flutter, I gather the little courage I have left to take the plunge and look around.

Knox's room surrounds me, looking the same as it did when he began the torture. But instead of the sunset, the lavender sunrise pours through the window.

I'm cuffed to the headboard, and my wrists are raw even though I don't remember him binding me in the first place. Despite the pain, I pull against them slightly. That movement is enough for me to realize something is off, and it's not anything to do with crows.

There's an arm resting over my abdomen. A face in the crook of my neck.

Knox is fast asleep, still shirtless, holding me close to him.

My nostrils flare at the sight of him, and I want nothing more than to be free so I can rip open his throat. I try to keep hold of the anger, crave its somehow healing presence, as fear claws to take its place. Static and numbness fill my limbs.

Cry for me.

Cry for me.

Cry for me.

A phrase uttered between every endless vision, every flare of pain that accompanied his touch. Imprinted like a song that won't leave my head.

My weakened crows only amplify every uncontrollable emotion in my chest. I'd do anything to be rid of it. For once, I'm craving my crows to be back at full strength to numb my emotions, even though I know they're the reason for the misery. Without them, I can't throw up my walls or bury my pain.

But none of that matters at the moment. Right now, I need to find a way out of here.

My cuffs are secured in a way that no amount of tugging will break me free. Not unless I don't mind breaking my wrists, but that's a last resort. If I want to escape before Knox awakens, I'll need a key.

I note Knox's trousers on the ground next to the bed. He must have taken them off in favor of sleeping in underclothes. His pockets might have what I need.

I slide my leg off the mattress until my toe reaches the loop of the belt. Knox unconsciously holds me tighter against his bare chest.

Whatever he feels for me is complex and diagnosable. A sick obsession. Is he really only marrying me to torture the love out of me? Or is it something more?

"Are you flexible enough to unlock your restraints with your feet?" Knox whispers into my neck, hot breath coating my skin. "Try it. I want to see what positions you can bend yourself into."

I try to hit him with the side of my body, but he quickly moves back.

Knox takes the trousers off my foot and throws them across the room. He straightens up and rests against the headboard next to me, admiring the window view with his arms behind his head. "S uch a pretty sunrise on a day like today."

"I need water." My voice is scratchy.

"You'll get all that and more today."

With his touch gone, I'm able to numb my emotions once again. Having crows is like taking shots of liquor. No wonder most proditors are so cold at times.

"They make life so much easier, don't they?" Knox says as if reading my mind. "You don't have to feel as deeply as a normal human anymore. I tormented you half the night, and now we can exist as friends once more."

"We're not friends."

"You're right. We've far surpassed that." He moves his hand toward my mouth, and I quickly move my head away. "The wedding is approaching."

"I'm not marrying you."

"Well, it's a bit too late for that. The guests are already en route."

It feels like the world is crashing down on me. "It's today?"

"Of course. There's no time to waste."

"Why is this so sudden?"

"Let's just say that our union is only the start of the plans I have for you."

Before I can question him further, there's a knock on the door.

"Behave today." Knox stands and throws on a silk robe before opening the door. "Welcome, ladies."

Before I can blink twice, a handful of servants tow in carts of makeup and hair supplies, none of them caring that I'm strapped to a bed. One of the girls draws a bath, and others get to work setting up the vanity.

"Knox, no," I bite. I could care less who hears. "Call it off."

Knox ignores my words and stands over me, unlocking my cuffs. "Do so willingly, or I'll erase your memories."

My lips part. He wouldn't do that, would he? I've always associated my loss of memories with Milo. But Milo isn't the one whose crows can erase memories. Knox's are. To forget that's in the realm of Knox's powers is foolish of me. If I couldn't remember Knox and what he's capable of, who knows the ways he could control me.

"Lucky for you, I prefer you with your memories. Your anger and passion. The blank slate you were after the last time was too unsettling. Too unmolded," he says. "Unsatisfying."

Once free, I shrug him off and stand on my own, walking toward a servant motioning to me. I ignore her at first and disappear into the bathroom, raking water into my mouth from the faucet.

For now, I need to do what Knox says. But when I think about last night, I nearly rip off the sink handle. My crows are loud, screaming at me to satisfy them. My strength is growing and they promise me more—enough to overpower Knox—if I comply. But they are as dishonest as he is. They may strengthen me, but they are not my friends. Though I crave them.

When I reemerge, Knox is gone, and I don't resist the women as they bathe me and wash my hair. The entire time, all I can think of is alternative ways to take out Knox. But it won't be today or even tomorrow—which means I have no choice but to marry him.

After I dry off, I sit at a vanity in a silk robe while the women get to work on my hair, makeup, and body jewelry. I can tell they want me to remove Milo's ring from my thumb, but I refuse. They'll have to rip it off by force.

I see Knox return through the reflection in the mirror, and he plops down sideways into a plush chair. His dark and sultry stare makes it feel as though the bands of my lace stockings are constricting all blood flow.

"Stop looking at me," I bite.

"Why not? You're mine, aren't you?"

"I'm not."

A few of the women approach him with a stack of clothing. He lets them strip him and help him change into a dark military-suit plated with silver. "Right now you're unwilling. But after today, you may have a change of heart. Power is enough to change the most righteous of people."

I notice how delicate the girls are while they dress him, the nervous bobs of their throats and the trembling hands, terrified of making one wrong move.

"Why do you assume I'll come around?" I ask while a girl puts earrings on me. "You've already promised me years of misery."

"Yes, well, maybe I was a bit dishonest. Words thrown out during a time of anger."

"What is it you really want, Knox?"

"Patience, Little Fennec. But let's just say, saying '*I do*' will be the most insignificant choice you'll make today." Knox chuckles while a girl straightens out his suit coat. "Now be a good girl and let the maids help you into your dress."

Chapter 32

Milo

My mother, Lucinda, Alarik, and I listen intently while Lleu reports Onyx's intel back to us. I can barely believe my ears.

Dune has been caught and likely won't make it much longer. *Damn it, Dune. You shouldn't have* run *off. I should have known better and forced you to stay with the group.*

Even more horrifying are Knox's plans for Margot. Yes, crow transfers are possible, but I've never heard of a human actually being able to use the gift of the crows, no less against proditors. That is far beyond even my father's knowledge.

Between Knox's powers and Margot's, my cousin will be the most powerful ruler our solar system has ever seen. Even my father, with all his claims to power and his right as a tyrant, had to bend to the strength and approval of the proditors. He placed every region under his boot, grinding them into submission, but he knew that an uprising within the proditors themselves would be the true threat. With Margot's crows, Knox could truly rule everybody with an iron fist.

My knuckles clench thinking about him marrying her. And if he erased her memories again, she'd be completely helpless.

Already, I worry about her ability to resist his demands. Knox will certainly break her mind far beyond being able to recognize her own morals. Her crows are too belligerent as it is. Without them, she would have been able to think rationally and would have known that going after Dimitri was too risky. Now? All bets are off.

Lucinda directs her attention at Alarik and me. "What will happen to her if she torments this proditor?"

"I've experienced her crows, or rather Knox's crows, and I know one thing—if she does their bidding, she'll likely never come back from it. They will always be able to control her, and she'll be too addicted to deny them everything they want."

Alarik chimes in. "There's always the possibility that Knox is wrong about Margot's ability to use the crows."

"Doubtful. He wouldn't risk being wrong with so many watching."

My mother nods her head a few times. "Then it looks like we have no choice but to save her. Knox and his crows have been polluting Margot's mind to bring her back to him, all for this attempt at galactic domination. Saving her will save millions. And who knows, if crow transfers from her are possible, what if other humans could hold her magic too? Not only will she be a human test subject, but even a unified front of proditors and Vicars would stand no chance against the army Knox could create."

Lucinda folds her arms. "It's settled. We'll send a large team. This is going to get bloody."

I sit up straighter. "Let me go with the rebels. You'll need me there."

She narrows her eyes and points a finger in my face. "You're out of your damn mind."

"I'm half proditor. My powers may be the only ones able to get through to her if she's stuck within her own head."

"If Knox is defeated, what then? I have no doubt you'll take back your throne."

I grimace. "If Knox is defeated, and I'm not there to take it back, then what? You'll let some corrupt Ashtanaban diplomat who is twentieth in line become your Colum? At least you know where I currently stand."

Lucinda presses her lips together, but she doesn't have a rebuttal for that. Just because the arbitors are dead and I'm imprisoned, that doesn't mean everything goes back to the way things were before The Arris Reign upon Knox's defeat. My father was a powerful Colum for a reason. To get both planets back to normal and properly overturn his laws will take some thinking outside of the box, and who better to do that than a rogue Colum no longer under the retribution of arbitors, who now sympathizes with Lavenai?

I continue, "Margot means everything to me. If I lost her . . . Well, you already know I'm willing to risk my own life to save hers.

I knew that when I entered the underground. It was my own crisis of not knowing what it meant to be an Arris anymore that pushed me to take that risk. Because I no longer knew what I had outside of her."

Lucinda tries to resist softening her angered face, instead throwing her hands up and cursing. "Do you understand what you're asking? You helped keep my planet enslaved for over a decade. By all accounts, I have every right to keep you locked up here the rest of your life."

"And what would that solve? Revenge?" I shake my head. "Yes, my father took over your planet. I've just upheld it. The least you can do is help me fix my ignorance."

She thinks for a while and I wait in agony for her decision. If she doesn't let me go, I will go against the soldiers and overpower them with the strength my crows provide. I refuse to stay locked underground while my wife suffers.

"Okay," Lucinda says. "Go save Margot."

Dressed in rebellion clothing and a respirator, I head out to where the rebels going on the mission stand by vehicles, their arms folded and faces furious.

Thankfully for them, it's unlikely I'll ever return to the underground. For years, I thought when I found this place I'd find a way to turn it to flames. It was one of my father's lifelong wishes for me to stop the rebellion if he couldn't. How disappointed he must be in me, watching from the stars.

And I couldn't care less.

"Milo, wait!" I hear from behind me.

My mother rushes toward me, her long hair down and trailing behind her. She hugs me, cradling the back of my head, and I wrap my arms around her. I refuse to believe this will be the last time I see her, but I squeeze her extra tight. Just in case.

"Good luck," she says. "And when you save Margot, give her a hug for me too."

"I will, Mom." I pull away and kiss her forehead. "Thank you for saving my life despite, well . . . everything."

"A mother's love never truly leaves. It's not something everyone understands."

I smile and give her one last hug as Alarik calls for me. My mother watches me go, waving goodbye as I make it to the vehicles.

Chapter 33

Margot

The rebel in me stares in the mirror, unfamiliar with the girl dressed in shimmering darkness staring back. The maids straighten out the layers of glittering skirts, and one pins a few stray curls out of my face, letting the rest of my hair tumble down my back. They've turned me into the Columess Knox envisions me to be—a ray of night with a crown of sun, a lethal force, *his*.

Dark crystals follow the paths of the suffocating bodice's metal boning. The long, elegant sleeves hug my mid-upper arms, leaving my shoulders exposed. Vulnerable.

Even in the backroom, I can hear a roaring crowd through the stone walls of the arena. I didn't consider how many Lavens would willingly attend this last-minute, gods-forsaken wedding. Some people can't help but join in on chaos.

The door opens behind me, and I expect Knox to appear in the reflection. To my surprise, Commander Aisil stands there, holding a silver box, his arms fidgety. He's in an olive uniform with medals above the right pocket denoting his rank, but he looks every bit as uncomfortable as I do in my dress.

"May we have a moment alone, ladies?"

The girls quickly gather their things and rush out of the room with their heads down. Aisil secures the door, and I spin to face him, the gown moving with me.

He studies me with a deep, somber gaze. "It's a beautiful dress, Margot. Forgive me for using your first name. It's just that—"

"That I'm always between titles and last names?" My tone is short with him. "What do you want?"

"Did you know I had a daughter once? She'd be a few years older than you, I think. It's . . . hard to remember sometimes. She didn't live through that first night."

"I . . . didn't know that." Why is he bringing this up now?

"I'm not sure anyone does. Not anymore. That secret died with my late wife. And Balistar, I suppose."

"Are you here to take me to the ceremony?"

"Eventually."

I frown. "What's going on?"

He doesn't respond at first. His fingers fiddle with the edges of the box that I can only assume contains a wedding gift. "Have you heard the story of Balistar's rise? The whole story. More specifically, my role in his takeover?"

I raise an eyebrow, confused. "I've heard rumors. That Balistar never would have been able to take over Ashtanabo without you."

"We had first met at a bar, which he'd secretly frequented outside of the Vicars' knowledge. I was a high-up commander for the

Colum who preceded him. Balistar and I were like-minded at the time. After he used his crows to comfort a man dying outside of the bar, I knew there was something special about him. That he could change the galaxy."

"And? You abused your power to help your friend take over two planets. I can guess the rest of the story."

"You must understand where we started from. This dichotomy between our planets was reversed for much of our history. We were overpopulated, hungry, and driven to the edges of our habitable areas out of necessity. While Lavenai thrived, Ashtanabo stalled out. While our Colum got fat upon his throne, his people died, and Lavenai ignored us, their Colum no better."

I open my mouth to respond, but he holds up a hand.

"This is no excuse. It's just the context. Wouldn't you have done the same in our position? In Ashtanabo, we were all tired, young, and foolish, dreaming of unity and prosperity. Times of peace, of comfort. Of days spent under the shade our ancestors never got to feel. Balistar came and promised that future, and we all believed it.

"Those days of naïve dreams did not last forever. As Balistar moved forward, he began to search for strength in the wrong places. Instead of relying on those of us who followed him, he turned inward. As he fostered his dark magic, he began to change. Though he hid it well, his paranoia grew. He saw betrayal around every corner, flinching at shadows. Even as one of his closest confidantes, I wasn't immune to that. So he did what he did to everyone else who threatened them. After killing the Ashtanaban Colum, he gave me a stern reminder of who was really in charge." I see the shake in Aisil's hand. The tick of his brow. "With new power, he needed practice. Balistar, my friend, turned his ravens . . . on me."

It's hard to feel anything through the numbness, but I see the twitch of his eyebrow, the spasms in his jaw as he wrestles through the memories I know all too well. At that moment, I understand him. A man of confidence and renown, turned into an anxious shadow, wanting nothing more than to live out his days upon the Imnicus in peace.

"Why are you telling me this, Aisil?" I take a step off the circular riser. "What is it you want from me?"

Aisil's eyes are as hard as iron. Whatever nervousness that filled his gaze just a moment ago has evaporated before my eyes, leaving behind the man that fit the stories I've heard. A commander who dismantled an empire and set up his own.

"I've been living these last years in a sort of daze. Meetings, missions, security checks. I was numb to it all, living out my pitiful existence out of habit alone. Until your infiltration of the Imnicus reached into my past and woke me from my slumber. Another Arris marrying a Laven girl? It's like a story from the gods themselves, even if Milo only did it for show.

"Milo was a soft boy carved into the likeness of his father, but I saw you shave off the crust of Balistar, one layer at a time. Hard stone made flexible by the touch of a gentle woman. It wasn't long before I felt that long-dead dream stir. I opened my eyes to find hope again. An Arris Reign built on peace, unity, and comfort, not fear and aggression."

I swallow hard. "And then Knox . . ."

"With all the subtlety of a gunshot to the temple, he killed the dream just as it was rising again."

Aisil hands me the present. Confused, I pop open the lid, revealing a dagger atop of a stack of thin black clothes. Clothes meant for fighting.

"Most say I'm a coward with a title, and maybe they're right," Aisil says, "but if this meager act can wash away even a drop of the blood upon my hands, it will have been worth it."

Drums beat and a crowd roars as I am escorted by guards out into the arena, a glass dome separating the people and the sky, a relic of a time long past. Evidence, if anything, of Aisil's perspective, that Lavenai was once a bustling paradise. Now, all the glass dome reveals is a sky of smog. Merth's arena hasn't been used since before my birth. There was once a time when sports games were held here. Concerts. All sorts of entertainment Lavenai has missed out on.

Balistar never touched the arena. He preferred his mayhem to be out on the streets to begin with. But Knox likes a good show. Theatrics. Performances. For him, if people aren't watching, if he can't feel their reactions, then what's the point?

There must be thousands of people in the stands. Some are Lavens, others Ashtanaban politicians and officials. To my surprise, it's the Lavens who are loudest, cheering in excitement. I frown. What could they possibly be happy about? Knox has killed forty innocent people in cold blood since taking the throne. There is no way they are this ecstatic about a wedding. So, what am I missing?

There are proditors too—lots of them. Onyx and Crux stand among them, ready to control anyone in the audience who acts out of line. There's a man nearby holding Vicar texts, who I can only assume is the officiant.

But the arena is far from set up for a wedding. The large post with wrist binds makes sure of that. Which means I'm correct in thinking that nobody is here to see a marriage take place.

They're here for a show. A bloodbath.

Knox is dead set on marrying me. If I'm not meant to be tied up and publicly executed, then who is?

Before I can get another thought in, the crowd goes quiet.

My blood runs cold as Knox steps into the arena with outspread arms, doing a full turn to take in the audience.

I look at the people as a glassiness takes over their eyes. A tremble of fear. They look around the arena and at the sky, seeing things that aren't really here.

Ravens. He's reminding them who is in charge. That whoever tries to act out of line will face dire consequences.

Knox visibly chuckles before his eyes lock on mine. I shudder as he studies my face and the dress he picked out for me.

He grins but doesn't come to me. Instead, he stops in place, directing his attention back to the crowd. I can't see it, but he must be wearing some kind of microphone.

His voice projects to the arena, "Order must be kept on this joyous day. A day that marks the true beginning of my reign and, of course, my marriage."

Thousands of terrified eyes are on me now, and I don't like this one bit.

Knox continues, "But I know the Lavens in attendance aren't here for any of that, and I intend to deliver on my promise to you. I desire peace between us, and this rogue rebellion has forced my hand to do what is necessary to drag them out of hiding. So, I will make a sacrifice of my own. One of unity, from me to you. Bring him out."

Confused, I look at another arena entrance where guards are pulling someone out into the field. The crowd finally releases cheers as a weakened body is dragged across the dirt.

Oh gods no.

Dune.

This is what Knox was hiding from me. This entire charade is a show of his power over every Laven and Ashtanaban. That he isn't just Colum over humans, but over proditors too. What can he do to Dune that he hasn't already? Bruises line his chest. His bare back is riddled with whip marks. Though some of them look years healed over, others appear new.

Knox watches my reaction for a moment, a dark and devious look on his face. He speaks to the crowd again, "Today, you will witness something that has never been done in the history of Vicars or proditors. And it will be done by none other than my soon-to-be Columess."

Knox walks across the arena to me and I feel frozen in place, even as he nears and gently takes my hand in his.

"What is this, Knox?"

Knox lowers his mouth to my ear. "You will see, Little Fennec."

Before I can protest, he guides me hand-in-hand to the post where guards are binding Dune's arms above his head. They knock him to his knees, and I see the hyssopite necklace around his neck. Whatever healing powers his crows give him are being suppressed.

The Lavens chant wildly and the Ashtanabans watch with amusement as Knox pulls me across the arena. I spot Onyx and Crux among the other guards, patrolling in case anyone gets ideas.

Once I'm a few feet from Dune, I stare down at the battered proditor. My heart shatters. He's going to die today, and there's nothing I can do to stop it.

"Ladies and gentlemen, for the first time ever, witness a human break into the mind of a proditor," Knox projects to the audience.

The blood drains out of my face. I look at Knox, laughing along with the cheers of the crowd.

My crows force a swell of disgusting joy into my chest, confirming my fears. That what Knox says is possible. He must have realized I had the ability after I overtook him with his own crows. Now he's using it for his own gain. "Knox, no. I-I can't."

As a show of passion, Knox wraps an arm around my waist, pulling me into his chest. But it's far from an affectionate gesture as he whispers, "You can and you will."

"I refuse."

"Perhaps you need just a little motivation of your own." His bare hand touches my neck, breaking into my mind.

Time stops, the crowd freezes, and the world around me turns a hue of blue.

Though milliseconds pass, Knox makes it feel like literal years. I feel everything—anger, bitterness, rage combined with love and lust. Bloodthirst and revenge. All of it combined with a mind-altering and indescribable pain and weariness.

When Knox lets me go, I gasp. Dune's sunken eyes come back into view. My hands shake in tandem with my shattered mind, which I immediately call to my crows to patch up. But not without consequence.

I crave pain like an internal hunger. The need to inflict it on others.

Control Dune like everyone has controlled you, our crows coo. *He's going to die anyway.*

From behind me, Knox takes my trembling hands and raises them to Dune's skin, speaking against my temple. "If you do this, Margot, no proditor will ever be able to control you again. You'll be too powerful, even for me."

Do this, and you'll be free, and now I'm not sure if I hear the crows or myself. *Nobody will ever be able to hurt you.*

As my fingertips touch Dune's face, I feel a rush of energy. I'll be the first person with human blood to break into a proditor's mind. I'll be unstoppable and uncontrollable, and by the wisp of energy running from my fingers to Dune's skin, I know that what Knox says is true. It's the perfect temptation.

I begin to lose who I am as I see Dimitri's face in the back of my head, placing my mind in further anguish. He couldn't protect himself against proditors. I couldn't save him. With this, I would never lose anyone again.

Just as I surrender control to my crows, the earth rumbles, and the wall of the arena explodes in a cloud of smoke.

But I've already plunged into darkness.

Chapter 34

Milo

A steel barricade blocks the vehicle entrance into the arena. The rebel in the driver's seat doesn't slow down. He drives straight at a concrete wall, switching to our backup plan.

A girl next to me passes some kind of launcher down the line of us to the boy on the passenger side.

"Okay, everyone. Make sure to brace and cover your ears. This isn't going to be a cakewalk," he says.

Alarik holds his firearm closer to his chest. I place my hand on the one on my belt. We're almost there, and within seconds, I will come face to face with Knox once again. This whole ordeal is going to be bloody. Lives will be lost on both sides. But to not save Margot means to surrender to a world even worse than the one my father upheld.

As we approach the wall, the boy up front leans out of the vehicle with the launcher and pulls the trigger.

The rocket is ear-shattering, discharging fast. I lower my body and cover my head, waiting until the boom has dissipated to raise it again.

There's a large hole in the wall, the rubble turning to a smoky fog that we drive straight into. Alarik curses as the car nearly tumbles over some of the debris. I hold on to my seat for dear life.

We, along with the other rebellion vehicles behind us, enter beneath the jumbotron of the arena as planned, since there is no civilian section above it. But as the fogginess slowly clears, the sheer size of the arena comes into view. Crowds of people are huddled in front of their seats. Some people are frantically trying to leave, but Ashtanaban guards prevent them from running off. Other guards are dead, crushed by the weight of the debris from the explosion.

"Go, go!" our team leader yells.

The doors open, and rebels promptly throw smoke bombs around the arena. I funnel out of the vehicle, and the screams of the crowd are deafening. If any of the other rebels are trying to communicate with me, it's lost in translation. I can't even see them anymore as I squint through the smoke, trekking forward.

Gunfire goes off in every direction, and I duck my head.

Only a few feet away, two guards lock eyes with me through the smoke, and I know it's begun. Before they can take aim, I rush at them, grabbing their torsos and slamming them to the ground. One of them screams enough that I might have shattered his spine. The other tries to grab for his gun, but I stomp down on his wrist and grab it myself.

A third guard sees me through the fog. I quickly raise the large gun, placing a bullet clean between his eyes. And as much as I don't want to kill the man whose wrist I'm crushing, I don't have a choice, so I do the same to him.

I keep low as I sneak past the battles around me. I need to find Margot first and foremost, but these rebellion smoke bombs are good. I can't even remember which direction I came from anymore.

A shimmer of something guides me into a more visible area.

As I near, I realize what that glimmering effect is—light reflecting off the jewels of a dress. A black wedding dress.

A shiver racks my body as I take in the sight. *Margot.*

She's a ray of darkness in the dusky wedding dress with her golden curls billowing around her. Even with the sounds and danger around her, she doesn't pay mind to any of it, stuck within a war of her own. Her hands hold Dune's face, and her eyes . . .

They're pitch black. I'm too late.

Wait, there's a twitch in the corners of her eyes. A hesitation. I reach out to her with my crows, but they retreat with a shriek, as if someone has just slapped them away.

A set of eyes catch mine, calm and cunning. Ones ready to embrace war and death.

My cousin stares me down like a lamb at the slaughter. Uncaring for the destruction among us, unsurprised.

I duck as a few bullets fly past me, straightening right back up. I have to save Margot. I stomp toward my cousin within the chaos.

Knox extends his arms, a splitting smile extending to his ears. "Milo, I'm so glad you could make it."

"Let her go, Knox."

He tilts his head. "By all means, try to take her."

I grit my teeth. If Margot can break into proditor minds, there is no telling what could happen if I try to touch her in this state. "I'll kill you for this. For everything."

"Hmm, a fight to the death between Colums. Between cousins. How poetic."

"You're a rabid dog, Knox. I should've put you down long ago."

He eyes the rebellion insignia on my clothing. "Tell me, cousin, does your allegiance sway that easily? Can one girl really change who you are?"

"She changed you," I spit. "Her very existence turned you into even more of a bloodthirsty maniac."

"On the contrary." Knox looks at her briefly before smirking back at me. "I changed her."

My jaw ticks, and I point the firearm at him. "She won't go through with it, even if she finds a path into Dune's mind. She'll resist."

"Are you so certain? A person can only be broken so many times. She's falling apart at the seams, Milo. She needs someone, me, to put her back together. I might be her pain, but within me is also her strength."

Rage fills me, and I do not hesitate. I begin to pull back on the trigger.

But Knox is quicker than I can process, a small throwing knife hitting the barrel of my gun. It misfires.

Toward Margot. *No.*

The bullet flies, hitting one of the chains holding Dune's arms above his head.

Knox wipes his brow. "Try it again, and I'll make it a fatal shot." Around his thigh is a band of more throwing knives. He has his own gun, but I know he won't use it purely to humiliate me. To show me he's stronger, even when bullets are on his opponent's side.

I don't know what else to do. "Margot, can you hear me? Let go of Dune!"

Margot's fingertips shake and I'm not sure if she can hear anything. Even the bullet barely took her out of the trance. She's teetering on the edge of a magic this universe has never seen before.

"It doesn't matter if she can hear you." Knox teases near her. "I can feel her crows, feel their joy at finally being unleashed. She's bathing in ecstasy, washing away her pain. Why would she stop? After all, you're partly to blame for her pain, Milo."

The gun shakes in my hands. "Stop."

"Milo, you can drop the good boy act now. You've always thought yourself as more righteous than me. But when will you admit to yourself that you're an Arris through and through? You'd slit a thousand throats to save her, wouldn't you? Are you really so much better than your dear cousin? We both would do what is necessary to get what we want. You just stand upon a pedestal of hypocrisy and sneer at my motivations."

I want to pump every last bullet straight into Knox's stomach as his words prod into my psyche.

The memory of my father stops me from doing that. His constant disappointment toward me. His favoritism of Knox. My father said it himself—that I didn't deserve to bear the last name Arris.

"You know what? You're right, Knox." I slowly lower the gun. "If you commanded me to kill everyone in this arena just to save her life, I would do it. I've spent my life filling graveyards. As much as Father didn't believe in me, I am his child through and through."

Knox raises a confused yet amused eyebrow. "Watch, Milo. Soon, she'll be my wife, and together our powers will be used to inspire the nations as Colum and Columess. Once she breaks into a mind as honorable as Dune's, she'll stand by my side willingly."

"You're forgetting one thing about Arris Law. Something that will delay your plans."

"What?" Knox scoffs.

"She's still my wife."

Chapter 35

Margot

The edges of Dune's mind are a fortress like any other, and all good fortresses have their flaws. Some have unmanned posts. Others have useless, dull spikes as defenses.

My crows are as unrelenting as Dune's mental shield. His crows shriek and caw while mine search for cracks in the bricks. Shifts in the foundation.

"Margot, stop." Dune's breaths are heavy, and I can hear the pain in his voice as I peck at his mind. There is a way in. I can feel it.

Near the top of the fortress, there's a window. One with small circular dents, as if someone once threw small rocks at it.

There, I tell my crows. *Glass.*

They caw and rush toward it in a storm. As their beaks try to shatter it, I wonder why a proditor would have a window on their fortress. What terrible memory hides behind it? Whatever it is, it makes his fortress vulnerable.

All my pain lessens as I get closer to invading his mindscape fully. I barely remember my own name. What my favorite color is. Yet I don't care. I can't even remember why I'm doing this, the prickles of euphoric energy dominoing down my spine as I ready myself to enter into the true fabric of a proditor's mind. The anticipation is intoxicating.

But a voice breaks through. My focus halts, and the crows freeze.

Audible words as clear as day pierce through my psyche like a gong being rung.

She's still my wife, the voice says.

Milo.

A wave of knowledge passes over me, and I can see the looming blood on my hands. The atrocity I am about to commit. What am I doing?

Focus, the crows say. *We're almost there.*

But I'm already too far out of the entrancement, a smog growing between the fortress and me.

No. This isn't right, I tell them. *I can't go through with it.*

You are our creation, the crows scream in agony.

I cover my ears and run into the dark abyss as far away from Dune's mind as I can. The crows chase me down, circling above my head in a relentless storm.

Before they can descend, I push all my energy into my hands and release my fingers from Dune's face in the real world.

The arena snaps back into view as their wicked cries fade in my ears.

I fall back onto the ground, the tulle skirts of my wedding dress surrounding me.

It takes me a minute to come to. Dune's breaths are fast, his head slumping in relief. I hear screams and gunshots but can barely see anything through the dust storm surrounding me.

For a second, I think I see Alarik rushing through one cloud with a gun and disappearing into another, sparks of gunfire letting loose.

My chest seizes as I turn toward nearby fighting, seeing Milo in a brawl with Knox. He's dressed in rebellion clothing, the insignia contrasting from the black tank. Knox's punches are faster than I can process, and Milo barely keeps up, dodging and deflecting what he can and absorbing what he cannot.

I want to stand, but my muscles do not cooperate. My mind may be back in the real world, but the crows' voices are growing loud again. I'm usually numbed by them, but now they release their healing properties from my mind. A life's worth of pain and agony floods back in. They dangle it over my head like an older sibling keeping a toy from a younger one. The worst part is that my mental escape still lies just feet away. The crows still call for me to break Dune.

I resisted once. If I would have broken through Dune's walls, I would be bound to Knox for eternity out of the sheer shame of it. Bound to the freedom and addiction he promised.

That thought alone drives me to stand. I cannot let him win, not after all of this. But as my knees gather beneath me, a crushing weight slams into me. My body tumbles before a body sits on my abdomen.

Crux stares down at me with cold fury, and Onyx stands behind him. I try to kick Crux, but the damn dress blocks my attempts. Not only that, but my own crows seem to be keeping my strength from me as a method of retaliation.

"You almost killed me once, and I never paid you back for the favor. I won't make that mistake again," he says.

He grabs my hands in one of his, pinning them above my head. I thrash against him, already lightheaded from his weight on my torso. Crux pulls out a dagger with his other hand and places it against my neck.

Onyx quickly steps forward, shaking Crux's shoulder roughly. "Crux, stop! This isn't part of our orders!"

Crux temporarily retracts the knife to shove Onyx back. "Knox is distracted, and I'm not losing this chance again." He looks back down at me. "I thought I knew why I hated you. That you reminded me of *her*, but that was only the tip of the iceberg. I hate you in isolation. You're a pathetic human. A Laven. Yet, favor chooses you at every turn. The crows even chose you. And you didn't even have lift a fucking finger while *we* were tortured for years to excel in training."

Onyx is frozen as he watches Crux make a small nick against my throat. Enough to draw a glimmer of blood. *Please*, I plead with my eyes.

But Onyx stays put, like his entire life is flashing before his eyes. Damn him.

Though Crux is touching my bare wrists, he hasn't put me in a trance or disabled my crows yet. If my limbs would cooperate, I could overpower him. I've done it before, on the Imnicus. But I'm still too weakened by my own stubborn crows.

"You're an ant. Crawling within our midst, with your little mandibles stuck in all of them. They're *obsessed* with you. Milo, Knox, even Dune tolerates you. *Why?*" Veins along his neck bulge in rage. "You're *nothing*. Mud under our fingernails."

Crux releases my hands and raises the weapon above his head.

Something in Onyx finally snaps. "Crux, stop it!" Onyx runs forward. He tries to pull Crux off me, but Crux is immovable.

No, I won't let it end like this. I have to think of something.

As Crux brings the dagger down, I whisper something to my crows.

And they are pleased.

Before the blade can sink into my chest, I use newfound speed and strength to grab his hands around the hilt of the dagger, and hold the knife inches from my chest.

I close my eyes as I battle his strength.

And I let my crows seep into his skin.

Dune's mind was a righteous fortress. Protected, guarded, well maintained. Finding a weakness was difficult, but everyone has one. As for Crux, his mind melts like putty. I find my opening without even trying, delving into human impossibilities.

Crux is catatonic within seconds, and all I feel is pure ecstasy. I take in every whimper of pain like wine. Every groan of agony is like strawberries on my tongue.

I feel his fears and use them against him. His pain is my weapon, so I make him suffer and enjoy every second of it. There's a Margot inside that screams for me to stop, but her voice is quiet, weeping as I push her down, down, down into the depths. It does not matter. Crux deserves it. Every bruise upon my skin is given back one-hundred fold.

The crows pull me back into the physical world against my will, as if there is nothing left to hang onto. I notice that Knox and Milo have paused mid-fight. Milo has gone bone white watching me. Onyx lies on his side, as if he were thrown violently across the ground. His eyes have widened.

I realize now that Crux is no longer above me, but I sit upon him. He lies beneath me with parted lips. Blood drips from his black, caved-in eyes.

I quickly scoot off him, my breaths quickening.

Oh my gods.

My crows killed Crux.

I look down upon my hands, thumbs slicked with hot blood.

I killed Crux.

Chapter 36

Milo

Crux's body is stiff, twisted in an unnatural position. His death was unnatural. Impossible. Crow magic can make someone believe they have died, as a form of torment. But the one rule it's always had is that it cannot kill. Yet I just watched Margot's magic kill someone, like turning a pillowcase inside out.

Margot stares down at him, horrified. From far off, Alarik stops suddenly after taking out two guards, his jaw slack at the sight of Crux.

I look at Knox, expecting his own show of horror that one of his closest friends is dead.

All he does is laugh in disbelief. "She really did it."

Yes, she did the unforgivable. The forbidden. The impossible. I'm terrified of what will come next.

Risking an ambush from Knox, I rush to Margot and kneel in front of her, careful not to touch her skin. "Margot, talk to me."

She doesn't hear me, too shocked by Crux's blood on her hands to process my words.

"Tell me what your crows are saying."

Again, she says nothing, as if I'm not even there.

"The crows are pleased with her, just like the Lavens are," Knox says. "After all, it was my last-minute advertisement of tormenting and killing a proditor that enticed them to willingly attend today's festivities."

I look at the crowd, cheering and clapping. Some leaping and pumping their fists. For the first time in their lives, they've seen their biggest fear taken out by somebody of their own kind. They're ecstatic.

Knox inspects his nails. "I suppose all that's left is to marry her."

"You won't," I seethe. "By Arris law, she is my wife."

"And you know what ends a marriage? Death."

I stand and tighten my fists.

"Milo, there is no getting out of this. She cannot save you, and you cannot save her. The crows have corrupted her. Don't believe me? Listen to your own."

I don't have to consult my crows to know he's telling the truth. Gray fills in the white space of Margot's eyes, which is not something that happens when the gift of the crows is used by someone with Vicar blood. The horror from Crux's death is slowly melting off her, replaced by a blank slate and morphing into a blanket of comfort as her crows free her of all pain. The addiction is already seeping in, and there's nothing I can say to stop it.

"Let's face it, even if I leave you alive, she will choose me. Not out of love, that much is certain. But she will choose me because only fear is stronger than love."

There is one way I could try to get her back. If I can risk touching her skin to put her crows to sleep, she'll be free temporarily. I think.

Sensing my thought, Knox steps between her and me. "That won't be happening, cousin."

Margot's weight finally drops. She catches herself on her palms, her breaths amplified. She lifts her head, finally looking at me. In that moment, the girl I'm staring at isn't the girl I know. Yet I can still see a glimmer of the girl I do know. The fighter still trying to claw her way to the surface despite everything.

Slowly, Margot stands in her dress, her posture crooked from the crows' exertion. To my surprise, she reaches back and unzips the wedding gown, letting it fall to the ground.

She stands there in sleeveless combat attire that I'm sure Knox didn't instruct her to wear under her dress. Her eyes are filled with poison.

"It seems I have a maid to kill." Knox shakes his head at the secret attire and her dagger. "Nevertheless, you've tasted freedom from pain now. You cannot go back, even if you want to. Our crows are too strong."

"Knox—" Margot starts, her voice weak. "I cannot be bound to you. I *will not* be bound."

I sigh in relief.

"Oh?" Knox tilts his head. "I don't believe that for a second."

Margot holds the knife up at him, but it's shaking.

Knox continues, "Maybe you just need me to free you from your last weakness."

Before I can process what's happening, my cousin lunges at me.

Chapter 37

Margot

"Milo!" I scream. "No!"

Milo moves quickly but not fast enough. A long dagger plunges into his shoulder. He curses loudly, his hands gripping Knox's forearms, trying to haul him off.

Knox is visibly irritated at missing Milo's heart, but he doesn't withdraw the blade. With his ravens giving him an edge over Milo, he knocks Milo back against the ground and pushes the blade in farther.

Though the blow is not lethal, Milo seethes in agony. His arm goes stiff and falls at his side. Unless he gets the blade out, his crows won't be able to heal him. And considering how many nerves are contained in that area, it won't be easy. He's defenseless against Knox.

That dagger isn't the only blade Knox carries. I need to stop him before his next attempt. Losing Dimitri was already hard enough. But to lose Milo too . . .

A whoosh grazes my ears. The slice of a crow's wing. I can feel them, building stronger as my anger rises. The ecstasy of killing Crux still rushes through me, and it's sickening me less and less. I feel as though I could fight an entire legion of men. My muscles feel harder, my mind sharper. Begging Knox to spare Milo won't be enough. I have to fight. If I'm as valuable as he says I am, he'll avoid killing me.

I sprint at Knox, grab his torso, and take him to the ground with me.

"Margot, don't!" Milo pleads, but when he tries to sit up, he hisses and falls back down.

As I roll away from Knox, he tries to grab me. I narrowly miss his grip and quickly gather myself enough to stand.

But he stands and follows after, the blade dripping with Milo's blood by his side. I swallow.

The arena is still in an all-out brawl around us. I see Alarik fighting off guards. Strangely, the only proditors that tried to step in were Crux and Onyx, and Onyx has long disappeared. Why haven't others come to aid Knox?

Knox raises his blade, inspecting the glimmer of metal and blood. "There's still time for you to surrender. Remember, Margot, without me and my crows, your heart is nothing but a forest of thorns and nightmares. Who else will protect you from them, if not me?"

I grip the handle of my dagger harder. "I-I will find a way to handle them on my own."

"Oh? Maybe I would have believed you before you killed Crux. But now that you've tasted true freedom, no matter how much you try to convince yourself of its horrors, you'll always crave it. The crows will only be satisfied for so long, and you'll need me to guide you to your next fix. Because do you think *he* will?"

Milo stares at me in terror while he cradles the blade around his wound, as if he can feel the shift in my crows. That Knox's temptation holds weight.

It does.

Because if I house these crows and the pain that accompanies them, I will always face their cravings. It's what they do—tempt you into violence, give you anesthetic and pleasure for obeying, then slowly remove that pleasure until all you feel is the excruciating ache of your thoughts and actions.

The reality of it hits me like a truck. Enough that a wave of dizziness passes over me, and my knees wobble. The life I will be subjected to, now that I have given into the crows fully, will be one filled with pain and misery. I will wake up and go to bed in torment, unless I periodically kill. No, not just kill. Draw it out. Take pleasure in it. My fears turn into vivid thoughts, courtesy of the crows, projecting what my reality will look like now that I'm forced to spend my life with them inside me.

I grab my head with one of my trembling hands, and my entire body shakes.

"Yes," Knox coos. "See?"

I think I'm going to be sick.

"Margot, it doesn't have to be that way." Milo speaks in labored breaths over the pain of his injury. "You know that they can be relieved by other proditors. By me."

Yes, but only for short times, the crows remind me. *We're always there. Asleep and awake. Morning and night.*

My ears ring as the choices swirl inside my head. Milo's voice. The crows'. Knox's. It's like a tornado I'm unable to stop.

Knox comes toward me, stopping only a foot away. He places his hand on my chin, raising my eyes to meet his. His face is fuzzy, going in and out of focus.

"So, what's it going to be?" he asks.

A sudden realization dawns on me, my thoughts finally giving me reprieve.

The dagger weighs heavy in my hand.

I swing it, the tip of it pressing into Knox' stomach. Time seems to slow as I pierce past his clothing and into the beginning of muscle.

That's as far as I get before his boot slams into my torso, knocking me back. But my strength has ignited, and I catch myself before I fall over.

A small stream of blood trickles down Knox's clothes. It's far from a deadly wound, but I think he gets the picture.

"Ah, so that's how it's going to be." Knox drops his shoulders, as if only mildly disappointed.

"Only one of us is walking away from this alive," I repeat familiar words. "And I meant it."

Knox presses his lips together before speaking, then he readies his stance. "So be it."

"He'll kill you!" Milo shouts, and I know he wishes with every fiber of his being to leap to his feet and take out Knox himself.

This is my war. I want to win it.

Knox flies forward, swiping his dagger a centimeter from my neck. I quickly avoid it by rolling backward and rising to my feet. *So, he will risk losing my powers after all.*

As Knox rushes at me, I feel my crows' addictive energy course through my veins. The strength they bring. I channel it for every block, every strike, and every swipe of my blade. It's the only way I can keep up with him.

And every time my strength wanes, I think of everything I've lost—Dimitri, my sanity. Even my own parents and their young faces frozen in time. I wonder if they'd be proud of me. Or if they'd be ashamed of the evil I gave into.

It doesn't matter now. I'll do whatever it takes to bring Knox down.

I stay on the defense as much as I can, using his body weight against him, but he's strong. Stronger than me no matter how hard I fight. Regardless of the skills implanted within me, I'm at a disadvantage. I haven't trained my whole life for this like he has. My human muscles are quickly losing their strength.

Unlike his proditor muscles that could probably fight for days on end if needed. For every misstep I make, he can make ten and still be in the lead.

In the corner of my eye, Milo heaves in pain, trying to pull out the knife as his half-proditor blood slowly heals him. He has to know that even he can't stop this.

Knox seems to catch notice of him too and gets a glimmer in his eyes. *No.* Besides the exhaustion trying to take over, how will I also defend Milo as he lies there helplessly?

The thought of Knox taking him from me is overwhelming. It's enough for me to take my dagger in both hands, aiming it straight for his neck.

Knox barely catches my wrists in time, but I don't stop trying to bring it down toward the hollow of this throat.

It doesn't seem to throw him off at all. "Do you know why my crows chose you, Little Fennec? It's because we're two sides of the same coin."

My arms shake from the exertion. I'm so close to nicking his skin. "No, Knox. You embrace the evil of your crows. I have done everything to resist it."

"Really? Everything?"

I know he's trying to trip me up. Remind me of the times I have gotten too close. The times I let myself dwell on the crows' seductions.

Knox twists my wrists and the knife drops from my hands next to my feet. I cry out from the pain.

He quickly pulls me into his chest, holding a chunk of my hair in his fist. "And that's why *I* chose you. What other woman would keep me so entertained?"

I close my eyes just so I don't have to look at him. With him holding me, I know there isn't an ounce of fatigue in his own muscles. Even if I manage to shove him away, my body is on the brink of giving out. I don't know how much longer I can fight.

His hand is on the back of my neck now, and I brace for the entrancement and all the ways he'll punish me.

But an entrancement never comes.

I open my eyes, and there is a confused look on Knox's face. The tone of his muscles has lessened slightly. Enough that I easily kick him in the shins and push away from his chest.

He looks down at his hands then up at the sky.

What is going on?

A figure emerges out of the foggy air and the sea of brawling bodies.

Anali . . . oh my gods.

I almost think she's a ghost until I see Oliver in the distance, taking down a hoard of guards with Desmond. How in the world did they get off of Ashtanabo? How did they get here?

Wait, if Anali is here . . .

Now I know why no proditors have come to stop us. In the visible areas around us, hooded men lay dead or severely injured across the arena. And based on the amount of blood streaking Anali's hands and face . . .

For a second, Knox's face changes. He almost looks like a different person. Similar to the first day I met him. When I still thought of him as a friend.

He follows my line of sight to Anali, and I can only assume he recognizes her from prisoner files. She's standing the perfect distance away for me to act.

Before he can even consider making the next move, I'm on him, grabbing his head.

I push all my crows into him.

He tries to fight me off while his limbs weaken, and I seep into the corners of his mind.

In my mind's eyes, white crows surround us. The crows that once willingly attacked him and sided with me. The rare few in him that avoided the sickness of their flock.

A reddened smoky void surrounds us, filled with trees burnt to crisps and lakes running with liquid silver.

Obsidian crows sleep by his feet. Others are barely awake, yet trying to hide within Knox's shadow, fearing for their lives as more white crows land on rotting trees and stony structures.

Knox's fingers grab at his blonde hair, clawing at his scalp. He's done this to thousands of people. He knows what comes next. "Release me!"

"Why do you fear my power?" I ask him. "You created it."

Knox looks around at the remnants of my own mind.

I continue, "Isn't this what you wanted? For me to be powerful enough to overcome proditors? I don't know when I started referring to your crows as my own. But I think even they like the ring of it."

"No . . . No!" Knox points straight at me. "I've fed them for years. Been enslaved to their own dark natures to keep them satisfied. Been loyal beyond reason. I will not be pushed aside for a human."

Unlike Crux's entrancement, this projection won't last long. I can already feel the edges rippling. "You deserve every bit of pain you gave me. This is the end, Knox."

"Is it? Do you really believe that, Margot?"

Knox does something even I don't expect. He brings his hand to his mouth and bites down. Blood dribbles down his palm and beneath his sleeves.

The top of the entrancement cracks like glass, and a flock of crows and ravens fly above his head. I see—Knox has never harmed himself before. That pleases them.

His lips are painted with his own blood. "You won't outsmart me, Little Fennec, and you know what?"

I take a few steps back within the entrancement. "What?"

"You won't outlive me either."

The real world flies back into focus and Knox is already running at me. I duck and roll too far into Anali's range of power, my powers weakening. *Dammit.*

Anali nods and tries to get out of my vicinity, but Knox is already on me again. I reach for Aisil's dagger from the ground beside me and point it at him.

He grabs the blade with his bare hand, as if he doesn't feel pain at all. As if he doesn't feel it cutting into his tissue. In fact, I think that pain is the only thing keeping his strength slightly immune to Anali.

Still, I don't let go of the hilt, no matter how much he tries to pull it from me. Blood from his hands drips down onto my face, rolling down my cheekbones like tears.

Anali's mouth is moving in the distance, as if cursing to herself. But her powers are strong. I can't imagine Knox will be immune too much longer. I must fight him off.

"If you won't be mine, you won't be his either," Knox seethes and catches my neck with his bloody hand, squeezing.

I finally unhand the blade, clawing at his wrists. No, no. I have to take him down. I can't let it end like this.

"You know, for a while there, I thought I might have even been in love with you. Who knows, maybe I still am. But it will be an honor to guide you to your end."

My vision goes black, and I swear I hear Milo shouting my name. It's the only thing that keeps me from losing consciousness. My body keeps trying to buck Knox off, even as my mind goes dark.

Suddenly, I hear Knox shout. I feel his hand leave my throat, and then his body.

I turn on my side and gasp for air. The arena slowly comes back into focus, and it takes a few blinks for me to comprehend what I'm seeing.

Anali is on Knox's back with her legs in a vice grip around his torso. Her arms grip his head for dear life.

"Let go!" He yells back at her and tries to pry her off.

Even if his powers are still active, Anali is the only human he cannot entrance. She's strong, not allowing her grip to falter for a single second.

"Margot, do it!" Anali yells.

Pushing through waves of dizziness, I stand and find Aisil's dagger, kicking it up from the ground, catching the hilt in my hand.

I run at Knox, and time stands still. I take in every step, every beat of my heart, and every drop of sweat on my brow.

Knox's lethal gaze is fixed on me, even as his arms still work to get out of Anali's grasp.

He's put me through unimaginable horrors and grotesque levels of pain. He's used me as his plaything for too long. Owned me as a child owns a doll.

So I barely believe my own senses when I feel my blade give way into flesh. When his shouts stifle into a squeaky grunt.

I don't stop, even as that familiar metallic scent takes over the air. Anali has dropped down from him, but he doesn't move, his lips parted as he stares down at me. I return the favor, taking in every flicker of his eyes as I push in deeper, crows roaring while I soak in his whimpers of pain.

He weakly lifts his hand to the back of my head, pressing his forehead against mine while I retract the blade slightly and reangle it. His breaths are so deep, it's pushing out blood from around the entry wound.

With one final movement, I press the blade into his heart.

He accepts it, a pained exhale leaving his parted lips. Knox is quiet, and I'm frozen. I stand there with his forehead against mine, watching his pale face. I expect him to fall over. Or for his arm to finally drop from my head.

But instead, with his face sheet white, he whispers, "I wish I could have known you . . . without them."

My crows laugh at him as I quickly withdraw the blade, paralyzed by his words.

I take a step back, and Knox finally falls to his knees.

A hand rests on my shoulder—Milo's—as we both watch him fall onto his side. He blinks slowly, as if looking into the window of another world.

Milo goes ahead of me, his shirt stained in blood. But unlike Milo's wound, well, there's not enough crows in the universe to fix a blade to the heart.

Milo kneels next to his cousin and pulls him into his arms.

As my foe begins to take his final breaths, my plan begins to take fruition.

As Knox's life dies out, so do my crows.

Chapter 38

Milo

I hold my cousin, watching him gasp for air, blood bubbling inside his lungs. Only the gods know why I'm trying to console him in his final moments, my hand holding his icy fingers. He sure doesn't deserve it.

Maybe it's for the boy that would have had a full life had he not been born with sick crows. A boy I haven't seen since my father died. But in this rare moment, I see him one last time. Anali Matsumoto had quieted his crows as if she were a living dove. Or maybe I am a fool for seeing that boy now, as he slowly bleeds to death in my arms.

Knox searches for my face. All I can see is fear. "Milo?"

"I'm here," I whisper, my throat tightening.

"Do you believe," Knox barely gets the words out over the blood filling his lungs, "that the gods will punish me?"

I swallow. "Yes."

Knox stares up at the purple sky. He chuckles and coughs. "I look forward to it."

Margot stands at my side and places a hand on my shoulder. The life in Knox's demented eyes fades out and his breaths finally stop.

For some time, I don't stop holding my cousin's hand, even as Margot kisses her little finger, then presses it against Knox's forehead. My chest aches, knowing that he deserves worse than death. He chose to stay true to the evil that he was. A man cannot be blamed for his nature, but there remains no excuse for submitting to it. A boy cursed by gods and crows themselves. I hope he suffers long past his last breath.

I finally unravel his dead body from my arms, and Margot covers his face with his capelet.

The crowd in the stands murmurs, most of them hard to see. They had ducked away in fear of Knox's ravens, which are now gone with his death. The fighting has stopped, the arena ground strewn with rebel and Ashtanaban bodies alike.

Alarik stands by a now-freed Dune, motioning to a large screen on the wall, and it's only now I realize this is being televised.

The planets are looking to me, Ashtanabans and Lavens alike. Even the rebels look to me for clarity. As does Margot.

By all accounts, I am Colum once again, my throne reclaimed—and I'm completely lost.

But the people need to be addressed before things get out of control. There's just one thing I have to do.

I turn to Margot.

"Milo, we should go before—"

"If I am going to become Colum again, it will not be under the government my father set up."

"But your father's laws are too set in stone." Margot takes my hands in hers protectively. "Will Ashtanabo's leaders even accept the changes you try to make? Won't you be subject to nymbing?"

"There is one loophole." I play with my ring that's still snug around her thumb. "When I first captured you, I legally married you to keep questions out of the arbitors' heads and never recanted the records."

Margot's eyes widen. "So that's why you said I was your wife back there?"

I nod. "There's a stipulation in the law that the two-Colum system can only be reinstated through marriage. A ruler for Ashtanabo and a ruler for Lavenai. I suppose my father always liked to put little loopholes into his own laws in case he himself got too boxed into them. Not only that, but you're a Laven. Your people will accept you."

"I-I . . ."

"Margot, I can't force you to stay married to me. But there isn't much time." I scan the arena, which is becoming more restless by the second. Another brawl may happen if I don't address the people soon. "Will you be Columess of Lavenai?"

Margot's lips search for words, but she doesn't find them. I can see the thousands of thoughts behind her eyes, the questions she wants to ask but has no time to do so.

Finally, she nods.

I sigh in relief and resist the urge to embrace her. Carefully, I grab the small microphone attached to Knox's attire and bring it to my lips.

Then I take Margot's hand, watching the jumbotron in the corner of my eye for a brief second before lifting our hands together in unity.

"Citizens of Ashtanabo and Lavenai . . . "

Chapter 39

Margot

The first week following Knox's death, and the announcement of the two-Colum system, is filled with chaos and confusion on both planets. We couldn't even fly to Ashtanabo because of the uproar from the regions' leaders. But after a televised legal battle that could have ended with Milo being nymbed, his argument was upheld by the judges.

It's official. I am Columess of Lavenai.

I know for years to come, Milo will be slowly dismantling the rest of Arris law through additional loopholes that will probably start miniature wars. But what other choice is there? Both planets and all citizens should be allowed to thrive without taking from the other.

On day eight, once it's safe, Milo leaves for Ashtanabo on his own. He leaves me behind with Lleu, Alarik, and Dune for my own safety until tensions cool.

It's that same day that I sit in my room within an Ashtana-ban-owned hotel on Lavenai, hours before I need to make a speech of my own on the jumbotrons, that I see Imory enter from the reflection of my vanity's mirror.

I rise, adjusting the skirts of my dress, and quickly run to her. She embraces me with the warmth of a mother.

"How do I do it? How do I make Lavenai trust me?" I ask because in all honesty, I'm terrified.

Imory squeezes me once before pulling away and resting her hands on my shoulders. "Don't you see, Margot? They already do. Word has spread about Margot Tavish—the rebel-turned-Columess. The girl who softened the heart of an Arris and saved their planet."

"And I don't suppose you had anything to do with that?"

Imory smiles and holds my hands in hers. "Billions of people are looking to you now. Even ones on Ashtanabo, believe it or not."

"Many Ashtanabans don't want their life to change. They're used to extravagant lives."

She laughs. "A leader will always have those who want to see them off their throne, whether the reason is just or nefarious."

"What if Ashtanabo is not as healed as we believe? Then what?"

"It will take time, and they know that. Probably a decade or more, if we're being realistic. But Lavenai has something it hasn't had for years—hope."

I nod. She's right. With Ashtanabo restoring itself, there is no need to fight over energy resources any longer. If Milo and I can work together as Colum of Ashtanabo and Columess of Lavenai, the planets can unite once more.

"How is Lucinda?" I ask Imory.

"Well, she's spent twenty-three years running a rebellion that has no more use. She's tired, I know that much. She keeps mentioning retirement after she helps reintegrate all her people back into life above ground."

I smile. Lucinda probably hasn't had free time since she was a young girl. "Well, she deserves some rest. Though, Lavenai will need its own army if we're to truly be separate from Ashtanaban rule. Some of the soldiers will stay temporarily, and maybe even some of the officers. But we need a new commander-in-chief. I was hoping to ask her."

Imory gives me one more hug. "I'll pass it along. You know she's never much for staying still."

Milo and I see each other often but briefly. Both of us are on the move from dawn to way past dusk dealing with affairs on our planets. There are speeches, meetings, and judicial issues that need to be taken care of on our separate planets. Until things are more settled, sleeping in the same bed, or even the same region, will be a long while away.

But there are rare moments when we're alone together. Where his lips are on mine, taking every ounce of each other before one of us is inevitably called away. Once, he followed me into a privy after a meeting in Dhuaan and practically ripped off my dress. We had barely finished when I heard a servant calling my name from a few halls down.

I crave him everyday. Miss his warmth. When I have a second to think about anything other than my people, I think of him and when we'll rule together yet separately from the Imnicus. Part of me still resists the words "husband and wife" or "marriage." I still wear his ring and he wears mine, but it doesn't feel official. Or maybe I'm still too much in shock to accept it.

Recently, Milo has been traveling between each region to meet with geologists, as well as to visit each temple point for assessments. Though Ralia's easternmost side is still in devastation, it seems like many of the points look promising enough to start immediate dismantling.

It will take time. More than anybody really hoped for, but even the Laven people are tired of the bloodshed. Nobody wants to repeat Ralia, especially by accident.

Just the other day, it was announced that Lavenai's air quality was clear enough in most regions for people to safely breathe without respirators. I'll never forget the smiles I saw on Laven faces as I announced it to thousands of onlookers. Seeing their joy was a dream I didn't realize I had.

As for my powers . . . My crows died with Knox. With them gone, my mind is free. Though the imprint still remains. They do not cripple me as Knox intended. Instead, they shape me like hard iron.

I can still fight significantly better than I once did. Knox's muscle memory may be gone, but my body managed to memorize it in the process. Dune often spars with me in the early morning before my endless day of duties starts.

Just before dawn, I find myself in a field in the restored Laven region of Staeziemie, staring down at a single stone grave. I can feel the eyes of guards from up the hill, watching carefully for assassins or wildlife.

I take a seat on the grass in a silver dress, letting it billow around me while the clouds pass overhead.

"Hi, Dimitri." Just saying his name burns the back of my eyes. "Sorry it's taken me so long to visit. It took a while to get your body transferred and the grass regrown. The entire surrounding half-mile is sectioned off for you."

I get more comfortable, placing my palms on the grass. "Anali and Oliver miss you. Well, Oliver especially. He's been busy paying off some debt to Joriel. I guess the deal he made to get back to Lavenai wasn't cheap. Funny considering how travel between Ashtanabo and Lavenai is no longer restricted. Then again, you know Joriel. Always holding people to their promises."

A breeze rustles the nearby trees.

"Anali volunteered to start as my personal bodyguard soon. I mean, you saw her. That girl can fight. She'll be able to disable any rogue proditors that come after me, which Milo says is an inevitability."

The sky grows rosier as the minutes pass. I enjoy the silence, even if eyes watch me from the distance. For months now, I've always been with someone, whether it be a maid, a delegate, or Milo himself. I'm enjoying this rare moment alone, which is few and far between these days.

But I would sacrifice all this silence if it meant Dimitri were truly here with me.

I close my eyes, imagining my cousin sitting next to me and listening intently. It's enough to bring red-hot tears to my eyes. "You know . . . I was really angry at you for a while. I mean, we made so many promises to each other about what our lives would look like if Lavenai were ever saved. And you had to go and—" I try to gather myself and wipe a tear from my cheek. "I met her, you know? The exact girl you described that you'd want to marry—red hair, rosy cheeks. She even had those damn freckles you like so much."

I imagine laying my head on his shoulder while we watch the sun rise on the horizon. "I saw Lucinda cry for the first time after we finally buried you. I don't think she knows I saw. Let's keep it our little secret, okay?"

I hear a whistle in the distance. Time is running short, and I need to be back soon. Lleu and Alarik are getting married today.

"Everyone knows you're a hero, Dimitri. I've made sure of it. You'll be in the history books for centuries to come."

I kiss my little finger and place it on Dimitri's grave. "You can rest now, Dimitri. Lavenai is saved."

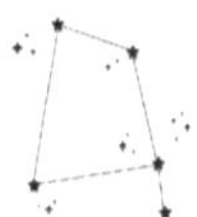

Lleu and Alarik's wedding may be the most I've cried from sheer joy in my life. It's also one of the rare days when it was the only thing on the docket for Milo and me, as we are both part of their processional.

It was also the first time I got to meet a Vicar, Erik Walsh. It felt nearly impossible to get word past Eskdale's magic that Ashtanabo was on the brink of change. But once we did, Alarik went on his own to speak with them and reemerged days later with his father by his side. The Vicars don't trust us completely yet, but hopefully things will change soon.

At the reception, I lay my head on Milo's shoulder at our table while we watch Alarik and Lleu share their first dance under the moonlight. She stares up at him with all the love in the world.

I hold on to Milo's arm as the chill of night passes through the air. "Onyx would have loved to be here for the dancing alone."

Milo stiffens. "He chose to disappear and not face retribution. That was his choice."

"Maybe he'll finally find what he is looking for."

"You're too kind to him, Margot."

I nudge his side. "Good thing he went into hiding on my planet then."

Milo laughs. "Then I assume Lavenai will make no attempt to arrest him?"

"We will not."

Milo drapes his arm around my shoulder and pulls me closer into his side. I take in every second of it, trying to banish the possibility of being pulled away from this rare moment with him. With my friends.

We leave hours later, after too many drinks and too much dancing. Our guards escort us to the gorgeous resort, but before they lead us to our bedroom, Milo dismisses them.

"They're supposed to stay with us until we're secured in our quarters for the evening," I remind him.

"It will only be a second." Milo takes my hand, and I laugh while he pulls me behind him through the halls.

He leads me through an arched door into an indoor garden. I take in the trickle of the fountains and the ceiling made of glass. It feels like we're standing right beneath the stars.

My heels click against the stone path surrounded by vines and violets. I look around in awe. "It's beautiful."

When he stops near the fountain, I turn to face him. He's always been handsome, but something about the night sky illuminating his silver-lined attire leaves me breathless. It is the first night we get to spend with each other as Colum and Columess, for real this time. We even chose Aisil and Lucinda to temporarily take over all of our duties while we're away at the wedding's festivities. So, unless there's planet-wide catastrophes, we'll be left completely alone.

Milo places his hands over the olive tulle of my bridesmaid dress. He rakes his gaze over my body. It's not a hungry gaze, but one of content disbelief.

He cradles my head and kisses me. The ache in my chest melts away, and heat rushes all the way to my feet. *Gods, I've missed him.* Honestly, the only time we've truly spent together like this was when my memories were still erased. And because that doesn't count, in my opinion, this may be the first.

Milo pulls away, looking deep into my eyes. His breath even hitches. "Margot, I have to ask you something."

"If it has anything to do with planetary relations, give me five more minutes. I need you."

"Do you know the moment I first fell in love with you?"

I'm taken aback. After weeks and weeks of nothing except working, I can hardly process his words. But I find an answer soon enough. "I sure hope it wasn't the first moment you saw me."

He laughs. "No. Trust me, I hated you through and through."

"Then when?"

His face reddens. "It was when I saw you dancing on that stupid table."

Now I'm the one laughing. "You're joking."

"Shortly before, I kept referring to you in my head as 'my wife' by accident and would curse at myself every time it happened. So, when I saw you dancing with Onyx . . . well, let's just say I wanted to strangle him. But more so I wanted to curse myself. Because no matter how much I tried, I couldn't see you as a Laven in that moment.

"As time wore on, I tried to deny that looming feeling in my chest. But I found myself watching you more. On one hand, I couldn't believe you were Laven, but on the other, I couldn't believe you were mine."

My pulse flutters. His words are bittersweet. Our story will always be painful to remember, but right now, I choose to remember the pleasant times.

"I never expect you to fully forgive me." He looks away, ashamed. "But I hope you can learn to live with me."

Milo gets down on one knee and pulls my old ring off his pinky finger.

Part of me is in disbelief—our love is impossible, yet here we are. While we're already married by law, this is different. He wants me to choose him. Willingly.

"Margot Tavish—will you marry me?"

Every memory from the beginning until now plays like a film reel. Every painful one and every sweet one. He's broken my heart a hundred times and mended it a hundred more.

"Of course I will." A tear falls down my cheek. "I love you."

Milo smiles the biggest I've ever seen. He slides the ring onto my ring finger.

As he rises, I slip his own ring off my finger, and he looks down between us as I put it in my dress's pocket.

"What are you doing with that?" Milo asks.

"I'm going to give it to Dune for safekeeping. For the wedding."

"You know, I never took you as a ceremony kind of girl."

"Then you still have a lot to learn about me." I pull him in for a kiss.

I may be Margot Tavish, a Laven. A Columess. But most importantly, I am his.

Epilogue

Milo

"Are you nervous?" my mother asks me, her arm linked with mine while we wait for the coordinator's instructions. My suit is lightly armored, more for show than functionality, with an equally silver cape that just barely touches the floor.

Dune and Alarik stand in front of us. Dune has his long hair pulled back into a bun and his suit finely tailored. Alarik's hair was getting as long as mine last month, but now it's cut halfway down his neck. Apparently, his Vicar mother prefers it ear length, and that was their compromise.

"No," I lie, but part of it is true. I'm not worried about the hundreds of cameras, the thousands of people in attendance, or the billions watching from their homes. All of whom think this is simply a renewal of vows to further show unity between our planets. It's more than that. "Did you see Margot this morning at breakfast?"

My mother laughs. "She'll show, my sweet boy."

"Of course she will." I swallow the lump in my throat. It doesn't matter how many times I've seen Margot. How many times I've kissed down her body or held her in my arms as we slept. I don't deserve her love. Or her forgiveness. Gods, she could do so much better than me.

A woman with a clipboard and a mic'd headset rushes into the marble arched hallway. "It's time, Colum."

My mother pulls me forward, and my legs feel like jelly. It isn't until I feel thousands of eyes on me at the threshold to the Vicar cathedral that I take in a deep breath and let my crown control my posture and demeanor.

Sunlight streams through the ultra-high window, warming my skin as I walk next to my mother over the glossy gray flooring. Delegates from every region on both planets are here, as well as members of the rebellion, sitting on carved stone pews. Golden bowl-like light fixtures hang from the ivory-antler chandeliers.

Once at the altar with my proditors, my brain goes hazy. I look over the thousands of people to watch the bridesmaids. Most of them are girls from the rebellion whom I don't know, but when the maid of honor walks out, Alarik's chest rises and falls deeply.

Everything goes quiet after Lleu is in place at the altar, and the tune of music changes. My heart beats quicker and quicker until it stops completely. If it weren't for the pressure of the cameras, I might be on the brink of collapse.

My bride emerges, her arm linked with Lucinda's. Everyone stands and even my crows are crazed with excitement.

Oh gods, she's beautiful.

Margot takes her first step to the sounds of harps and violins. Her dress is made of bejeweled tulle, off-shoulder sleeves, and an intricate bodice with boning. She looks like glittering stars, her curly blonde hair shimmering and pinned back around her face by decorative silver pins.

I bite my lip to try and stop it, but I can't. A tear runs down my face, and I try not to think of the billions of witnesses. But as I watch her more, I forget all about them. She's mine. A girl that nobody else can have. I feel Dune's comforting hand on my shoulder.

I nearly shatter when Margot looks at me and smiles, holding back cheerful cries of her own, hand gripping the bouquet of flowers genetically modified to look like glass. Though she manages to stop her emotions from spilling out, Lleu fails considerably, her makeup already ruined.

As Margot reaches the steps, Alarik's father, Erik Walsh, begins his speech, asking Lucinda permission to give Margot away. To my surprise, she doesn't hesitate.

I know it has taken a long time for her to trust me. Even after Margot gave her the position of commander-in-chief, the former rebellion leader could barely look at me for months. Now that the things I said I'd implement to save Lavenai are coming to pass, she has lightened up some. Especially after the air became breathable once again.

I take a few steps down the stage, taking Margot's hand and leading her up the steps. Her hand is warm in mine as she ascends with me. Once she's in place, Lleu adjusts the long train of the wedding gown.

Erik Walsh starts his speech, "We're gathered here today, not only to celebrate the wedding of Milo Arris and Margot Tavish, but also to commemorate what this means for Lavenai, Ashtanabo, and the dissolution of the Arris Reign as a whole. What it means for our populations and for the entire galaxy."

Erik goes on and recites passages from Vicar texts, but I barely pay attention.

Already, I feel extra protective of Margot. Of course I always have, but with each sentence that passes from Erik's speech, the feeling grows stronger. Even just the thought of someone glaring at her makes me murderous. I avoid looking back at the crowd for that very reason. Tensions are still high with a select few, even if the public show of our union will ease things temporarily.

At one point in the speech, Dune hands me Margot's wedding band. Lleu takes the bridal bouquet and hands Margot my ring with a lettering now engraved on the inside, one for only our eyes. I tried purchasing her a new ring after I proposed, but she refused. She said that she liked the one I originally got her, no matter the reason.

Erik turns to me, "Milo Arris, son of Balistar Arris, do you take Margot to be your soulfully wedded wife, bound by the stars, entwined by the crows, as long as you both shall live and well past eternity?"

"I do," I say, and slip the ring onto Margot's finger. It's only now that I see her hands shaking. I rub her hand with my thumb for a moment to calm her nerves. She thanks me through her eyes.

"And Margot Tavish, daughter of Enzo Tavish, do you take Milo Arris to be your soulfully wedded husband, locked by the moons, enraptured by the seas, as long as you both shall live and well past eternity?"

"Yes, I do," Margot says and places my ring on my finger. It's been so long since I've worn this ring with my others that it now feels foreign, but I don't mind. I like that she laid claim to it. That she wore my ring as long as I wore hers.

Erik smiles. "Then I now pronounce you Colum and Columess. Husband and Wife. You may kiss your beautiful bride, Milo."

Margot's hands find my face, and my own hold her waist. I bring her into my chest as our lips find each other. I hear the cheers, the music, and the celebrations already starting. It takes everything in me to keep the kiss tame and to be mindful of the cameras. I'll make up for it tonight.

In no time, we're whisked off to the reception, and then a ship to our honeymoon afterward. Alarik will take over my duties for the week, as Aisil recently retired, and Lucinda will handle Margot's. But for now, it's just my bride and me.

Once we wave goodbye to the cameras and the ramp closes, I secure the doors and push Margot against the wall while the ship readies itself to take off.

"Milo! Shouldn't we wait?" Margot gasps while I kiss across her neck.

"I can't wait any longer. I need you right now." I try to bunch up her skirts, but they're too long. I spin her around and work on undoing her bodice's long row of string. "Gods, you don't even know what you're doing to me in this dress."

"Then why remove it?" Margot jokes. Her giggle fades as she rests her forehead against the wall while I work at the laces. "I love you, Milo."

"I love you too."

"Do you think the ceremony will ease any leftover tensions with officials?"

"Not completely," I say. "But it helped."

"And the Ashtanaban elite who hid that the planet was regaining its health? What did you do with them?"

I pause untying the string. "Let's leave it at that."

Margot says nothing as I loosen the rest of her bodice and pull her dress down. Some things may never change about me. But now I don't have to do it at the ideals of my father, but the ones of myself. Those who endanger our planets must be punished.

I pull her away from the mountain of tulle and lace and back her into one of the seats, pulling her underwear down her sleek legs. I kiss the tops of her thighs then between them.

While I take her, body and soul, I know that the road ahead of us won't be an easy one, but together, Lavenai and Ashtanabo will live in peace as long as she and I both do.

Nobody can take our worlds from us, not with proditors and Vicars on our side. In a way, my refusal to give up my throne could seem selfish. As well as using loopholes through my marriage to

Margot, and her new position as Columess of Lavenai, to abolish the laws on arbitors.

The burden I carry is enormous, and the compass of morality heavier than I could bear. One wrong move, one bad day, and the power I hold could become too much. I could destroy civilization as I know it.

I stare at my wife, her face relaxing as I finish pleasuring her. It's she who will keep me in balance. To ensure that I won't ever be consumed by power the way my father was. And if for some reason she grows power hungry too, well, I know Lucinda would never let that happen.

The planets are saved. All we can hope for is continued peace with the planets beyond as our technology advances. And that they will never take from us as we once took from each other.

To Arris Reign.

Acknowledgements

I can't believe this series is complete (for real this time. I promise I will never rewrite this series again, *Lady of the Colum* lovers).

I couldn't have finished this book without some amazing people standing by my side:

To my husband, thank you for encouraging me while you left me content editing suggestions. And thank you for not being scared to tell me the truth. Your honesty has been instrumental in making these 2nd editions the best they could be. Commander Aisil thanks you for advocating for him to have his moment.

To my beta reader, Ola, for leaving me such in-depth comments, I probably should be paying you. Our friendship started with Atticus, and I am so glad you found these characters and loved them as much as I do!

To Taylor, my editor, thank you for proofreading these books with care and finding errors my brain never would have processed. You're the best!

And to all the readers who are the reason I do this. I might be a small author, but you guys build me up like I'm a NYT bestseller. I hope to deliver more of what you love about my books in the future.

About the author

Abelia Sumpter holds a Bachelor of Science in Nursing and discovered her love of writing while preparing for her national licensure exam. Her passion for storytelling began much earlier. As a child, she wrote screenplays and created short films with her friends. She currently lives in Ohio with her husband and owns a vision board the size of a novel.

TikTok: abeliasumpter
Instagram: abeliasumpter